7

DEAR REBEL

DEAR REBEL

Mary Nichols

CHIVERS

British Library Cataloguing in Publication Data available

This Large Print edition published by BBC Audiobooks Ltd, Bath, 2007. Published by arrangement with the Author.

U.K. Hardcover ISBN 978 1 405 64230 9
U.K. Softcover ISBN 978 1 405 64231 6

11432188

Printed and bound in Great Britain by
Antony Rowe Ltd., Chippenham, Wiltshire

CHAPTER ONE

'Lieutenant Stone, I am no Royalist, I am for Parliament.'

Alys stifled her gasp of astonishment at her father's blatant lie when she felt Prue's warning grip on her shoulder; best wait and see if the ruse worked and their uninvited visitors could be persuaded to leave without searching the house. They must not find her brother who, weary from the chaotic fight at Edgehill and the King's march towards London, was resting in an upper room.

'I pay my taxes as soon as they become due,' Lord Carthorne went on. 'And, tell me, do I look like a Cavalier?'

Alys knew that the lack of lace on his burgundy satin doublet and breeches was due not so much to religious conviction, but to the fact that since her mother's death he had paid little attention to his appearance.

'No,' admitted the lieutenant, who was himself dressed in a plain buff leather coat cut straight and worn over woollen breeches and hose. His short cropped hair was covered by a sugarloaf hat which he had not removed. The soldiers who accompanied him all wore breastplates and the pot helmets which had given them the derogatory name of Roundheads. Some of them were armed with

1

swords on their shoulder belts and others had carbines and powder bags hanging from their waists. Although they did nothing but guard the doors, their appearance terrified the whole household.

Lord Carthorne's family and servants had just sat down to dinner in the great hall when the small troop of militia had arrived, demanding money and men to help in the defence of London. King Charles, who had been victorious at Brentford, was almost at the gates and was expected to try and take the city by storm at any time. For months the citizens of London, a hundred thousand of them, including women and children, had been ringing the city with forts and ditches and now, when the danger was at its greatest, trained bands, the men who would defend the city, had gathered in force at Turnham Green, ten miles distant, to try and halt the King.

Lord Carthorne had been prepared to stay and welcome him, but Benedick, arriving unexpectedly, had advised him to leave. 'Go to Oxford,' he had said. ' 'Tis safer than going home to Waterlea Manor.' How her brother had come through the defences around the northern perimeter of the city, Alys did not know; he had been too exhausted to answer questions.

Through her reverie she became aware of the conversation going on between her father and the army officer, and that there was some

2

talk of looking round the house to decide how many men could be quartered in it. She turned to Prue, still standing behind her chair waiting to serve her, and whispered, 'Go and warn Benedick.'

Prue, dear reliable Prue, hurried to obey, but was stopped when she had almost reached the door by an imperious command to halt.

'Where are you going, woman?' the lieutenant asked, striding over to the old servant and making her quake in her shoes.

'She is going to fetch more glasses,' Alys said, answering for her maid. 'I am sure you would wish to slake your thirst and drink with us.'

'Aye, I would, my lady,' he said. 'We've been at this task all day and my throat's as dry as summer hay.'

'Then please sit,' Lord Carthorne said. 'Tell your men to take their ease.' Then to Prue, 'Go, do as your mistress bade you.'

Prue scuttled away and Alys breathed a sigh of relief. Benedick would leave by the back door and scale the wall behind the house, to return to his fellow Cavaliers, and goodness knew when she would see him again. Her brother, who was full of life and enthusiasm for the King's cause, was her hero, her idea of what a fighting man should be. He was fearless and as good a horseman as could be met anywhere, besides being a first-class swordsman. If all the King's men could be like

3

him, she thought, the war would be won in a matter of days. She smiled to herself; perhaps if the King was victorious they would all be together again very soon . . . Her thoughts ran on in pleasurable vein, so that she was only half aware that the soldiers had all taken seats at the table and were helping themselves to the bread and venison which her father had had specially sent in from the country, though that would soon be in short supply; the carts which brought it would be stopped at the defences and, even if they were allowed to proceed, would be stripped of their cargo. Fish was still plentiful, coming as it did from the Thames, but even the price of that was soaring.

'Wine?' Lord Carthorne said. 'Or would you prefer ale or sack?'

'Wine will do very well.' The lieutenant did not trouble himself to use his lordship's title.

Prue returned, pink-faced and breathless, with a tray of glasses and a new bottle of wine, which she handed to one of the menservants to pour. Only the tiniest inclination of her head told Alys that her mission had been accomplished.

'Where do you hail from?' Alys asked the lieutenant.

'South Lincolnshire, m'lady,' the man said, and Alys was pleased to note that he had not entirely abandoned his manners. 'East of Grantham.'

4

'I thought so, your accent gives you away. My father's house is at Waterlea. Do you know it?'

'Aye, my lady.'

'We have not been there since the winter began. I do hope all is well there—'

Her father gave her a look which stopped her in mid-sentence. 'Why should it not be?' he queried. 'The area is in the hands of Parliamentary troops and they will make sure there is no trouble. And we have nothing to fear from them as long as we pay our taxes.'

'Quite so,' the soldier said, drawing deeply from his glass. 'Though I fear those will become more burdensome as the war goes on. Armies have to be paid and fed and they need arms and ammunition and supplies of all sorts. Free quarter is nowhere near enough, especially when you consider how many men make up an army and all crammed into one small area.'

'How many men make an army?' Alys asked.

'It depends, my lady, but as an example there are twenty-four thousand at Turnham Green at this moment, waiting in readiness to stop the Royalists.'

'That many?' Alys queried mildly, wishing she could send a message to Benedick to let him know what he and his comrades faced.

'Yes. The King will never take London. Even if he were to break through at Turnham, he will not enter the city; the gates have been shut, the portcullises let down and every man is waiting to arms.'

Alys could not stifle her cry of dismay, but he took it for fright and smiled thinly. 'Have no fear, my lady, you will be safe enough. I will quarter my best men here to help defend you.'

'Oh, but that will not be necessary,' Lord Carthorne said quickly. 'There is but little room and, besides, we have nothing to fear from the Royalists.'

'I thought you said you were for Parliament?' the officer said, putting down his glass. 'If you have been deceiving me on that, it will go ill for you.'

'No, no, I did not mean that we welcomed the King,' Lord Carthorne lied again. 'I told the truth, we are for the cause. Why, my daughter, Alys, is betrothed to one of your captains.' He ignored Alys's cry of 'Father!' and went on, 'You may know him; Sir Garret Hartswood, of Eagleholm.'

'Indeed, I do,' the lieutenant said, looking at Alys with new interest, taking in her small even features and stubbornly pointed chin, her blue troubled eyes and long golden hair combed back over slim shoulders, without cap or combs of any sort. Her bodice was of blue silk and heavily embroidered, but it was not new and did not necessarily reflect Royalist convictions. 'He is my commanding officer.'

6

'If you doubt me, I have the betrothal document here.' Lord Carthorne stood up and went over to a heavy oak chest standing against a wall and, unlocking the padlock, opened it and brought out a parchment tied with ribbon. 'Here it is, signed on the last day of July 1638, over four years ago.'

Alys did not hear the man's answer; she heard no more of the conversation because her mind was in a whirl. Sir Garret lived in one of the few large houses close to her father's country estate. She also knew that there had been some talk of a betrothal, but that had been before her fourteenth birthday, and she had not taken it seriously. She had been a mere child and he, even then, had been a full-grown man.

She remembered him as being very tall, though she herself had not then finished growing and that might have been an illusion. He had been dark, she recalled, and he had dressed sombrely, though not as strictly as the Puritans, and he had looked down on her in a patronising way which, even then, had made her bridle. She had seen him little in the intervening years and not at all since the troubles began to brew between King and Parliament. Her father had always promised her he would not force her into a marriage that was abhorrent to her, and his statement now had shocked her to the core. He could not mean it; he was just playing for time,

7

trying to make the Roundheads leave them in peace.

'Why has the wedding not yet taken place?' Lieutenant Stone asked. 'Your daughter is well-grown and comely.'

Alys listened to her father's answer and her heart sank. 'She was young and Sir Garret was content to wait until she grew to womanhood and could understand the solemnity of what she was undertaking. Besides, I was having her educated and he was not against that. And since the conflict began he has, of course, been away from home and I have not been able to raise the dowry we agreed. But now he has asked that the contract be honoured and has generously waived half the dowry. We are, even now, preparing to leave, as you can see.'

He was referring to the boxes and bags which were already piled inside the main door, ready to be loaded on to a carrier's wagon, just as soon as one could be found. John, their steward, had been sent to comb London for one and pay whatever was asked, and, if a horse was not to be had to pull it, then the combined efforts of the servants would have to do so.

Alys smiled to herself with relief. How clever her father was to explain away the signs of imminent departure in this way. If they were allowed to leave, they would be long gone by the time it was discovered their destination was Oxford and not Lincolnshire.

'I doubt you will be allowed through the defences,' the lieutenant said, watching a servant refill his glass. 'Not without a pass, that is.'

'Perhaps you would be kind enough to furnish us with one.' Lord Carthorne smiled.

'But why leave the city, when Sir Garret is here?'

'Here?' Alys repeated, her heart sinking. Now her father would be caught out in his lie, and they had sent good men to the tower for less.

'Oh, yes, did I not tell you he is my commanding officer? Where else would he be but with his troops?'

'The wedding is to take place at Waterlea,' Lord Carthorne said in a last desperate effort to convince him. 'When Parliament has thrown the King back from the gates of London, the war will be over and Sir Garret will come home. We go to make preparations.'

The lieutenant stood up and his men followed suit. 'I must ask you to remain here until I have spoken to Captain Hartswood. He will say whether you are to be allowed to leave, and, if he agrees, a conveyance and a pass will be found for you. In the meantime I will leave two of my men on guard, to protect you; every army commander is out looking for quarters today and some are not so well-behaved as these.' He bowed to Alys, turned on his heel and left, followed by his men, two of whom took up their station on the other side of the screen which stood between the large hall where they had been dining and the front door.

'Now what are we to do?' Prue whispered.

'If we could trick the men into relaxing their vigilance, we could leave before the lieutenant gets back,' Alys said, after making sure the soldiers were out of earshot.

'How can we distract them long enough to get our belongings and all the servants out of the house? Besides, John has not returned with a conveyance. Would you have us abandon everything and walk?'

'Why not?'

'No,' Lord Carthorne said. 'We must agree with whatever is asked of us. It will be safer.'

'Even if Sir Garret comes here himself and insists on marrying me?'

'Yes.'

'I won't agree. I refuse.'

'The document is legally binding, as you well know. And if you disgrace me by making a fuss, then we shall have to devise a suitable punishment for you. I have been far too easy with you and I am rewarded with rebellion.'

'Father, he is a Roundhead!'

'So, does that make him inhuman? This war will end one way or another, but life will go on just as before, and there will be marriages and children born and old men, like me, will die; nothing changes.'

'Father, I care not for this war. It seems to me that one side is as bad as the other, but at least with the King we knew where we stood, and he will surely win, having right on his side, and he will punish all those who fought against him as traitors. Would you have me a widow almost before I can become a wife?'

'You will obey me.'

'But you promised me I would not be forced into a marriage I did not want. Why have you changed your mind?'

'I have not changed my mind, but I expect you to change yours.'

'Well, I never will,' she said defiantly. 'But if it helps us to escape from our immediate trouble, then I will remain silent. Once we are clear of London, we can go north for a while and then turn towards Oxford.'

'We had best finish the preparations,' Lord Carthorne said, turning to the servants to give orders for the packing of everything they could carry—plate, utensils, pots and pans, chests full of clothes, bedding curtains, linen, everything that had always been included when the household moved from Waterlea to their Chelsea home close by the Thames. When everything had been packed, then the servants had to put together their own belongings. In the days before the war, the grooms and coachmen would have been busy preparing the horses and coaches, but, though there was a carriage left in the coach house, there were no horses; his lordship's fine animals had been taken to pull gun carts.

'What is the use of all this packing?' Prue said, somewhat irritably. 'If we are given passes, we will never get through with more than the clothes we stand in. We might as well resign ourselves to that.'

'Are you suggesting we should leave everything to be looted?' Alys asked.

'If we leave it here, the Roundheads will have it; if we take it with us and get it through the barricades, the Royalists will plunder it, so we will lose it either way.'

Alys thought her maid had a good point. 'In that case,' she said. 'I shall tie my jewellery round my waist under my skirt and put what clothes I can into a bundle and shall be ready.'

'And that is how you intend to meet your bridegroom?' queried her father. 'He may have waived the greater part of your dowry, but that does not mean he will want you penniless.'

'Then he will either continue to want or tear up that document.' She pointed towards the parchment, still in her father's hand.

He looked at it as if he had forgotten it, then put it back in the chest and relocked it. 'You will not find him so easy to shake off,' he said, smiling ruefully. 'Though I wonder if he realises what he is taking on. You are more a rebel than ever he is.'

'Why did he want to marry me so

particularly?' she asked. 'He's old to be still single, so why has he never married before? Is there some mystery about him, some dark secret in his past that stood in the way? There must be a dozen ladies just as worthy and just as rich, so why me?'

'Riches do not enter into it,' Lord Carthorne said. 'He is already very wealthy, being a merchant adventurer and having inherited Eagleholm and the title from his father. His estate is nearly as large as Waterlea Manor.'

'And together with Waterlea Manor, it would be vast. Has he, perhaps, his eye on that, Father?'

'Don't be foolish, child; Benedick will inherit Waterlea in the fullness of time.'

'And if Benedick is killed fighting for the King, or if the Royalists lose this war, then the estates of the vanquished will be forfeit to the victors.'

'Then we will make sure there is a Carthorne at Waterlea, whoever wins.'

'You have not explained why an old man wants to marry me, if indeed he still does when he finds out how wilful and disobedient and completely unsuitable I am.'

'He is not old, Alys, he is barely thirty.'

'That is old,' she said stubbornly.

'His father and I were firm friends in the far-off days of our youth. We always said we wanted our two great houses to unite and the

13

arrangement was made when Thomas was on his death-bed.'

'And Sir Garret agreed to it?'

'Indeed, yes, he promised his father.'

'Without even seeing me?'

'He saw you several times as a child. The betrothal was agreed when you were almost fourteen and near full-grown.'

'But you stipulated that I had to agree?'

'I did not!' her father said indignantly. 'What sort of a father would he think me, that I had to ask my own child what she should do? It would have made me look very foolish indeed.'

'But you promised me I would not be forced into it.'

'I can hardly force you into making marriage vows, my dear, but I expect to be obeyed. Surely, you can see that it is for your own good? I would not ask you to do anything which would bring you hurt, would I? Wait until you see him and talk to him, then you will come to think better of the arrangement.'

'I will not!'

'Enough! Go and prepare your own belongings ready to leave. Whatever happens, we will not be staying here. You heard what Benedick said; it's too dangerous now. Go, my dear, and we will talk about Garret when we have more time.'

Alys turned to go to her own chamber. Behind her, she heard her father sigh and say,

'I have spoiled the child, so I have only myself to blame if she rebels.'

Alys climbed the oak stairs to the upper floor and went to her room. She had never felt more rebellious in her life and for two pins she would change into some of Benedick's old clothes and run away to join the army. She would fight for King Charles, just as he was doing, and if she died in battle she wouldn't care. Anything was better than marrying that Roundhead and living a life without joy. He probably uttered a prayer with every breath and sat about on the Sabbath doing nothing but read the Good Book. Why, even the King—and he was as godly a man as any— approved of games after Church on Sunday. The wedding ceremony would likely be such a travesty of what it ought to be, it would hardly be a ceremony at all. She smiled wickedly; supposing she insisted on a High Church wedding, would his conscience be so affronted that he would refuse to go through with it?

She pulled aside her bed curtains, intending to fold the covers, ready to pack them in the great trunk which stood in the middle of the room, and let out a gasp of astonishment, for Benedick was lying across the bed with his hands behind his head and an easy smile on his handsome face.

'What are you doing here?' she said. 'I sent Prue to warn you there were Roundheads in the house.'

'I left, but there are so many enemy troops about, I dare not try and go through them, so I came back. I'll leave with you.'

'We have to have a pass, and the lieutenant says Sir Garret Hartswood is in London and Father—'

'I heard,' he said. 'I was standing on the stairs.'

'Oh, Benedick, supposing they had seen you?'

He laughed. 'I can take care of myself, and anyway Garret is an old friend of my childhood—he would not harm me, nor you either, being his betrothed.'

'He is a Roundhead, Benedick.'

'So? He is a man and you are beautiful. Play his game, sister dear, it could help us all.'

'You are as bad as Father. I tell you, I will not marry him.'

'Not even for the sake of your family?'

She smiled suddenly. 'I have only to wait until the King wins the war and he will punish all those who fought against him.'

'He can't punish every Roundhead soldier.'

'He will send their leaders to the block and I will be rid of my unwanted suitor.'

She turned towards the door as they heard voices coming from the hall below. 'Stay there,' she said, pulling the curtains around the bed and enclosing Benedick again. 'Don't move.' She left him and tiptoed to the head of the stairs. Lieutenant Stone had returned and was accompanied by a senior officer, whom Alys knew at once was Garret Hartswood.

She could only see the top of his head when he removed his hat and was surprised to see he wore his dark hair long enough for it to curl on his shoulders. He bowed to her father and spoke softly, so that she could not hear what was being said, but there was no arrogance about him and when he stepped forward she could see that he wore a light brown tunic with darker brown facings and trousers tucked into wide-topped boots. His sash was a vivid orange splash across his broad chest and at his belt hung a sword which would have been the envy of any of the King's courtiers. She melted back into the shadows as he glanced upwards, but curiosity made her stay on the gallery.

This was the man her father had contracted to make her husband, and she realised her memory had played her false. He was neither old nor ugly, but that made no difference; he was probably cruel and heartless, the sort of man who thought wives were chattels and could be treated as such. Well, she would not marry him, not for anything, and the sooner he realised that the better. She stepped forward, intending to go down and confront him, but stopped when she realised he was taking his leave without asking to see her, and suddenly she was angry. How dared he treat her so offhandedly! Was she or was she not betrothed to him? Was he so conceited, so confident that he could be under the same roof without asking for her?

'Good.' She heard Benedick's soft voice behind her. 'Father has fobbed him off. Be thankful for that, little sister, because otherwise we might all have ended in the Tower. Go and finish your packing. And find me some of John's clothes. I'll disguise myself as a servant and ride with the baggage.'

Alys hurried to rejoin her father, to learn that they had not only been given a safe conduct through the defences, but that Garret had provided them with a large cart pulled by six strong horses to convey their luggage, and well as two smaller nags to harness to the coach. The animals were only on loan and were to be stabled at Waterlea until he came to fetch them. He sent his greetings to his bride and asked forgiveness for not waiting to meet her, but he had pressing business to see to in the defence of London.

'He is a true son of his father,' Lord Carthorne said. 'A courtier, for all his misguided loyalties. We need a few like him on our side.'

'Well, I am glad he is not,' Alys said stubbornly; it was easier to hate an enemy than an ally. 'Do you know that Benedick has returned? He couldn't get through the defences and says he means to travel as one of the servants.'

Her father shrugged, knowing there was nothing he could do about it, and turned to give orders to the servants, who were more interested in the family squabbles than in preparing to leave. Although his voice was as strong as ever, fine lines round his eyes and mouth told how tired he was, and his drooping shoulders revealed how low his spirits were. And it was not just the war, for he could come to terms with that and be as warlike as the next man in defending his home and family, but to be brought before the bar of the House of Lords and chastised like a naughty schoolboy was more than he could take.

Alys felt deeply sorry for him. She went over and slipped her hand into his and smiled up at him. 'In Oxford, surrounded by friends, you will be able to forget Waterlea, Father, until after the war is finished. By that time—'

'By that time the whole village will be a watery wilderness,' he said bitterly. 'Or else the commoners will have starved to death and men like Jan Van Hildt will be lords of a land which is not theirs and can never be theirs. Waterlea is my home and your home, and, yes, Garret Hartswood's home too. It is our heritage and the fen should be left as it has been for centuries. The Dutchmen are trying to change the face of the countryside, and all for gain.'

His sympathy towards the fen folk, who had rioted over the loss of their common land during the draining of the fens, had led to his being accused of not pursuing the true course of justice. When the new landowners had come to him demanding he punish the culprits he had been too slow to act and the miscreants had escaped into the fen. Jan Van Hildt, a Dutchman who had invested heavily in the drainage and been awarded two hundred acres of the reclaimed land, had sent a complaint to the House of Lords. As a result Lord Carthorne had been required to give a bond of two thousand pounds to be more diligent in the future and to prosecute the wrongdoers. The order of the Privy Council required him to do all in his power to promote the drainage works and he dared not disobey.

'The men will know that you have no choice,' she said. 'They will understand.'

'Perhaps,' he said gloomily.

'Let's think of Oxford and how pleasant it will be to stay there for a while. They say the King's court is as glittering there as it was at Hampton Court. You will be able to hunt and hawk and we will be able to go to the play, just as we did before these stiff-necked Puritans spoiled all the fun.'

He smiled and patted her hand and they finished the packing in great good humour.

They left the next morning. Benedick came down the stairs wearing a servant's smock and breeches tucked into woollen stockings. He had shaved off his moustache and little pointed beard and pushed his lovelock, now without its ribbon, under a plain felt hat, and was hardly recognisable as the heir to Waterlea Manor.

The cavalcade set off through the streets of London, which were thronged with soldiers and citizens preparing to defend the capital against the forces of the King. Everyone who could remotely be called a Royalist supporter had been imprisoned or was in hiding and it was only because of his lie and the protection of Captain Garret Hartswood that Lord Carthorne and his entourage were still free. Even so, their nerve-ends were tingling as they made their slow progress along the embankment. Watermen and ferrymen jostled for room on the water with cargo boats and gilded barges. Fishermen sat in their small boats, hauling in nets full of gleaming fish, and along the shore the hawkers tramped barefoot crying their wares.

'They seem to be unconcerned about the siege,' said Alys, who had elected to ride in the wagon beside her brother.

'Why should they be? The Thames is their life in more ways than one. They make their living on it and they can escape by it if they have to. It's because of the river that a siege cannot work. The King will have to attack and fight through the streets until he has retaken it.'

The cart turned north, its wheels rumbling

on the rough road. 'And will he?'

He shrugged. 'I think not,'

'Benedick, this is the first time I have heard you mention the possibility of defeat.'

'I said nothing of defeat,' her brother said. 'I expressed a doubt that he could take London, especially now the town has been fortified.' He pointed. 'Look at those defences and the new forts. It would be madness to attempt it.'

'Will he try?'

Again he shrugged. 'How should I know, sister? I am merely a cavalry captain, I am not privy to his innermost councils.'

'But you are close to him? We will find a welcome at court if we go to Oxford?'

'Yes, I have said so, have I not? But the King is not often there, you know. He prefers to lead his men in battle.'

'Oh, Benedick,' she said. 'When will the fighting be at an end? Will life ever be normal again?'

He shrugged. 'Who knows? I do not think there can be a swift victory, for neither side is disposed to give an inch.'

'Halt! Halt there!'

Alys lifted a corner of the canvas covering the cart and peered out, as a horse galloped up from behind them and stopped the coach in which her father rode.

'Who is it?' Benedick asked, as their driver drew the wagon to a stop behind her father's carriage. 'Can you see?'

'No, but best get down out of sight.'

He huddled down behind a bundle of linen, while Alys crawled over boxes and baskets until she was sitting beside Prue just behind the driving board.

'It's Captain Hartswood,' she said, watching the officer as he leaned into the vehicle to speak to her father. 'Why has he stopped us? You don't suppose he knows about Benedick, do you?'

Prue shrugged. 'Why should he, my lady? There is no one with us who would give him away.'

A moment later, the captain left the coach and strode over to them. Alys scrambled up on to the driving seat beside their driver, showing rather more of her ankles than was seemly, before straightening her taffeta skirt and pulling her cloak more closely around her shoulders. His expression was serious, but there were signs of humour and warmth in his brown eyes which she had not been close enough to see the day before. She wanted to hate him, wanted nothing about him to be likeable, but here he was smiling at her and making her tremble in a way which had nothing to do with fear. She told herself it was anger which made her hands shake, anger at the way he was able to order them about and the fact that there was nothing they could do about it. 'Your father said you were travelling with the servants, my lady,' he said. 'I can hardly believe my eyes.'

'Is your sight defective, sir?' she asked, sharply sweet.

He shifted his gaze, which had been fastened on her face, to the back of the cart where Benedick was only partially concealed. 'No, my lady, there is nothing wrong with my eyes. I see what I see.'

'Why have you stopped us?'

'There has been a change of plan, my lady. It is unsafe for you to continue on to Waterlea.'

'Why?' she asked, remembering, just in time, that he thought they were going home to Lincolnshire.

'We have reports that the Marquis of Newcastle intends to march his army south to join the King and he is expected to take Lincolnshire on the way. You must turn aside and go to Cambridge. You will be safe there.'

'Supposing we do not wish to go to Cambridge?'

'I have spoken to Lord Carthorne and he agrees. I suggest you travel with him; it will be safer should the cart become separated from the coach.' He reached across and took her hand in a grip which was firm and unyielding. Like the man, she thought-he would not know how to be gentle. 'Let me help you.'

She wrenched herself free, determined not to allow him even that small act of chivalry, and jumped to the ground. It was unfortunate that one of the horses chose that moment to step backwards in the traces for its haunches sent her sprawling. Garret acted instantly, pulling her from under its great hooves and carrying her to safety. He set her on her feet, but his arms remained around her.

'Are you hurt, my lady?' He was rock-steady, like a mountain, and just as immovable, but his voice was unexpectedly gentle. She was shaking and weak with shock and allowed her head to drop on to his broad chest, where she felt the strong beating of his heart. She stood in his encircling arms and it was as if the world stood still and she wanted the moment to last forever.

Angry with herself for her weakness, she pulled away from him; she must not forget that he was an enemy and one did not take comfort from an enemy. 'Not at all, Captain.' She managed a light laugh. 'The horses, like me, are impatient to be on the move again, so let us be on our way.' She marched purposefully over to her father's coach and dared not look back.

'If you will be so good as to stay with his lordship, my lady, I will escort you all to safety,' he said, handing her up. Although she allowed him to help her this time, she did not speak to him as she settled on the seat beside her father.

Lord Carthorne smiled ruefully as they

began to move again. 'So much for Oxford,' he said.

'Yes, but it is good news. The King's armies are on the march and if they take Lincolnshire, we can go home and . . .' She stopped and smiled because it might also mean the hateful marriage need not take place.

'We are supposed to be loyal Parliamentarians,' her father reminded her. 'Sir Garret is concerned for our safety, and he is going to take us to Cambridge.'

'You mean he is going to stay with us all the way?'

'Yes. He says it is fortunate that he has to join Oliver Cromwell there.'

'Then we must elude him,' she said.

'No, child, that would be most unwise. We will accept Sir Garret's protection and be thankful.'

'But what about Benedick? He has to rejoin his company; he can't pretend to be a servant forever.'

'It was his own idea,' Lord Carthorne said flatly. 'He must take the opportunity to leave whenever it shows itself.'

'I think Captain Hartswood recognised him,' Alys said. 'We must help him to escape, otherwise . . .' She dared not think of all the dreadful tales she had heard of what befell prisoners. If they were not mercifully killed, they were branded or maimed or made to

26

fight on the other side against their own kin.

'They have been friends since childhood. Whatever you may think of him, Alys, Garret Hartswood is an honourable man. He won't hurt Benedick.'

'You have more faith in him than I have, Father. In war it is a soldier's task to kill and Garret Hartswood will have no compunction about it. I just hope Benedick kills him first.'

'Child, how can you say such a thing?'

'Easily. I hate him and I want him dead.'

'Be silent!' her father commanded. 'There is enough hatred and killing in this war without you adding to it. Besides, you do not know what you are talking about. I have always been too easy with you.'

Alys knew he was thinking of the accusations of leniency he had been made to face so recently and hung her head in shame to think that she had added to his troubles. 'I am sorry, Father. I will speak of it no more.'

'Good. I will have peace within my household whatever is happening outside, and that will also be so when Sir Garret becomes a member of the family.'

Alys did not answer, but silently promised herself she would prevent that at all costs.

CHAPTER TWO

Alys rode in the old unsprung coach the whole of the first day, with the horses going at no more than walking pace because of the need to stay with the cart. By the time they reached the wayside inn, where they stopped for the night, her body felt bruised from the jolting and she was so cramped and cold from sitting that she resolved to walk part of the way the following day. It might also give her an opportunity to speak to Benedick.

He was still pretending to be a servant and, to her amusement, had developed a limp to avoid being pressed into military service by the sergeant who rode with Garret. 'I hope he does not forget which leg he is supposed to have injured,' she said to her father. 'You can be sure it will be noticed.'

'By whom? Garret is too busy to pay attention to our servants.'

'I am not so sure. I think he has eyes in the back of his head. Every time I try to go back to the wagon, he seems to be watching me.'

*　　　*　　　*

Except for Sergeant Wally and Lieutenant Stone, the small band of men who accompanied Garret were new recruits,

28

Lincolnshire men who had been living in London and were returning to their home county to take up arms in its defence. They were cheerful and willing, as yet unable to appreciate that the war was not the great romantic adventure they imagined it to be and that they were unlikely to win glory and riches. Aldous Stone was different. Aldous, who had come unscathed through several fights, including Edgehill, was well aware of the dangers and he knew, as Garret did, that the peaceful countryside through which they passed could hide a skirmishing party from the other side. He was growing more and more impatient with the slow pace of the great cart-horses which pulled the wagon, and fidgeted in his saddle.

'Can't you make them hurry those animals up?' he grumbled. 'We shall be on the road till doomsday, at this rate.'

'They are going as fast as they can,' Garret said mildly. 'The poor beasts are half-starved.'

'Then why not tell Lord Carthorne to abandon some of their belongings?' Aldous went on, looking over at the canvas-covered cart. 'What are they carrying in that wagon, the entire contents of Waterlea Manor?'

'We need not concern ourselves with what they carry.'

'We are sitting ducks. Let's leave them and ride on.' They were entering a wood and both kept a sharp look-out as they made their way between the trees. 'My flesh is beginning to creep.'

Garret smiled; his lieutenant was always one to look on the gloomy side, but the man's grumbles made him question why he was riding at a snail's pace to stay beside a lumbering old cart and a coach which had seen better days. He had only to order his men into a canter and they would leave them far behind. And why was he thinking of marriage when he had more important things needing his attention? 'If we did that, they would be preyed on by every scoundrel for a hundred miles,' he said. 'The King's men need money and anything which can be turned into money, and they do not pick and choose.'

' 'Tis plain as a pikestaff they are Royalists, so why not leave them to take their chances? We have more important things to do. The whole of the eastern counties could be overrun while we dally.'

'Would you have me leave my bride in danger?'

'She does not behave like a bride,' Aldous said, more outspoken than was wise under the circumstances; the captain was known to have a temper which was enough to terrify braver men than he was. 'Besides, it will not do your prospects any good to marry a Royalist, however comely she might be.'

Garret laughed aloud and looked over to where Alys walked alongside the horses, picking her way over the ice-hardened ruts and talking encouragingly to the animals, who twitched their ears as if they understood. The hood of her cloak was thrown back and rapiers of sunlight, piercing the branches of the trees, glinted on her hair, making it look like a golden halo about her head. 'She only thinks she is because her young puppy of a brother has taken up arms for Charles,' he said, refusing to be rattled. 'Besides, think what a pleasant task it will be to convert her.'

Alys had moved back to walk alongside the wagon and now appeared to be talking to herself, though he knew perfectly well that it was not a one-sided conversation, and if he did not stop it others would notice it too. He did not want to antagonise her further by having to acknowledge her brother for what he was and make him a prisoner. He ordered Aldous to keep a sharp look-out to their rear, and rode up alongside her.

'My lady, I must ask you to return to the coach.'

'Why? I am enjoying the walk.'

'We must make all speed through the trees,' he said. 'They could hide an enemy on the look-out for booty such as you have with you.'

She looked up at him, and there was defiance in her eyes. 'The horses cannot go any faster and if you are afraid of being ambushed then ride ahead. We did not ask you to escort us.'

'My lady, I must insist. If anything happens, you would be safer in the coach with your father.'

'Why are you concerned for my safety? Could it be that you have your eye on booty too?'

He reached down from the saddle, picked her up round the waist and laid her across his horse in front of him.

She squirmed, trying to free herself. 'Put me down! Put me down! How dare you molest me thus?'

'Molest you, my lady?' he asked mildly. 'Why, you are naught but a spoiled child. I do but chastise you.' And he smacked her rump to illustrate his point, but it was only a gentle tap. Then he urged his horse to walk forward to the door of her father's coach, which he ordered brought to a stop.

'My lord, I would deem it a favour if you would keep your daughter by your side for the remainder of the journey,' he said, setting her down at the steps of the coach. 'She does not appreciate the danger we might be in.'

'You . . . you . . . !' Alys was so furious she could hardly speak. 'Are you so afraid of a handful of Royalists that you have to bully a defenceless girl?'

He was about to say she was far from defenceless, but thought better of it, and instead spurred his horse to the head of the column and there rode in silence, fuming.

*   *   *

The next afternoon they rode into Cambridge, where Garret's efforts on their behalf procured a house for them inside the new defensive earthworks at the castle end of the town, which they were obliged to share with half a dozen soldiers. Not until Garret left them to settle in did Alys feel it was safe to look for her brother. She found him in the stables behind the house.

'My comrades will think I have deserted,' he said. 'I must go back to them.'

'There are Roundhead soldiers in the town,' she said. 'Do take care.'

'They are too busy fighting the students and each other to notice me,' he said. 'I can slip away without being seen, but I'll have to take one of the horses.'

She nodded. 'If Captain Hartswood asks, we'll pretend it was stolen.'

'He recognised me when we left London, I'm sure of it.'

'Why didn't he have you taken out, then? You don't believe in this idea Father has, that he would not harm you, do you?'

He shrugged. 'I don't know. I haven't spoken to him since the troubles began, but we cannot assume too much. I know that if I met him in battle I would do my best to kill him, and I must suppose he would do the same to me.' He flung a saddle over the best of the nags and bent to fasten the stirrups. 'Now, bid me goodbye, for I must be off. I have already said my farewells to Father.'

'You will take care?'

'Of course.'

She flung her arms around him and he hugged her, but then they heard footsteps approaching and he pushed her away from him and retreated into the stall, hiding behind the horse he had been saddling. Alys turned and put herself between Benedick and the door as Garret was silhouetted against the light from outside.

'What are you doing in here, my lady?' the captain asked, ducking below the lintel to join her.

'I am sending a servant to my cousin in Peterborough, to fetch her here where it is safer,' she said, gathering her wits.

'I assume you are sending the young fair-haired one with the limp,' he said, pretending not to notice Benedick.

'Have you anything against that?'

'None, except I cannot allow him to take the nag. Horses are too valuable to risk. He is young, he can walk.'

'It will take him weeks,' she protested, then, remembering that Peterborough was hardly more than a day's ride away, added quickly, 'He has an injured leg.'

Garret smiled slowly. 'He can take his time,

there is no need for haste.' He turned towards Benedick and now there was no doubt he knew who he was. 'Go, my fine fellow, run my lady's errands and be sure to remember her messages to her cousin.'

Benedick came out from hiding, grinning boyishly. 'That I will.' He removed his bundle from the back of the horse and strode towards the door, forgetting his limp.

'Do not go towards London,' Garret said, as Benedick reached the door. 'The King was halted at Turnham Green and has withdrawn to Oxford. The country between here and the capital is firmly in the hands of Parliament.'

Benedick paused a moment, then shrugged and strode across the yard and out of their sight.

'Is it true?' Alys asked. 'The King did not take London?'

'Prince Rupert was all for storming the city while they had the advantage, but the King was afraid if he let his nephew have a free hand he would set the city on fire, and the King was sensible enough to see that would do his cause no good at all. He restrained the Prince and that gave the trained bands time to gather and turn him back.'

'His Majesty was thinking about the safety of his subjects; he cares about them.'

'He cares for nothing but money, but we will not argue about that.' He took her arm to escort her back to the house. He was head and shoulders taller than she was and she was very conscious of his power as he walked beside her. A simple order, given to his troops, and he could have her slain or imprisoned, and he need only justify it by saying she was an enemy of the state. Why he had not arrested Benedick she did not know, but she felt sure it was because he had some use for him, and not because of simple humanity. 'It is a pity that my time in Cambridge is limited,' he added. 'We could have spent some of it getting to know each other.'

'To what purpose? We have nothing in common and if you think I shall ever come to know you enough to—' She stopped suddenly because he was looking at her so intently that it was almost like having her secret soul uncovered; she could not meet his gaze. 'If you are leaving,' she added hastily, 'then I am glad.'

'There is a war to be won, otherwise . . .'

'Are you so sure you will win it?'

'There is no doubt of it; we have God and right on our side.' He paused, expecting an argument, but surprisingly she said nothing and he went on, 'Your father has asked me to supper. We shall be able to talk more easily over good food and wine.'

'I shall take supper in my own chamber,' she said.

'As you wish.' They had reached the door of the house and he made her a superficial bow, before striding off down the hill towards the town, where he had quarters in his old college.

Alys went indoors, determined to avoid all contact with him in the future. She did not want to get to know him; she had no interest in him whatsoever, and the sooner the King won the war and punished the traitors, the sooner she would be rid of him. When she said as much to her father, he was angry, and even angrier when she said she meant to take her supper in her room.

'You will not disgrace me,' he said. 'You will be a dutiful daughter and sit by him and make yourself pleasant.'

'Pleasant to that . . . that . . . Puritan Roundhead, never! I will sit beside him if you order it, Father, but I cannot like him. He is our enemy.'

'Not all Roundheads are Puritans, child, and he is not our enemy, he is the enemy of the King.'

'It's the same thing. Had you forgotten your own son is fighting for the King?' She stopped suddenly, seeing his frown and the tightening of his lips, which meant that if she went on she could expect to be punished. 'I shall go and change before supper,' she added meekly.

She called to Prue and hurried up to her chamber, where she flung herself on her bed and fumed with frustration. 'I wish I were a man,' she said. 'I would be off fighting with Benedick.'

'But you are not,' her maid said mildly. 'God has seen fit to make you a beautiful woman and to give you the opportunity to be loved and cherished, first by your father and then by your husband.'

'Husband! If you mean that Roundhead captain who thinks he can beat me into submission—'

'Beat you, my lady? Why, 'twas but a love tap.'

'Love! Do you think he knows the meaning of the word? He loves conquest, that is all, and I will not be one of his conquests. And I do not want to talk about him, I will not even think about him.' Garret Hartswood must be banished from her life and then he would disappear from her head, where he seemed to be entrenched. If she could not persuade her father to give in to her, then she must make Garret Hartswood find her so unattractive he would no longer want her.

'I will make myself ugly,' she said aloud. 'He won't want an ugly wife.'

'What is ugly?' Prue asked mildly. 'To some men it is one thing, to others quite another. In the King's court, plain clothes and unrouged cheeks are ugly; in a Puritan's home, just the opposite.'

'Then I shall hide my face under paint and wear my most elaborate dress. Fetch out the plum-red velvet with the ermine trimming, the one with the low neck. That should offend his sensibilities. And I'll wear all my jewels.'

'All, my lady?'

'Yes, why not? I'll wear the emerald necklet and the gold chain, and I'll put the gold circlet with the pearl drops in my hair and wear all my bracelets and rings. How many have I?'

Prue went to a small velvet lined box which stood on a table in the corner of the room and began laying the jewellery out. 'Ten rings, my lady.'

'One for each finger, that's good. He will set me down as empty-headed, vain and selfish, without an ounce of sense. And if I also behave badly, he will not want me for a wife.'

'And I shall be ashamed of you,' Prue said bluntly. 'And as for your poor father—'

'He will understand.'

'I hope so,' said her maid unhappily, as she helped her mistress to dress. She became even more miserable as Alys set to painting her face with carmine and using soot from the chimney around her eyes. The effect would have been grotesque but for the fact that it was impossible to disguise Alys's natural beauty.

'There!' Alys said with satisfaction. 'He cannot find me attractive now.'

She ignored Prue's entreaties to wash it off and, hearing Garret arriving and being greeted by her father, she sailed downstairs and into the assembled company.

If she had expected Garret to display his displeasure, she was wrong. He seemed not to notice her appearance and treated her with inbred courtesy, ignoring her own lack of good manners. They had been at the table only a few minutes when she realised that it had not been such a good idea after all; her father was miserable and ashamed of her and the servants were finding it difficult not to laugh aloud. But it was too late to change and she found herself playing the part to excess, wishing it could all be over and done with. To the servants who waited on her she was rude and unfeeling; she found fault with the food and she drank too much, waving her goblet about as she talked, so that Garret, sitting beside her, was obliged to duck on more than one occasion.

'Alys, do be careful,' Lord Carthorne said. 'You will spill your wine down Sir Garret's doublet.'

'Oh, I am so sorry, Captain,' Alys said, bowing to him and contriving to push his plate into his lap.

The dogs were on to the spilled food in a second, as he sprang to his feet and the plate clattered to the floor. 'Enough!' he said. 'The entertainment does not please me.' He took Alys's arm in a grip that hurt and propelled her from the room.

'Let me go, sir, let me go!' she shouted. 'You have no right—'

'I have every right.' His voice was grim. 'You have humiliated your father in front of guests and servants and while they may have no control over you, I have.'

'You! You will never control me, never! Not you, nor any Roundhead traitor.'

'I will pretend I did not hear that.' He pulled open a side door and pushed her out in front of him.

'Then I will repeat it.'

'I advise you not to, because then I will have to have you arrested as an enemy of Parliament. Think of your father before you speak again on that subject.'

'Where are you taking me?' she asked, as he dragged her across the moon-bathed yard towards the stables.

He did not answer as he pushed her, struggling helplessly, towards the horse trough, which stood at the stable door. She managed to shriek 'No!' before her head was firmly ducked under the water. It was icy cold and sobered her immediately. He held her under for a moment and then pulled her head out.

'How dare you? How dare you?' she spluttered, but her protests were feeble and she was immediately ducked again. When she emerged the second time, she tried beating her fists against his chest in silent desperation. He laughed and caught her wrists, easily holding her away from him.

41

'I have caught a wild cat,' he said. 'And she must be tamed. Would you like me to throw you in?' He indicated the trough with a nod of his head.

'It's freezing!' She no longer struggled.

'That I know.'

'Is this the way to treat the daughter of your host?'

'If the daughter of my host is also my bride and needs to be taught a lesson, then I must, for my own pride's sake.'

'Sir,' she said, trying to maintain a dignity long lost, 'I have not agreed to be your bride. I find you not to my taste.'

He laughed suddenly. 'Oh, you want a taste, do you?' He pulled her roughly against him and pressed his warm mouth on her cold lips, forcing them to part. He radiated heat and she was shivering, which was not only due to the cold of a November evening and the icy water, but also to a tingling sensation which was centred somewhere in the pit of her stomach and spread outwards, giving her an inexplicable urge to press herself even closer to him. He released her at last and then the cold of the atmosphere took over and her whole body shook.

'Now, is it to be a ducking or an apology?' he asked mildly.

'I will never apologise to you.'

'Not to me—I care nothing for your insincere utterances—but to your father.'

'Oh.' Her voice was low.

'Well?'

'I will say sorry to Father.' Her teeth were chattering and she could hardly get the words out. 'But in private.'

'Not good enough. It must be now and in front of the whole assembly.' He paused as she wrestled with her pride. 'That or a ducking.'

'Very well.'

He turned to take her back to the house as Prue came running out. 'Oh, mistress, what has he done to you? Let me help you.'

'Later, later,' Garret said. 'Go and ask my lord to join us in Lady Alys's chamber.'

Prue dared not defy him and ran back indoors.

'Now let's take you in before you die of cold,' he said, addressing Alys. 'Take me to your bedchamber.'

'No.'

'Very well.' He swept her up into his arms. 'Which is it to be, a ducking or your chamber?'

'My chamber,' she said in a very small voice. 'It is the door opposite the head of the main stairs.'

He strode indoors without setting her down and carried her up the stairs and into her room. He dragged the covering from the bed with one hand, set her down by the fire and wrapped it around her. Then he piled more logs on the embers from the basket by the fender, making the flames roar up the chimney. Alys sank to the hearth, staring into the flames.

Prue joined them and found a cloth to wipe her mistress's face and dry her hair. 'There, there, my chick,' she said, glaring at Garret. 'I'll put you to bed and make you one of my herbal drinks to ward off the cold, just as soon as the captain leaves us.'

'I'll leave when I am ready,' he said.

'You'll not stay with my babe before your wedding night,' Prue said. 'I'll die before I allow it to happen.'

He laughed. 'Have no fear. I have no wish to fight you too.'

Alys was exhausted and humiliated and she was frozen to the marrow. All she wanted was to be left in peace; she had no more strength for fighting. 'Prue, be silent,' she said. 'Go and make up that foul-tasting medicine of yours.'

Reluctantly Prue turned to leave, passing Lord Carthorne at the door.

'Good heavens, what has he done to you?' her father asked, striding across the room to the hearth.

'My lord, I have been teaching your daughter some manners. Now she has something to say to you.'

His lordship looked from Atys to Garret, then back to Alys.

'I thought you said I had to say it in front of

the whole assembly,' Alys said.

Garret smiled. 'I could not be so cruel, and I must leave the wild cat with some of her pride. Besides, underneath I think you are really no more than a kitten.'

'Even kittens have claws,' she said.

'What is all this about?' Lord Carthorne asked.

'Father, I apologise for my behaviour this evening,' she said sincerely. She did not need the captain to tell her that she had behaved badly, and, even though it was his fault, she wanted to make amends. 'I am truly, truly penitent and it will not happen again.'

'I'm glad to hear it,' her father said. 'Though why you did it, I cannot think.'

'Oh, the reason is not hard to find,' Garret said, smiling at Alys. 'My lady thought to turn me against her, but she could have saved herself the trouble. I have no wish to marry a spitting cat.'

'You are cancelling the contract?' his lordship queried. 'I can promise you tonight's behaviour is not at all like Alys; she is usually docile and obedient and altogether gentle and charming. Everyone loves her.'

'I promised my father on his death-bed and signed the contract myself; it cannot be cancelled.' He looked straight at Alys. 'Besides, I think I shall enjoy taming her.'

'Leave me, all of you, leave me,' begged Alys. 'I am tired and I want to go to bed.'

45

Garret bent over and, taking her hand, raised it to his lips before bowing to her father and leaving the room.

'Really, Alys!' Lord Carthorne began, but stopped when he saw the tears running down his daughter's cheeks. He bent to pat her hand. 'I will leave you now to ponder on what you have done; that, I think, will be sufficient punishment. Goodnight, my child.'

He left the room and almost immediately Prue returned, carrying a cup containing a dark, bitter-tasting concoction whose ingredients she would not divulge except that it contained rue and poppy seed. When she had made Alys drink it, she helped her undress and climb into bed, and by that time the young lady was almost asleep. 'Sweet dreams,' she said, stroking the girl's forehead with cool hands. 'You will learn from today's events that there are easier ways to get your own way, but first you must know what it is you want.'

'I do know.'

'Do you?' the servant asked, but Alys was already asleep and did not hear her. 'I think not.'

*　　　*　　　*

Alys had time to reflect on her behaviour and Garret's during the next few weeks because he left Cambridge the next morning to join

Oliver Cromwell in the defence of the eastern counties. To her father she was penitent and anxious to please, knowing how badly she had behaved, but that did not mean she felt any differently about Garret; her stubbornness was no less because she had decided not voice it. As Prue had said, there were other means to achieve her end and she would bide her time.

They spent Christmas in Cambridge, waiting daily for news of Benedick and hoping for a Royalist victory. Alys told herself it was the only way she was going to be rid of the Roundhead. If she could further the King's cause in any way, she would do it, she decided, even if she had to take up arms herself. There was no more talk of going to Oxford, though the King still had his headquarters there, but neither were there any plans for returning home to Waterlea.

Cambridge was being fortified against attack: a ditch had been dug round the eastern side and all the bridges, except one, destroyed. Tales of troop movements and distant battles reached their ears from soldiers passing through, biased according to the allegiance of the tellers. The fairs and markets continued as usual and it was at these that they heard pedlars and traders tell of hardship among the people who were having to finance both armies; of horses being commandeered, money demanded with threats, soldiers

47

requiring free quarter. Parliament could not raise taxes without the King's consent to a bill, but they did it by issuing ordinances which had the same effect: the people had to obey or have their goods impounded. The King, as ever, was very short of money to pay and provision his army, and had to rely on the generosity of his followers.

'It's unfair,' she said to her father, one afternoon in January. 'The King is poor because he cannot get at the funds which should rightfully be his.'

'The King is poor because he is a spendthrift.'

'Father, are you turning Roundhead?'

'Of course not, child; the King has a divine right to rule and no one can question that. Whatever anyone does, he will still be King. I support him as every loyal Englishman should. Have I not said I will send gold and plate to help him?'

'You have? When and how? Has a messenger come? Have you heard from Benedick?'

'No, I have heard no news of your brother. Last year Oliver Cromwell prevented some of the colleges from sending their gold and plate to aid the King, but now a group of worthy individuals are got together to try again with their private wealth and I have promised to add my small offering.'

'Then I will too. The King shall have all my

48

jewels.'

'They are part of your dowry, Alys.'

'I would rather throw them away than give them to the Roundhead cause, and that is what will happen if I marry Captain Sir Garret Hartswood. If he must have me, he will have me penniless.'

'Why are you so against him?'

'Because he has taken up arms against God's anointed King and, more than that, against my brother and all loyal Englishmen. I want to see the King victorious and soon, and if my jewels can help to bring that about then I give them gladly.'

'Very well. I will find out when and how they are to be sent.'

Alys packed her valuables in a roll of lint and laid them ready, but, before Lord Carthorne could find out how to send them, Oliver Cromwell returned at the head of his cavalry and suddenly the town was swarming with the troops, many of whom were garrisoned in the colleges. Trying to do anything in secret was going to prove very difficult.

'They are using the lovely college windows for target practice,' her father told her. 'And they arc trying to terrorise the townsfolk, though, to give them their due, the citizens of Cambridge are a match for them. It is hardly safe to walk about the town. I pray the troops are only here for a short time because there will be nothing of value left if they are allowed to continue.'

'Surely now is the best time to send off the plate; it will be less likely to be missed, and if it is the soldiers will be blamed. Do go and find out what's happening, Father.'

They were not being very closely watched, although Lieutenant Stone was quartered with them and, unlike Garret, he would not turn a blind eye to efforts on behalf of the King. Lord Carthorne was obliged to be very careful that he was not followed when he left the house, late one afternoon. When Aldous Stone asked where he had gone, Alys said her father had arranged to meet old friends from his student days.

He seemed satisfied with that and had left the house when her father returned with instructions about the transport of the plate. It had to be taken to a blacksmith's on the south side of the city whence a cart would leave at dawn, accompanied by half a dozen horsemen disguised as peasants. Sending a larger escort would invite attention.

'I dare not go out again so soon,' he told his daughter, 'and it would be unfair to send a servant, so I must ask you to go.'

Alys agreed readily and, as soon as it was dark, their valuables were loaded into a basket and hung from the pommel of her saddle. Dressed in a dark doublet and skirt, and with a long thick cloak about her, she mounted and walked the horse out of the yard and on to the road which led down the hill into the town. At the crossroads she turned away from the bridge, which was guarded by sentries, and took the road south, leaving behind the sounds of revelry and fighting and musket fire which had become commonplace since the arrival of the troops. 'Let them remain thus occupied,' she prayed.

It was a dark night and the road was bad; the mare had to pick her way very carefully and Alys realised it would be folly to ride at more than walking pace. She strained her ears for sounds of others on the road, but there was nothing to be heard except the rustle of the leaves in the trees and an occasional owl. It was good to be doing something positive, better than sitting at home waiting to hear what others were doing. If only they could have news of Benedick, she would be content.

Her brother would be in the thick of any fighting, she knew, but there had been no big battles for some time; it was as if both sides were waiting for the other to move first. She had heard that there had been attempts to end the war by negotiation and both sides had met at Oxford to discuss peace, but it had come to nothing. Parliament blamed the King's supporters, whom they called 'delinquents', and not the King himself. Provided he withdrew his protection from his followers, they would agree to a peace. When Alys had first heard this, she had thought immediately of Benedick; without the King's protection, he would probably die on the scaffold. Death in battle would be preferable to that. But the King had refused the terms and she had breathed a sigh of relief.

She could see a light further along the road and pulled the horse up to make sure it was coming from the blacksmith's, then she rode slowly forward. There was a large covered cart at the open door and horses stood ready saddled and hitched to a railing nearby.

'Stop where you are!' The command, coming suddenly from the darkness behind her, startled her and her horse reared. She brought it under control and the voice continued. 'State your business.'

'My business is with the loyal smithy,' she said, giving the password her father had told her. 'I have the means to shoe a few horses.'

'Good. You may go forward.'

She rode into the yard and dismounted. The man who had challenged her followed, carrying a musket, which he put into a sling on one of the horse's saddles. 'I hardly expected a lady,' he said. 'But no matter. You have brought the goods?'

'Yes, in the basket. Be sure they reach their destination safely.'

The mare was relieved of her burden and Alys remounted. 'Good luck, my friends,' she said. 'And if, by chance, you should come

52

across Benedick Carthorne, tell him I am thinking of him and looking forward to our reunion, when the war is won.'

'Aye, mistress, we will tell him that. Now, best be off and keep a sharp eye about you; there are those who would betray us.'

'I will, have no fear. I wish I were going with you.'

The men laughed good-humouredly and waved to her as she left and was swallowed up in the darkness again. Now that her task had been accomplished, her taut nerves relaxed, and she felt suddenly drained of energy. By the time she arrived home, she was almost asleep in the saddle. Prue ran out to help her dismount.

'Come indoors and straight up to your chamber,' she said. 'Sir Garret has arrived and we told him you were ill with a chill from the ducking he gave you. You must get into bed in case he wants to see for himself.'

Alys giggled as she hurried in at the kitchen door and up the back stairs. 'He no doubt thinks I am being my usual rebellious self and making excuses not to see him.'

'You cannot avoid him forever, my lady. He is not one to give up easily.'

'And neither am I.'

'Did you find the smithy?'

'Yes. The valuables are on their way and if they help to send Benedick home even one day sooner, then it will have been worth the sacrifice.' She opened the door of her chamber and caught her breath in surprise, for Garret sat on her bed, holding aside the curtain to reveal the bed with its covers smooth and uncrumpled. She recovered herself quickly and demanded, 'What are you doing in my bedchamber, Captain? We are not man and wife yet, nor will be if it pleases God to release me from you.'

'I came to offer sympathy for your illness,' he said, standing up and letting the bed curtain fall back into place. 'But I see my sympathy is misplaced.'

'My lady was overcome by the heat,' Prue said. 'She went out for some air.'

He looked at the fire, whose embers were low, and at her heavy cloak and mist-dampened hair and, to her annoyance, smiled. 'It must be heat which puts the colour in your cheeks and the sparkle in your eyes; if I had not been told you were unwell, I should have said you were exceedingly healthy.'

'Fever,' Prue said. 'I should keep your distance, sir, for it could be contagious.'

He laughed aloud. 'With a guardian like you, Prue Newman, she needs no other protection. Do you stay by her and watch over her.'

'That I will.'

'And see if you can put some sense into that empty head of hers.'

Alys picked up her jewel box, the nearest

thing to hand, and flung it at his head. He ducked and it landed on the floor at his feet, open and empty. She stood and stared at it in horror, sure that he would guess what had happened to its contents, but he appeared more amused than concerned, and picked it up before closing it and replacing it on the table at her side. Then he turned to leave. 'Goodnight, my lady.'

As soon as the door had closed on him, Alys sank on to the bed and shut her eyes. 'He knows I went out. Do you think he is curious enough to try and find out where I went?'

'Better have a tale ready, mistress.'

'A secret lover,' she said. 'That should settle him. I'll pretend to be reluctant to tell him and when he forces it out of me he will be so angry that he will cancel the marriage contract.'

In the event Garret did not ask. In fact, he showed annoyingly little interest and when he called again two days later he spent his time talking to her father, whose company he found congenial. She sat in the same room and listened to them but took no part in the conversation. Her father seemed to be able to pretend to be in sympathy with the Roundhead cause without actually saying so, or betraying his Royalist sympathies. If she had not known him better, she would have accused him of facing both ways at once. He had managed to steer the conversation away from the war and they were talking of home.

'The fen folk are an independent lot,' her father was saying. 'They care nothing for the war and the reasons for it. As long as they can carry on in their own way, fowling and fishing and grazing their cattle on the commons, they do not even want to know who rules them. They attack Royalist and Parliamentarian indiscriminately if they see their way of life threatened. They support Parliament only so long as Parliament appears to support them in their fight against drainage and enclosure. If you let them down, Garret, they will turn on you, and there are none so ferocious when roused to anger.'

Garret smiled. 'I know, I am one myself.'

'Not a fen commoner.'

'No, but I, like you, have lived close to them all my life, and I understand why they have been quick to seize advantage of the times to upset the drainage works. There is some truth in their claim that, because of the war, they have no legal remedy.'

'And they are right. No one will listen to them.'

'And is that why you have failed to punish the ringleaders?'

'I cannot punish those I cannot find; there are more hiding places in the fens than we could find in a year of Sundays. Besides, the men say they flooded the fens to prevent the Royalist advance and that is a strong

56

argument in their favour.'

'I believe the Lords did not agree.'

'No,' Lord Carthorne said morosely. 'I was treated to a lecture and heavily fined. It has impoverished me, I can tell you. I have had to part with a great many valuables, which is why the cup you drink from is only pewter.'

'Let us drink to happier times,' Garret said, raising his goblet. 'And may we both have what we most desire.' He looked over the rim of his drinking vessel at Alys, searching her face with brown eyes which seemed to lay bare her most secret self. She tried to stare him out, but in the end it was she who looked away. Murmuring her excuses, she stood up and left the room. Much as she enjoyed listening to the conversation, she could not stay in the same room with Garret Hartswood; he unnerved her with his gentleness and charm at the same time as he angered her with his arrogance and pride. She went to her own chamber and did not hear him leave.

*   *   *

He would come back, she knew, but when he did not put in an appearance for several days she found herself looking out for him, pretending that she needed to be prepared so that he could not catch her unawares. She became edgy and unable to concentrate on the daily tasks she had set herself. She wandered through the house and around the yard, not daring to go far for fear of being caught in the skirmishes between town and gown which were a feature of Cambridge life. She was sitting by the window one day, playing a plaintive tune on her recorder, when Garret cantered up to the door and, dismounting, hurried up the steps and into the house without waiting to be shown in by a servant. It annoyed her to think that he could make himself so much at home, but she did not have time to voice her irritation, because he strode up to her and flung a lint-wrapped bundle into her lap. She recognised it immediately.

'Open it, my lady,' he said angrily. 'See that all is safe.'

Slowly she unwrapped the cloth and laid bare the emerald necklet, the gold circlet with the pearl drops, the bracelets and the ten bejewelled rings. She looked up at him, trying to gauge how much he knew, and was surprised to find there was more amusement than anger in his eyes, though his voice was clipped. 'Do not deny they belong to you,' he said, reminding her of that first disastrous evening in Cambridge. 'Remember I have seen them before, every one of them.'

'I do not deny it,' she said as calmly as she could. 'But where did you find them?'

He laughed bitterly. 'Now you are going to tell me you lost them.'

'No. They were stolen.'

'When and by whom?'

'If I knew that, I would have had the thief arrested and recovered them, would I not?'

'Do not sully that beautiful mouth with untruths, my lady. They were captured by our soldiers on their way to Oxford, together with your family plate and other valuables from misguided members of the University. It is well I recognised the jewellery and took charge of it, otherwise you would have lost your freedom, if not your head.'

'And Father?' she asked in a small voice, suddenly realising what a dangerous game they had been playing.

'His plate has been returned to him and I do not want to see it again except at his table when I dine with you.'

'Thank you.' The words of gratitude were bitter on her lips.

'I have to rejoin Captain Cromwell now and we shall be kept occupied for some time, I think. I will send word when it is safe for you all to go home to Waterlea. In the meantime, I bid you good-day, my lady.'

From the window, she watched him mount and ride away, a tall, upright figure, proud and unbending and yet . . . She shook herself. He was her enemy, she must not allow herself to forget that.

CHAPTER THREE

All through the spring of 1643, while Lord Carthorne and his family stayed inactive in Cambridge, unable to do anything without attracting the attention of the Roundhead garrison, Cromwell and his cavalry, which included Garret, sped hither and thither all over the eastern counties, putting down pockets of Royalist resistance. Cromwell crushed a rising in Lowestoft and towards the end of April he took Peterborough, with much damage to the cathedral. In May he was ordered to secure Lincolnshire for Parliament.

'I heard in the town that he had bombarded Crowland,' her father said, one day towards the end of that month, when the air was balmy, trees were bursting into leaf and the hawthorn was heavy with blossom. 'But the town was well fortified and the defenders refused to give in.'

'Good for them!' Alys said. 'I wish there were more like them.'

Now the fighting was taking place in their own county, they became eager for news, concerned for their own people, particularly when they heard that Cromwell's troopers had attacked a party of Royalists just outside Grantham.

'Could we not go home and find out,

60

Father?' she asked. 'Must we wait for Captain Hartswood to tell us when to go? After all, it is our home and we ought to be there to defend it and protect our people. There must be others like us, if only we knew where they were and could organise them.'

'You, daughter, will do nothing. I fear for you if Sir Garret finds you involved in any more plotting; you have tried his patience grievously and never forget he has the power to send you to the scaffold.'

'You would think,' Alys mused, 'that he would be put off marrying me. Instead he seems determined to master me.'

'As any red-blooded man would be.' He added, 'You are storing up trouble for yourself, my child, if you oppose him. It would be better to acknowledge him master now, because if you don't he will treat you harshly and without affection when you are married.'

'Affection! He is incapable of it.'

'He was always a dutiful and affectionate son, and good sons make good husbands. He treats his servants fairly and generously and he has helped many a villager unable to pay his taxes, not to mention paying for Ingram Martin's son to go to school. And he brought back our plate and jewels when he could have denounced us. He would not have done that if he had not been betrothed to you.'

'He is hoping one day to take over Waterlea Manor and all it contains, including those

61

same valuables.'

'How can he do that? Benedick will inherit Waterlea.'

'*If* Benedick lives and *if* the Royalists are victorious, but what will happen if Benedick is killed? Why, Captain Hartswood might even deal the blow himself.'

Prue who was sitting beside her doing some mending, dropped her needle and crossed herself, uttering a fervent prayer for Benedick's safety.

'And if the Roundheads win, then Garret Hartswood would expect to be awarded the Manor by a grateful Parliament,' Alys added, driving her point home.

'Then we must make sure there is always a Carthorne at Waterlea Manor,' her father said firmly. 'If it is not to be Benedick, then it must be you and your children. I will hear no more from you on the subject.'

'All the more reason to return home,' she argued. 'We can't even be sure the Manor has not already been taken over by the Roundheads, can we? Perhaps that is where the captain is at this moment, acting lord of the manor already, Father. Had you thought of that?'

'I must confess that I should like to go home.' Prue murmured. 'Winter is behind us and the countryside is so beautiful in the spring when the birds are nesting and the young animals can graze to their hearts content in the meadows.'

'If the whole lot is not under water,' her father said gloomily, thinking of the rioters and the destruction of the newly constructed banks, which had led to his being summoned to the House of Lords.

'And that's another reason for going back,' Alys said. 'Father, you cannot stay away any longer.'

Faced with the pleas of his daughter and her maid, Lord Carthorne gave in and went to see the garrison commander for permission to travel.

Once again the trappings of the household were packed away and once again the horses were hitched to the coach and wagon, which had been standing forgotten at the back of the stables throughout their stay in Cambridge.

They left the town in the early afternoon and headed for Huntingdon, where they stayed the first night at an inn, setting off again at cockcrow the next morning. The second night was spent at Stamford, and the third day they continued on towards Grantham, before turning off to the east, intending to stay at a wayside inn for the night. It wanted an hour or two before it became too dark to travel and Alys begged her father to go on. 'Don't let's stop now,' she said. 'We can be home tonight if we keep going.'

'I shall certainly feel safer once we are off

the high road,' Prue said. 'We could easily be run down by a company of galloping horsemen.'

Alys laughed. 'What horsemen?'

'Oliver Cromwell's cavalry. They would not stop for a slow-moving cart and an old coach drawn by the skinniest pair of nags you have ever seen.'

Alys laughed. 'When I think of how we used to travel, with wagons and coaches and outriders and the best horses in the eastern counties, I am ashamed of being seen thus.'

'You would prefer to arrive home in the dark, is that it?' Lord Carthorne said, smiling at her. 'You may be right. Let us continue.'

He put his head out of the door of the coach and called to the driver to go on. After a few miles they turned north again. This road, which led nowhere except to Waterlea and the village beyond it, was full of potholes and in some places disappeared altogether, but Alys's spirits rose as they were bumped about in the swaying vehicle. She was going home to the flat, wet land of her childhood, with its swirling mists and dancing reeds, where the kingfisher darted and the heron paddled, where the otter swam and men did their hunting on stilts.

In London and Cambridge she had had to live within the constraints of her place in society; in Waterlea there were hardly any. She could go out alone to walk or ride or punt a boat without anyone raising an eyebrow; she could milk a cow, pluck a fowl, skewer an eel with the best of the fen women and had been known to kilt up her skirts and walk on stilts to rescue a stranded calf or collect ducks' eggs laid on a bank. Here she had learned to shoot and fish and chase her father's hounds after fallen wildfowl. Sharing the hazardous life of the fen folk, she also shared their freedom.

It had not, until now, entered her head that her freedom stopped short of marrying whom she chose, that in this one thing she differed from the young women of the village. Well, she would not give in, she would not!

Her father had pulled aside the leather curtain above the door to peer into the gathering dusk, but Alys did not need to see to know where she was. The oaks, poplars and birch grew sparser as they left the uplands behind them and were replaced by alder and willow. The smell of damp peat filled their nostrils, but it was the smell of home. The grey light of dusk, streaked with purple and blue, had a luminosity which never failed to move her. Some hated it, calling the air foul and noisome and unhealthy, but to those who had lived there all their lives it had a special quality, a magic which drew them back however far they roamed.

The higher stretches of the fen through which they were passing had been criss-crossed with dykes, so that each April the land drained of its own accord, leaving strips of rich pasture, which were called summer grounds because they were only dry in the summer months. Until the intrusion of the gentlemen adventurers and the undertakers, the wet lands beyond that had given a living to reed-cutters and basket-makers who farmed the osier beds. On lower land still was the fen itself, the home of fish and fowl and few men. No one had paid rent; the fens had been held in common and, in that sparsely inhabited district, there had been room for all. Now that was changing; the reclaimed land was being allocated to those who had invested in the undertakings and they looked to see a return on their investment in the form of rents. In making some areas drier they were drowning others, and the shape of the landscape was slowly changing.

Lord Carthorne gave a sudden growl of annoyance. 'I knew it. Jan Van Hildt's new pasture is under a foot of water. It has almost reached the road. The fools! The fools! Don't they know I cannot protect them any longer?'

'But, Father, it's nearly summer,' Alys said. 'Where has all the water come from?'

'From the New Drain, where else?'

The drain had been dug in a straight line with ten foot high banks to contain the water flowing down from inland hills, so that the land on either side, which was lower than sea level, could be drained and cultivated. It was this land which had been enclosed and allocated to Jan Van Hildt, who had put it to the plough and was attempting to grow arable crops. He had built himself a grand house on the edge of Waterlea village.

The villagers hated it and its owner; he was a foreigner who had had the temerity to set himself up as a farmer with land wrested from its true holders. His cole-seed and hemp grew on *their* commons and his cattle waxed fat on pasture they and their forefathers had used for centuries, and they rebelled. The King might be lord of the soil, but that did not give him the right to dispose of it to strangers.

'It's Ingram Martin who is at the bottom of this, you can be sure,' Lord Carthorne said. 'Oh, the fool!'

'You cannot prove that,' Alys said.

'I shall have to try or forfeit my bond.'

Five minutes later, they crossed the moat and rode under the arch of the gate into the courtyard and drew up at the door of Waterlea Manor. The house, with its mullioned windows and tiled roof, had been built on the foundations of an abbey given to Lord Carthorne's ancestor at the time of the Dissolution. He had ordered the abbey to be torn down and rebuilt as a manor house, using the materials of the original edifice. A small chapel and the great hall, used by the monks for dining, had been left unchanged. As befitting the status of the owner, the rooms were huge and draughty and needed prodigious amounts of peat and sea-coal to warm them, but the house had an atmosphere of grandeur, a feeling of stability, of permanence, as if the comings and goings of the mortals who inhabited it through the centuries had left it untouched.

It had been home to Alys all her life and since her mother's death she had been its mistress, but she often thought of the monks who had once walked its cloisters and slept in the row of small cells at the back of the building which were now used as storerooms.

London, Cambridge, Garret Hartswood and Jan Van Hildt were all forgotten as Alys jumped down and hurried into the house, delighted to be home again. A torch was taken round to the wall brackets and candlesticks, fires lit in all the rooms and the kitchen embers stirred back into life to provide the travellers with something hot to eat. Alys roamed the great hall, inspecting the tapestries, the long oak table, which was still gleaming from the beeswax polishing it had had, the sideboard with its stacks of plates and dishes, the matching aumbry, his lordship's armchair and its cushion, the stools and fire irons. 'Oh, it's so good to be home!' she said. 'And nothing has changed; there isn't a stool or a hanging out of place.'

'Did you expect there would be?' Prue asked.

It was then Alys realised she had been wrong about Garret occupying the house. When she enquired, she was told that he had been home to Eagleholm once or twice in the last two months, but had not come to the manor. Eagleholm, which Garret had inherited on his father's death, stood on the far edge of the village, not more than two miles away. Its builders had made use of Peterborough bricks and the discarded remainder of the abbey's stone, and the house was an ivy-covered mixture of both. It was not as large as the manor, but was, nevertheless, a substantial residence. From the upper rooms of the manor its tiled roof could easily be picked out from the small flint and clunch cottages with their thatched roofs which made up the remainder of the village.

'Why should he?' Prue said. 'There was no one here to visit, was there? And by all accounts he has been kept very busy by Captain Cromwell.'

'They could have been here and razed it to the ground.'

'To what purpose? If, as you say, he wants Waterlea Manor for himself, he is hardly likely to ruin it, is he? No, my lady, while he has an interest here, the house is safe, never forget that.'

Alys, alerted by her tone, looked up sharply. 'What do you mean?'

'Simply that you should think carefully

before you do anything to anger him. While he has his heart set on marrying you, we are safe: you, your father, the servants, even Benedick. You have their lives in your hands.'

'And if the King's men come? Will that still be so?'

'*If* they come, which I beg leave to doubt, then Lord Carthorne's loyalty to the King will protect us.'

'And we might fall between two stools,' Alys said gloomily, 'and both will destroy us.'

'It is unlike you to be in low spirits, my lady. Come, cheer up, tomorrow you will be able to go for a ride on a good horse. I am told they were all well hidden when the commissary officers came looking for them.'

Alys, never dispirited for long, laughed aloud and jumped into bed. 'Goodnight, dear Prue. Wake me early, because I want to ride while the dew is still on the grass.'

*   *   *

Alys, riding out while the sun was still only just above the distant horizon, colouring the wide expanse of sky in shades of pink, forgot about her low spirits of the previous day. The path was narrow, but clearly defined, and she walked her horse along it, sniffing like a dog at the scent of the morning air and filling her lungs with it. The pastures either side of her were bright with gossamer; clumps of reeds stood unmoving in the still air, their stems criss-crossed with dew-laden spiders' webs. It was good to be home; the war seemed a long way off and although, in one way, she would have liked to be riding with Benedick, in another she was glad of the solitude, the absence of soldiery; particularly, she told herself, Garret Hartswood.

But the tall cavalry officer would not be banished from her thoughts and she found herself weighing up the arguments Prue had used in favour of the marriage; they were unanswerable. If, as Prue had said, the safety and happiness of all those she held dear depended on it, she had no choice but to marry him. Her only hope of a reprieve would be if the King were victorious. Even then, she decided, she would not want the captain punished by death; it would be enough to exile him in disgrace.

Her thoughts ran on as her horse skirted the flooded fields. She noted that the villagers' own strips were also under water and the sails of the water-lifting engines at the dyke edges were slowly turning, scooping up the flood water and tipping it into the drainage channels. She smiled, remembering the trouble that these mills had caused between neighbours when they had first been introduced. The courts of the Commissioners of Sewers, who looked after the maintenance of the banks and dykes, had been kept busy with complaints that one man had dried out his land at the expense of another. But they had been minor matters compared with the universal drainage which had been causing so much trouble of late; *they* were disputes among local people and had nothing to do with foreigners.

She passed Jan Van Hildt's house, isolated by flood water, and rode down through the village with its row of cottages strung out along the road edge like beads on a necklace, until she reached a broad expanse of green in front of the church. Here she pulled up, because there was a troop of pikemen and musketeers drilling across it and blocking the way. The war had come to Waterlea.

She had been watching them for five minutes when their sergeant spotted her, but, instead of speaking to her, he went into the church, to emerge a minute later accompanied by Garret. If he was surprised to see her, he did not show it as he strode over to her.

'Good-day, my lady,' he said, taking her bridle. 'When did you arrive home?'

'Last night. And if you are going to say we should have stayed in Cambridge, you may save your breath. The Carthornes are not ones to hide themselves away when danger threatens. We came home to be with our people.'

'Very commendable, if unwise,' he said. 'But, as you see, the men have taken to arms in the defence of their homes.'

She watched him stroke her horse's neck; it was almost a caress and she found herself watching his brown hands and the thought came unbidden into her mind that he loved horses and he could be gentle with things he loved. Would he be gentle with her if he loved her? She pushed the traitorous thought from her. 'Did they do it willingly, and did they have any choice about which side they fought on?'

'They will fight with a will if it becomes necessary,' he said. 'And I advise you, my lady, not to try and interfere.'

'I?' she queried, pretending innocence. 'How can I, a mere woman, interfere in the raising of an army? I am simply riding out for the exercise. Would you deny me that?'

'No, my lady, ride while you can. Were you going anywhere in particular?'

'No. Why do you ask?' she countered, deciding that the reason her heart was beating so furiously was because she had not been riding for weeks and the unaccustomed exercise was making her breathless.

'You were not coming to see me?'

He was smiling up at her, teasing her into a sharp retort and, indeed, there was one on her lips, when she remembered Prue's advice and changed her mind. Softly, she told herself, softly now. Aloud she said, 'Captain Hartswood, I had no idea you were here, so I cannot, with honesty, say I was coming to see you, but if you wish me to visit you, then I will do so—another day.'

'Alas, I regret that day may be some time off,' he said, and it was almost as if he meant it. 'I ride to join Cromwell after I have seen to these minor local affairs.'

'Local affairs?'

'You cannot be unaware that the summer fields are flooded.'

'What has that to do with the army, Captain?'

'The Lords have required the enforcement of the law and the execution of the Riot Act if necessary. The sluice gates are to be opened again to allow the land to drain and anyone who tries to stop the repair of the banks and dykes is to be arrested. I have been appointed deputy sheriff to carry out the Lords' instructions and these men are here to see there is no trouble.'

'Does my father know of this?'

'He was absent from home and something had to be done.'

'He was absent from home because you took us to Cambridge and advised us to stay there,' she snapped. 'You did it for your own ends! You did it to gain power over these people. You think you can set these men against their own neighbours but, be sure, you will not succeed.' She was so angry she forgot all about her intention to go softly. 'My father is the justice here and he is the one to enforce the law, not you, and he does it with the help of the local constable. You take too much upon yourself.'

'I have my orders and cannot disobey.'

'We will see about that.' She tugged the reins out of his hand and dug her heel into her horse's flank. 'I bid you good-day, Captain.'

She did not pull up until she came within sight of the manor, and then she stopped because a gleaming black coach was standing at the front door with an elegantly clad postilion waiting beside the lead horse. 'Jan Van Hildt,' she murmured aloud. 'He wasted no time.'

She rode round to the stables, dismounted, and left the horse for one of the grooms to attend to, before going into the house. She could hear Van Hildt's loud, complaining voice as soon as she entered.

'You are a justice, my lord, and it is your duty to punish de offenders, and yet dey hide behind your coat-tails, knowing you vill not turn to see vot goes on behind your back.'

'I have been away from home, Master Van Hildt,' his lordship said. 'And the coat-tails have not been here to hide behind, and by accounts I have received you have not been idle in my absence but have had several men put into gaol.'

'My husband was within his rights.' This was a woman's voice and Alys guessed the

Dutchman had brought his wife with him. 'With the justices absent and Sir Garret and his troops away at the war, there was no one to call on for help; you could not expect him to stand by and allow it to happen.'

'And what did happen?' Lord Carthorne asked.

'Why, the common rabble opened the sluice gates,' Lettice Van Hildt said. She had since her marriage taken it upon herself to speak on her husband's behalf, assuming his English was not up to the task, although whenever Alys had spoken to him he had expressed himself perfectly well. 'And when our men tried to stop them they held them off with weapons and said they were doing it on the orders of the Lincoln Committee. When all was flooded, they shut the gates to hold the water on the land. It has ruined our growing crops and the fodder in the barn. Are we to stand by and allow ourselves to be thus threatened?'

'Weapons?' enquired Lord Carthorne mildly. 'Where did they find weapons?'

'I mean mattocks and peat spades and suchlike, handy enough weapons in the hands of rioters.'

'They are the tools of their trade,' her father said.

'Trade! They have no trade, being dissolute, idle, and barbaric. They prefer to live in squalor, half sunk in disease-ridden

76

water, rather than work gainfully on dry land.'

'They are free men,' his lordship said. 'You cannot make slaves of them.'

'You cannot make civilised men of dem eider,' Jan Van Hildt said flatly. 'I haf appealed to the deputy shcriff and he haf undertaken to read a proclamation outside de church at Waterlea this day forbidding any furder interference vid de drainage vorks. He haf also sent soldiers to votch over de re-opening of de gates.'

'Deputy sheriff? I know of no such person. Who is he and where does he come from?'

'Captain Sir Garret Hartswood has been appointed in your absence, my lord,' Lettice put in. 'You would do well to associate yourself with the steps being taken to restore my husband's land to him.'

'Do not tell me what I should and should not do,' his lordship said, doing his best to conceal his surprise at this news. 'I do what I consider to be right.'

'And that, I suppose, is why you have been in conflict with your peers, my lord. We know that you have been required by the Privy Council to uphold the law . . .'

'And that I shall do, without any prompting from you, Mistress Van Hildt, but I cannot prosecute nameless faces. When I have proof of a man's guilt, then I will act.'

'Then I will give you a name. I give you Ingram Martin and, as for proof, we have the sworn statement of two witnesses who are prepared to testify that he incited the commoners to open the gates and to resist attempts to stop them, and that is all the law requires.'

Lord Carthorne looked up as Alys entered, smiling as if relieved by the interruption. 'Ah, you have met my daughter?'

Alys came forward and bowed her head towards the Dutchman. 'Good day, Master Van Hildt.' She turned towards his wife, whom she had only previously seen at a distance, and was surprised to find that she was beautiful. Much younger than her middle-aged husband, she had straight black hair tied into a knot at the nape of her neck, a style which on anyone else might have seemed severe, but which on Lettice Van Hildt emphasised her even features and perfect complexion. She had finely arched brows and green eyes which reminded Alys of a cat's: perfectly still, but watchful.

'My vife,' Jan Van Hildt said.

Alys bowed and smiled and received an acknowledgement which was something less than cordial, but, refusing to be put off, she spoke cheerfully. 'Will you take some wine, Mistress Van Hildt?'

'Thank you, but no. We were on our way to Grantham but, seeing his lordship's flag flying, we decided to call and tell him what had been happening in his absence.'

'Oh, and what has been happening?' Alys asked, feigning innocence.

'It is not someding to concern de ladies,' Jan Van Hildt said, ignoring the fact that his wife had been playing her full part in the conversation until Alys's arrival. Alys had heard that Lettice wore the breeches in the Van Hildt household and could not be silenced, certainly not by her husband.

'When the men are away from home, as many of them are now, then the women have to do the men's work as well as their own,' Alys said. 'They need to know what goes on.'

'That does not apply to you, because your father is here,' Lettice said. 'And I am needed because my husband does not always understand the language.'

'What is good for you is also good for me,' Alys said. She turned in surprise as Lettice began to laugh. It was an empty sound, without humour. 'Did I say something amusing?'

'No, oh, no,' Lettice said, wiping tears from her eyes. 'It was just the thought of something we have in common—pay me no heed.'

'Please share the jest, that we may all laugh,' Lord Carthorne said. 'There is little enough to amuse us these days.'

'Oh, no, my lord,' Lettice said. 'It is something that only another woman would understand.'

'Den, be silent or take your vimmen's prate

somevere else.' Van Hildt turned back to Lord Carthorne. 'My lord, I called vom friendship to you and your family, I haf no vish to see you brought down to de level of de commoners—'

'I will not be threatened, Master Van Hildt.' Lord Carthorne's voice was clipped with suppressed anger. 'Given proof, I will punish anyone who breaks the law. And I will certainly go to the reading of the proclamation.'

'Good. Ve vill see you dere.' The Dutchman took his wife by the arm, bade everyone good-day and left the house. They could hear him arguing with her as they climbed into the coach and were driven off.

'My life,' his lordship said, smiling broadly, 'what a spitting cat she is! I am glad I am not married to her.'

'Father, I saw Sir Garret while I was out riding,' Alys said, 'and what Master Van Hildt says is true. He has been made deputy sheriff and I saw him drilling soldiers ready to put down the villagers. We ought to warn Ingram Martin.'

'I can hardly do that, child. It would be playing into the Dutchman's hands.'

Alys conceded that he was right, but that did not mean she could not do something herself. As soon as he was occupied elsewhere, she ran out to the stables and saddled her mare again, ignoring the protests

80

of the groom who had only just finished rubbing her down.

A trap had been set for the fen men and she could not let them walk into it. They would not understand why his lordship was suddenly becoming ruthless, why the blind eye he had turned up to now had suddenly begun to see.

She rode through the village, turned the mare away from the higher ground and set off towards the fen, where the reeds swayed like the tide of the sea. But the fen was not all water; it was criss-crossed by well-worn paths and once she was among the reeds she had to follow them or be swallowed in a quagmire of mud. The soft clop of the horses' hooves, cutting into the bright green turf, revealed a rich black soil—the most fertile in the whole of England, some said. Here, at the very end of the path, lived Ingram Martin and his wife, Hannah.

A dog barked and a pair of ducks suddenly took to wing, rising majestically into the clear air. She heard a shot and the cock plummeted down. She rounded a bend, marked by a clump of willows flanked by waist-high reeds, and came face to face with Ingram Martin, who had a smoking fowling piece in his hands.

He was about forty years old, thick-set and dour, with a thatch of dark, tangled hair and brown eyes which showed no sign of surprise at seeing the daughter of the lord of the manor riding out alone. 'Good day to ye, Lady

Alys,' he said, bending to take the bird from the dog's mouth. 'You're home again, then?'

'Yes, and glad of it, though unhappy to see the devastation. I came to speak to you.'

'And that you are doing.'

'About the drainage works.'

'I have nothing to say about those that a lady should hear.'

She laughed. 'Then I will do the talking.'

'It's not a fittin' subject for a woman.'

'Does Hannah agree with you?'

'Hannah is my wife,' he said, as if that answered her question, as to his way of thinking it did. 'But come and speak to her if you will.' Without waiting for her reply, he turned and walked towards the tiny cottage, whose foundations had sunk on one side so that it looked as though a giant hand had tried to tip it into the fen, and it hung precariously balanced on the bank. Before it stretched a wide expanse of mere water, too deep even for stilt walkers and too treacherous for horses. One of Ingram's ways of earning a living was by punting travellers across to where the path continued on the other side. No one needed the ferry in the winter when even the paths were under water, but in summer his services were in constant demand; crossing Waterlea Mere by ferry could cut ten miles off the journey to the next village. Beyond that was Holland Fen and Lord Lindsey's undertakings and, still further east, more fen and then the sea. But there were also great tracts where no man lived, where only the most adventurous fowler would go, where the water covered deep pits and the way was unmarked, and where bog suddenly replaced water and could ground a craft out of sight or sound of help. Ingram was one of the few people who knew these places and he was wise enough to avoid them.

Inside his home, it was warm and cheerful; a kettle sang on the fire and the table was laid with pewter cups and wooden bowls. Hannah Martin, a year or two younger than her husband but already the mother of two grown sons, turned as they entered and, seeing Alys, tilted her head down in a gesture which did duty for a curtsy. To the fen folk, all men and women were equal.

'Lady Alys wants to talk about the drainage,' Ingram told his wife. 'Best perhaps she talks to you, or I might be more outspoken than I should be.'

'I came to warn you,' Alys said, addressing them both. 'My father has been charged with neglecting his duty and not punishing those who spoil the drainage undertakings. He must carry out the orders of the Privy Council and punish offenders.'

'What is this to do with us?' Ingram asked, hanging the duck on a hook on the wall out of reach of dog and cats. 'We live alone out here on the fen's edge; we know nothing of drainage.'

'No, I knew you would not,' Alys said, humouring him. 'But Jan Van Hildt has witnesses ready to swear you were the ringleader and if you show your face you will be arrested and my father will not be able to prevent it. He has been forced into promising to bring law-breakers to book.'

'The law-breakers are those who take what does not belong to them,' he said. 'Land, fish or fowl.'

'It would be better to go to law than try and take back the land by force,' Alys went on.

'There is no law in these times, my lady,' he said. 'The King says one thing, Parliament another, and the fen man is left without redress. If we complain we are denied the right to a remedy in the courts by those who would not have us win, and if we fight we are punished.'

'I know, and I am sorry, but breaking down the banks and opening the sluices will only make matters worse.'

'It was lack of repair which made the banks crumble,' he said, with some justification. Since the conflict began between King and Parliament, and with so many local workers joining or being pressed into military service, there had been a shortage of labour for maintenance. Dutch and French workers had been called in to help, but were ill-received by the local populace and few stayed long.

'They were being repaired and strengthened when we left for London,' she said. 'And I know my father hoped that would be the end of the trouble, but now we see the floods are worse than before. Someone waited until he was gone to deal another blow.'

'And you think that someone was me? Why should we rise up, when we know Sir Garret will uphold our claim just as soon as Parliament wins the war?'

'Captain Hartswood has been instructed to put down any trouble when the sluice gates are reopened and he has a troop of militia to support him. You are wrong to put your faith in him.'

'He must obey his orders, just as your father must obey his, and we must all obey our consciences.'

'Sir Garret would not do anything to harm us,' Hannah said. 'He understands and he will find a way.'

'You are for Parliament?' Alys asked.

'We are for ourselves,' Ingram said, confirming her father's view that they took sides only so long as it furthered their own interests. 'Lady Alys, you must look elsewhere for your troublemakers.'

'I am not looking for anyone,' she said sharply. 'I came as a friend to warn you, but if you do not choose to listen, then so be it. I bid you good-day.'

He did not answer and she left to return to

her horse. She had the reins in her hand, but had not mounted, when Hannah came from the house towards her.

'My lady!' Alys paused and turned towards her. 'Pay no heed to him, my lady—he don' seem to be able to tell friend from foe these days. We are grateful for the warning and I will try and see that he heeds it.'

'I understand,' Alys said, putting her hand on the woman's arm. 'And so does my father, but he has to do the bidding of the Privy Council, even though it causes him grief. He has to be there when the proclamation is read and the gates shut. It would be better if your husband stayed away. It would be better if he could not be found for a few days.'

She remounted and set off for home, taking the road which went past the Van Hildts' house. She doubted if Ingram Martin would heed her warning, and she dreaded to think what might happen to his wife if he were sent to prison. If only her father could regain the upper hand, he would make sure the punishment was a light one.

She was so engrossed that she did not see Lettice Van Hildt dismoun'ting from a horse at her gate until she was almost upon her.

'Riding again so soon, my lady?' she enquired. 'I feel for that poor animal.'

'The mare is strong,' Alys said, reining in because her way was blocked.

'Then I doubt you will have her much
86

longer; Sir Garret is taking all the horses he can find. Cromwell is a Colonel now; he has been ordered to secure Lincolnshire for Parliament and he does his work thoroughly. Your father is a Royalist and his son serves the King. Are you not afraid?'

'Afraid of whom?'

'Captain Garret Hartswood. He has only to give the order and your whole family will be arrested.'

'And you expect him to give the order?'

'I could persuade him it is his duty.' The woman's green eyes regarded her maliciously. 'Especially if you protected the rioters, and that is what you intend to do, is it not? I watched you ride into the fen and you did not go there for your health.'

'I often ride alone—anyone in the village will tell you that.'

'It is a habit I would not continue, if I were you. Garret does not easily forgive; cross him—or me—and you will live to rue the day.'

Alys did not answer, but put her horse up on to the bank beside the road and went along it a few yards before returning to the hard surface. She did not look back.

'She is jealous,' Prue said, when Alys told her of the encounter. 'It's no secret Sir Garret used to see a great deal of her—before she married the Dutchman, that is.'

Alys laughed. 'So that's what she meant when she said we had something in common. I

87

would love to tell her how wrong she is. She is welcome to Captain Hartswood.'

'You lie, my lady,' Prue whispered.

'And one day you will go too far,' Alys answered. 'Go and help Anne in the kitchen; I don't want to see you again today.'

Not in the least cowed, Prue left to obey; she knew her mistress better than the young lady did herself. And one day soon, Alys would have to admit she had been wrong about the captain.

CHAPTER FOUR

Garret did not like the task he had been given any more than Alys did, but Jan Van Hildt was a very influential man and his complaints to the Lincolnshire Committee and the Commissioners of Sewers could not be ignored. Even when troops were needed to fight the war, some must be diverted to quell what could become a riot if it were allowed to go on, and the nearest militia was the local trained band, which he had himself been recruiting. He did not need Alys to remind him that he would be setting men against their near neighbours if there were trouble, and he sincerely hoped Ingram Martin would do nothing to stop the gates being closed.

Another worry was the fact that Lord

Carthorne would see his appointment as deputy sheriff as a direct slur on his own ability to put down trouble. Coming so soon after his appearance before the Privy Council, this would humiliate him before his own people. He wished fervently that the Carthornes had remained in Cambridge until it was all over. He could do nothing about his orders, but he could go and see his lordship and try to set matters to rights.

As soon as he was free, he rode to the manor, only to find that he was not Lord Carthorne's only visitor. His lordship was talking to the local constable, who had the unenviable task of assessing the village property owners and tenants for their taxes— a fifth of their annual income and a twentieth of the value of their property. Lord Carthorne had made a strenuous appeal against his assessment and was arguing heatedly with the constable, with whom he was normally on the best of terms.

'I am glad you have come, Captain Hartswood,' he said, as if welcoming the interruption. 'Perhaps you can confirm what I have been telling the constable.' Then to Alys, 'Pour the captain a glass of ale, my dear.'

Alys did as she was bid, but she could not bring herself to answer Garret's smile with one of her own. It was all very well for him; the taxes her father paid helped to keep him and his men in food, clothes and quarters. She would hardly expect him to back her father against the constable.

'I have provided horses and free quarter and three haywains of fodder,' Lord Carthorne said. 'The constable refuses to take the value of that from my taxes.'

'My lord, I cannot.' The constable looked pained. 'You know it is not in my power to do that.'

'And do not forget that I have duties to perform as a justice. I need relief for that.'

'My lord,' the man said, fidgeting uncomfortably, 'that is all the more reason you should not be favoured more than anyone else. If the lord of the manor will not pay his taxes '

'It is not a question of *will* not,' his lordship said. 'I cannot pay what I do not have. Remember I had to give a bond to the Lords of two thousand.'

'Yes, my lord, but that has nothing to do with it.'

'And speaking of that,' Lord Carthorne went on, ignoring the interruption, 'what have you done about arresting Ingram Martin and the other troublemakers?'

'Ingram Martin has hidden himself in the fens and, without help, I cannot winkle him out, but as to the others, most of them have taken up arms with Sir Garret, and I cannot arrest them.'

Lord Carthorne turned to Garret. 'Is this

90

so?'

'Yes, my lord. And those that are left will give you no trouble after the reading of the proclamation. That is why I have come to see you, to explain. In your absence, I have been appointed deputy sheriff.'

'So my daughter tells me.'

'It was none of my seeking, I assure you, but there was no one else and Master Van Hildt has a right to protection.'

'And what about the villagers' rights?' Alys demanded, unable to keep silent. 'Have they no redress?'

'They do not help themselves by breaking the law,' he said, then, turning from Alys to Lord Carthorne, went on, 'I have arranged a settlement, which I think is fair to both sides, and, when the villagers gather this afternoon, I shall put it to them.'

'Why do you interest yourself in the affair?' Alys demanded. 'Could it be that you are in the pocket of Mistress Van Hildt?'

'Alys, be silent!' her father commanded. 'Does it matter who arranges the settlement, as long as it brings peace to the village?'

'How can you talk of peace?' the constable said, while Alys fumed. 'Had you forgot we are at war?'

'No, I had not forgotten, but we should not be fighting one with another in this small village.' His lordship turned back to Garret. 'What is this settlement?'

Garret smiled. 'The villagers are to be permitted to proceed to a legal trial of their title to the land, and in the meantime Master Van Hildt and his tenants will pay rent to the Lincoln Committee which will hold it, pending a final settlement. In return, Master Van Hildt is to be allowed to repair the banks and fences without let or hindrance, and to reap his crops.'

'And do you think the villagers will agree to that?' his lordship asked. 'They have little faith in legal proceedings.'

'Master Van Hildt has agreed to relinquish the land to the village if he has not secured a legal judgment or ordinance of Parliament come Michaelmas next year.'

This was something new, and even Alys was forced to concede it might persuade the villagers to agree. 'Will he secure such a judgment, think you?'

Garret smiled. 'You know how long court proceedings take, even at the best of times, and when there is war, and so many other cases to be heard, Master Van Hildt might find the delay is such he cannot meet the conditions. And as for an ordinance, do you not think Parliament has enough to do without bothering about the problems of one small village?'

'Very clever,' Alys said. 'If it works.'

'Master Van Hildt has entered into a bond and the villagers have been authorised to seize the land if he refuses to pay it.'

'Speaking of the Committee,' the constable said, trying to bring the conversation back to the subject which had brought him to the Manor. 'About the taxes . . .'

'Come back when you have thought again,' his lordship said. 'I have already paid all I can afford, so do not come asking me for more. Go and tell your masters that and see what they say.'

'Thc manor will be sequestered; you know that, my lord, especially as your loyalties are well known.' The constable turned towards Garret for support, but Garret was looking at Alys. 'I beg you to pay at least something towards the upkeep of the army. It will cost you far more in fines to keep your property intact.'

'My lord,' Garret said, dragging his attention back to the matter in hand, 'the constable is right. Please agree to pay something. Half perhaps?'

'I am not empowered to accept that,' the constable said, equally stubbornly.

'Then go away and get the agreement of someone who is,' Alys said sharply. 'My father is worn out by everyone—soldiers, commoners, the Committee, Privy Council—all making demands on him. His purse is far from bottomless. Come back when you have more favourable terms.' She called to their steward, who was waiting on the other side of

93

the screen. 'John, please show the constable out.'

He went reluctantly, knowing he would be in trouble for his failure, but there was no gainsaying Lady Alys, when she had the bit between her teeth.

When he had gone, Garret turned to leave, but Lord Carthorne detained him. 'You will do what you can for us?'

'I will, my lord, though it may be little enough.'

'And you stand by the marriage contract?'

There was a long pause during which Alys held her breath and dared not look at Garret.

'Is it still your wish?' Garret spoke at last, but he was asking Lord Carthorne, not Alys.

'Mine?' queried his lordship. 'Dear man, of course it is. And it was your father's wish too, spoken on his death-bed. And you agreed.'

'I did.' The words were clipped and unemotional.

Alys was incensed enough to turn and face the man who had uttered them. His expression was stiff, his jaw rigid. 'Your father could not have foreseen that we would be on opposite sides in this war—'

'War, war, war,' his lordship interrupted her. 'I am tired of hearing about it. I want to see you married before I join my Maker and sooner rather than later because my days are numbered . . .'

'Father, you must not talk like that. You are

94

not old or sick.'

'No, but I am tired, so very, very tired. I have no strength to deal with the running of the estate, nor the dispensing of justice, nor even the household accounts. It is all too much.'

'What has this to do with a marriage contract made five years ago?' she asked, while Garret looked silently on.

'I will die happy if I know you are provided for and, if Sir Garret can look after my business affairs until Benedick returns, then perhaps the Carthorne family will have a place in the new order of things.'

'In other words, we will lose the manor if I do not fall in line, like an impressed soldier?'

Both men were silent and she felt the anger rise in her throat like bile, but her father was looking at her with a plea in his eyes which silenced any thought she had of defying him. He took her hand in one of his own and reached out with the other towards Garret.

'Give me your hand on it.' As the young man obeyed, he joined the two hands and held them in both his own. 'Forget the war, forget what divides us and think only of what unites us; the friendship of our two families, our common desire to better the lot of the people of Waterlea. And a love of justice. Keep Waterlea Manor safe for Benedick to come home to.'

'And will it?' she asked, conscious of the

warmth of Garret's hand and the coldness of her father's. 'Will it keep the manor safe for him if I marry the captain?'

Her question had been addressed to her father, but it was Garret who answered. 'The subject did not arise when we talked of the marriage contract and for me it is not part of the agreement.'

'No,' she snapped. 'Because you will have it either way, won't you? How does it feel to have everything you wish for simply by taking it? Does it make the possession of it all the sweeter?'

'Are you speaking of the manor or yourself?'

'Either. Both.'

Lord Carthorne tugged at their hands. 'We have been through all this before, Alys. I am tired and I do not want to hear any more. You will obey me and accept that what has been arranged for you is for your own good.'

She hung her head, defeated, and Garret smiled slowly. 'I do not wish to force a marriage on your daughter if it is not agreeable to her,' he said.

'No more. I have spoken my last word on the subject.' His lordship dropped their hands and leaned back in his chair.

'I have to rejoin my regiment at once,' Garret said. 'My fate is in the hands of God, but if it pleases Him to spare me, we can be married when I return.'

Alys could not stop herself making one last effort to annoy him, simply because she knew she was beaten. 'I shall insist on a proper ceremony,' she said. 'I won't make do with any Puritan mockery of a wedding, and I shall dress as befits the daughter of a lord of the realm.'

He bowed and lifted the back of her hand to his lips.

'Kiss her properly, man!' Lord Carthorne commanded. 'Are you a soldier or some mincing courtier leading her in a dance? Go on, take her in your arms.'

Alys looked from Garret to her father and back to Garret, who shrugged and smiled, as if to say, 'We had better humour him', before drawing her towards him and, taking her chin in his hand, tilting her face up to his. She tried to remain wooden, to let him see that she acquiesced only to please her father and not because she wanted his kisses, but when his lips met hers she found herself going limp in his arms and then a fire raged through her as he pressed his body against hers. She lost sight of time and place and forgot her father, forgot everything but her own traitorous desire.

'Until we meet again, my lady.' There was a promise in his voice, a promise of more sensuous things than a kiss, and she trembled at the thought of it. But then she pulled herself together. He did not really want to marry her; she had proved herself his enemy.

And why was her father so insistent? She did not really believe the fate of the manor rested on it.

She smiled at him, a smile meant to convey that, although she had agreed, she would not make life easy for him. A rebel she was, a rebel she would remain. 'I will make the arrangements,' she said. 'Tell me, when do you expect to return?'

'That is for others to say. I will try and send you warning of my coming.' He inclined his head to his lordship and strode quickly to the door. His going left an empty space in the room and an empty space deep inside Alys which she would not acknowledge.

*   *   *

It was obvious that the villagers had been warned. Not a single one attended the reading of the proclamation, except the trained band, and there were no dissenters to the shutting of the gates. If Jan Van Hildt had been hoping for arrests he was disappointed. Alys was thankful that Ingram Martin had heeded her warning and for a few weeks, while the flood receded, there was peace in Waterlea, if nowhere else.

As the summer progressed, there was news of battles being fought all over the country, and Parliament was not having it all its own way. In June, John Hampden, one of their most loved and respected leaders, was mortally wounded; Lord Fairfax was defeated at Adwalton Moor; and in July the Royalists inflicted a crushing defeat at Roundway Down in the west country. That same day a great train of arms and ammunition bound from the north to the King in Oxford managed to get through unimpeded. In Yorkshire, only Hull held out for Parliament.

But the hated Roundheads would not give in easily and Oliver Cromwell was more determined than most. His orders had been to secure Lincolnshire for Parliament and that he intended to do. At Waterlea, the villagers gathered round every itinerant pedlar, every passing traveller, to hear the latest news, wondering how long it would be before they were hurled, willy-nilly, into the thick of the fighting. Those villagers who could use them were given muskets and ammunition, and the women, including Alys, began setting by great stores of food and provisions.

They had almost completed making their arrangements at the manor when Garret arrived, accompanied by Lieutenant Aldous Stone and a troop of horsemen. 'I am sorry, my lord, but we need quarters,' he told Lord Carthorne. 'I must make use of your stables and any spare rooms you may have. Newcastle is already at the county border—he must be prevented from marching south to join the King. If we cannot hold him back at

Gainsborough, he will be here in two or three days at the most.'

'So soon?' queried Alys, coming into the hall at that moment, carrying a basket which she had filled with yellow flag and sprigs of sweet willow gathered from the fen.

He turned towards her and smiled. She did not want him to smile at her; it reminded her of his last kiss and made it difficult for her to hate him, even though she persuaded herself he smiled out of courtesy and not because he was glad to see her.

'Yes, my lady, and because Waterlea Manor is the only house of any size hereabouts and can be easily defended, we must make what plans we can to defend it.'

'We have already done what we could,' his lordship said. 'We have gathered in provisions and cleared the moat so that the water runs free and deep, and the drawbridge pulleys have been greased and run easily.' He smiled suddenly. 'I cannot remember when we last hauled that up.'

'And have you guns?'

'A few fowling pieces and I have a pistol.'

'Good. Keep them well-primed.'

'And who are we to be aiming at?' Alys asked sharply.

He turned towards her and his brown eyes looked at her in a way which made her tremble. He would stand no nonsense from her but, perverse as always, she could not stop herself from goading him.

'You, my lady,' he said, 'will aim at no one except to preserve your own life. Others will come to defend the manor.'

'More of you! Are we that important?'

'In the scheme of things none of us is important,' he said flatly. 'We do our duty for the greater good of all.'

'How can you say it is your duty to fire on your fellow countrymen? How can it be right to do battle against your King? Would you kill your own brother were he on the other side?'

'Had I a brother, an' he were so misguided as to choose the wrong side, yes.'

'I have a brother,' she said quietly.

His voice softened. 'Yes, my lady, I know. I pray he is many miles away at this moment.'

He did not wish it any more than she did, even though they had not heard from Benedick since he had left Cambridge. She watched, with mounting horror, as a small cannon, called a saker, was brought on a cart, dragged into the courtyard and manhandled to an upper room, where it was set up at a window with its muzzle pointing northwards. Ammunition was piled beside it and powder and tinder set near at hand. A larger demi-cannon was put in the yard facing the drawbridge. Aldous was sent to scour the countryside for horses in any condition as long as they could stand, and to fetch in fodder and oats, saddles, bridles and horseshoes. His instructions were to pay for what he took and, when the money ran out, to offer promissory notes.

The commoners had little to give or sell, but Jan Van Hildt was obliged to surrender all but one of his working horses and his wife's riding mount, which raised a storm of protest from Lettice. In a fury, she arrived on foot at the manor to see Garret. He was overseeing the work of the men in the courtyard and their voices carried clearly to Alys where she sat at the open window of her chamber, looking out across the summer landscape.

'The animal will be no use to you,' she told him. 'It is a lady's mount and unused to a heavy saddle; you'll break his back if you set an armoured man on him.'

'There are other tasks for horses beside carrying soldiers, Lettice.' His use of her given name confirmed the story that they knew each other well.

'You'll never make him pull a cart! Oh, my poor Diamond! How can you be so cruel? Remember how we used to go riding together and you used to say he could almost walk under the belly of your great Bruno? And yet he carried me well and he is fast. But he is also skittish, not a good cavalry horse at all.'

'He is a sturdy little animal,' he said. 'And if it makes you feel better, I will try and keep him with me and my groom shall look after him.'

'And I may have him back when you have finished with him?'

'If he survives—if we all survive.'

'Oh, Garret,' she cried. 'Don't speak of not surviving—I cannot bear the thought of never seeing you again, it would break my heart.'

His voice was low as he answered her and Alys did not hear what he said. But she did not care, she told herself. He meant no more to her than a buzzing gnat who had constantly to be brushed away. She had more important things to think about at that moment. Who, for instance, was that lone rider she could see away in the distance?

Seen from the height of her first-floor window, the landscape was not as flat as it appeared at ground level. The manor was set on a slight rise which sloped down to the village, and that was higher than the surrounding fen. Its jumble of thatched roofs was dominated by Garret's house and the church. Further on, she was able to pick out other landmarks: a group of alder denoting land a little higher than the surrounding fen, the shining water of the mere and islets where the water birds nested, a cottage built atop a bank, a row of willows along the line of a dyke. But they did not concern her now because her whole attention was concentrated on the horse on the path leading from Ingram Martin's cottage. The rider must have crossed on the ferry from Heronlea, the next village to the north.

North! Was he the forerunner of the Royalist army they were expecting? The white horse was walking very slowly and its rider was half slumped over its neck, so that it was impossible to see what he was wearing. If only she could see more clearly!

Garret, who had walked to the stables with Lettice, had now returned to the courtyard below her window. 'Clear that dung up!' he shouted to one of the men. 'His lordship's courtyard is not a stable yard. And move that fire away from the house, the smoke is drifting in at the windows.' He glanced up and saw her. 'Good-day, my lady,' he called. He was smiling and his voice was cheerful, as if his meeting with Lettice had lifted his spirits. 'What see you?'

'Nothing,' she said, wondering why she lied. 'All is quiet.'

As soon as he had turned to other things, she jumped up and ran down to the hall, where his perspective glass lay on a table near the door. Picking it up, she returned to her window and trained it on the solitary figure.

The rider was clearer now and was obviously injured. It was impossible to make out his features because his red-gold hair was long and tumbled over his face. Judging from the blue doublet, over which he wore a breastplate, his darker blue breeches and the lace on his boot hose, he was not a

Roundhead. Alys gasped when he appeared to slip sideways, but he hauled himself upright with an effort and continued towards the manor. Perhaps he had brought news of Benedick. It meant death or imprisonment if he rode in openly; she had to stop him.

With thumping heart, she lowered the glass and looked down into the courtyard. Troopers were hurrying hither and thither, obeying Garret's orders, while the servants attempted to do their usual daily tasks around them. Her father was sitting on a bench talking to his steward, trying to pretend that the activity around him did not exist. She saw Prue go across to the barn and speak to one of the farm workers.

She picked up her most voluminous cloak, ran down the stairs and replaced the perspective glass on the table, then she shook out her skirt and made herself walk slowly out into the sunshine and cross the yard to where Garret stood talking to his lieutenant.

'Captain Hartswood,' she said, hoping he would not notice how flushed and breathless she was. 'You will be taking my mare, I suppose?'

'Yes, my lady, I fear I must.'

'Today?'

'I wait for orders.'

'I shall miss her sorely. May I have one last ride, just to exercise her for the last time?'

He smiled at her unexpected civility. 'Very

well, my lady, but do not go far.'

She thanked him prettily and turned to go. He called her back. She did not want to delay—the injured man was getting ever nearer and would soon be spotted—but she could not risk Garret's suspicion, and so turned back. 'Sir?'

'If you ride as far as the high road, see if you can see anyone upon it, will you? It would be as well to be forewarned.'

'Very well.'

She escaped at last and found Prue gossiping in the kitchen with the cook. 'I am going out riding,' she told her in a whisper. 'When I come back I shall have someone with me who will need a hiding place. It will have to be my chamber, it's the only room which won't be searched. Prepare it for a guest and tell no one else.'

'But, Lady Alys—'

Alys did not wait to argue, but went to the stables and stood impatiently while her mare was saddled for her, then rode out over the drawbridge as if she had all the time in the world. Not until she had covered the meadow in front of the manor did she dare to put Beauty to a gallop.

The rider was on the outskirts of the village, still with his head down on the horse's neck. She pulled up beside him, dismounted and ran over to catch his bridle.

'Sir! Who are you, that you ride into

Waterlea Manor in such a careless fashion?'

He raised his head slowly and there was a ghost of a smile as he said, 'Waterlea Manor. I thought I would never get here.'

'Why were you coming to the manor?'

'Benedick sent me, said you would look after me until I healed. He said it would be safe.'

'Benedick! You know my brother?'

'We were—are—comrades in arms. My name is Damian Forrester, lieutenant of His Majesty's loyal guard.'

'You can't ride on to the manor,' she said, noticing the torn sleeve of his doublet and the congealed blood on his exposed left arm. 'It's full of Roundhead troops. They are fortifying it.'

'To be honest,' he said, speaking slowly and with an effort, 'I care not. I must get off this animal before I fall off, and I would rather it were within a few paces of a bed.'

She turned suddenly at the sound of a vehicle approaching from the village. 'Get down!' she said, pulling him from the stallion. 'Hide!' He was too weak to resist her, as she half dragged him down a bank and under a wooden bridge which spanned one of the dykes. 'Stay there.' She left him sitting on the ground, leaning against one of its posts, as she returned to the road, unsaddled his horse, threw the saddle down into the ditch beside him and then drove the horse over the bridge into the meadow, in the hope that anyone passing would assume it belonged to one of the soldiers. Exhausted as the horse clearly was, he pricked up his ears when he realised his burden had been taken from him and trotted over to a drinking trough in the corner of the meadow, where the dappled light of an overhanging willow partly hid him.

A horse and cart rumbled round the turn of the road and she heaved a sigh of relief. It was being driven by one-eyed Simon, one of her father's old servants, who had been sent out with the cart by Aldous to collect fodder. He was returning with a load of hay. She moved into the road and hailed him.

'Simon, stop please, I need your help.'

Seeing his much-loved mistress, he grinned from ear to ear as he obeyed. 'Aye, my lady Alys, anythin' is better 'an helping them scoundrels what hev tek over the great house. I never thought to see the day—'

'Yes, yes,' she said impatiently. 'Can you keep a secret?'

'Course I cen.'

'Then get down and come with me.'

He obeyed without question and together they helped the injured man up and into the back of the cart. She wrapped her cloak about him and covered him with the hay.

'Drive the cart right into the barn,' she told Simon, 'and don't let the soldiers start unloading it. Do it yourself and make sure our friend is found a safe hiding place. Then find me and tell me where he is. Do you understand?'

'Aye, mistress, I understand, but if them troopers was to find him—'

'They must not.'

'My lady.' The lieutenant's muffled voice came from beneath the hay. 'I'd as lief fight them in the open than skulk around like a thief in the night.'

'That would be foolish indeed,' she said. 'There are dozens of them. You will be looked after and your wound tended, but you must lie still and do as you are told, otherwise you put us all in danger. I will see you later and we can talk of Benedick and how he does and the progress of the war.'

She mounted her own horse and set off alone in the direction of the high road, intending to do as Garret had asked and see if anyone was coming. It also meant that when she returned to the manor, she would be seen coming from the right direction. Behind her, the cart continued on its way.

She was singing as she rode into the courtyard half an hour later; singing for sheer joy, for devilment, for the opportunity to do something, however small, to help the King, and not even the sight of Garret, standing beside the demi-cannon, could dampen her spirits.

'Here is the mare,' she called out to him.

'She will make a brave mount for a cavalry officer, though if she knows whose side she is on she may not be so willing, being a well-bred animal.'

He laughed up at her as she passed close to him. 'My lady is in good spirits.'

She reined in, better not to appear in a hurry. 'Why not? It is a beautiful day, and peaceful.'

'Yes, here it is peaceful.' He smiled up at her in friendly fashion. 'I could wish it were always so. Did you see aught on the high road?'

'Nothing at all, Captain, nothing at all, except a gooseherd and she had seen nothing, so she told me. Perhaps the war has passed us by, after all.'

'I pray that it has,' he said. 'I go to join Cromwell at North Scarle as soon as my men are ready, but I will be back.'

Was he hinting that she should hurry with her preparations for their wedding? She had done nothing about them, hoping he was too busy to think about it. She rode on past him, feeling a small twinge of guilt because he had trusted her and she had not deserved it. More fool he, she told herself as she dismounted, left the horse with a groom and then went to the barn. Did he think she would change her allegiance to suit him?

The men had all gone into the kitchen for their dinner and the barn was deserted. She walked to the edge of the great pile of new hay and called softly. 'Lieutenant Forrester! Where are you?' There was no answer and she repeated his name.

'Do you want the whole Parliament army down on us?' said a voice from the door.

She turned with a startled cry on her lips. 'Oh, Prue, it's you.'

'It's as well it was no other, my lady. Have you no more sense than to call his name?'

'But I must find him, he might be stifled under all that.' She pointed to the hay.

'So he might have been if Simon had not had sense enough to fetch me.'

'Where is he?'

'In your chamber; that's what you wanted, isn't it?'

'Oh, Prue, you are an angel.' She hugged her servant. 'Let us go to him at once.'

'You are mad, do you know that?' Prue could be very outspoken when she chose; in her own eyes, her long service with the family gave her that privilege. 'If Sir Garret finds out, not even the marriage contract will save you.'

'Do you think I care a jot for Garret Hartswood, when a loyal soldier of the King needs help and brings news of Benedick?' She hurried ahead of her maid towards the house.

'He certainly needs someone, but a chirurgeon or an apothecary would be more appropriate.'

'Is he very badly hurt? Oh, he isn't going to

die, is he?'

'A flesh wound to the arm. He lost a great deal of blood which weakened him, but that has done him no harm.'

'And his arm?'

'It will heal. I have soothed it with unguent and bound it up and given him one of my potions to make him sleep. I do not think he will die.'

'You are better than any chirurgeon, Prue.'

'I have taken his clothes and hidden them and put him in one of Master Benedick's nightshirts.'

'Good.'

'Good!' Prue's voice was almost a squeak. 'My lady, it is not good. You will live to rue this day, I can tell you. You should hand him over to Sir Garret.'

Alys stopped in her tracks so suddenly that Prue, trying to keep up with her mistress, nearly collided with her. 'How can you say such a thing? Benedick bade him come here, he told him he would be safe. Garret would—'

'Would what, my lady? He will only make a prisoner of him until the end of the war.'

'Not while I can prevent it.' She began climbing the stairs to her chamber. 'He shan't find the lieutenant.'

'Where will you hide him?'

'Where he is now—in my room. I will have a truckle bed in your room.'

'My lady!'

Alys turned with her hand on the door-handle of her room. 'Why so startled, Prue dear? You often had me in your room when I was little and frightened or sick, you know you did. Now, go and make my bed, I want to talk to our guest.'

Prue clicked her tongue in disapproval but went to obey, and Alys, her eyes bright with excitement and her step light, went into her bedchamber.

The young man lay fast asleep in her four-poster and, although his complexion was pale, he was breathing easily. She sat on the side of the bed and watched him. He was young, hardly more than twenty, but handsome, she decided, and he must be very brave to have come so far when he was wounded, especially as he must have ridden through the Parliamentary lines.

He opened his eyes and smiled at her. 'My grateful thanks, my lady, for all your help.'

'You are welcome. But tell me, how were you wounded? Was it in a fierce battle?'

'At Burleigh House. That rogue Cromwell stormed us.'

'Was Benedick with you?'

'No, he had ridden on with the King, we were only a small party.'

'When did he tell you to come here? How did you know about us?'

'Benedick spoke of you often, and of his home, and he said if I ever needed help, I would receive it at Waterlea Manor.' He smiled. 'And so here I am and he did not exaggerate when he said his sister was beautiful.'

She blushed crimson. 'Benedick was not always so free with his compliments. Now, you must stay here in this room and keep silent as a mouse, because there are Roundheads quartered here.'

'But you are allowed to keep your home?'

'Yes, but we must be very careful. Only Prue and I will tend you. I dare not even tell my father you are here.'

She left the bed to go to the window and look out across the fens, to the line of the distant road. There was nothing to be seen except a shimmering mist, and nothing to hear but the insistent quark of a wild duck among the reedbeds of the fen. There was no sign of Garret and his troops. She turned back to the bed to speak to the lieutenant, but he had fallen asleep.

He slept a great deal in the next few days, while she went about her usual tasks—helping with the butter making, mixing herbal remedies with Prue, rendering down fat for candles, mending linen, all the things a good mistress had to know how to do, however many servants she had—while trying not to arouse anyone's suspicion that she was sleeping anywhere but in her own bed. Prue, in spite of her disapproval, would keep her

114

secret, but she was not so sure of the other servants. And, for his own sake, she wanted the fact that they had a guest kept from her father, until the Royalists arrived.

The invalid mended quickly and in a few days was pacing the room like a caged lion. He *was* caged. He grumbled and spent hours at the window, gazing out across the village at the fen landscape.

'Please come away from the casement, Damian,' Alys begged him. 'Someone will see you.'

'Who is there to see me? The place is dead; no one, nothing stirs. Where are our troops? Why have they not come? The war might be a thousand miles away.'

'It is only a few miles, you said so yourself. The fighting has been going on all over the county. I heard Gainsborough had changed hands at least twice.'

'And who holds it now?'

'I believe, the Royalists.'

He laughed. 'There, did I not tell you it would soon be over? Cromwell will be beaten, here, in the stinking fens he loves so much.'

'Garret is with Cromwell,' she said, before she could stop herself.

'And who is Garret?'

'He is the man I am betrothed to marry.'

He turned suddenly and grimaced with pain. 'A Roundhead? You mean your father expects you to marry a mortal enemy?'

'Yes.'

'You jest.'

'I do not. The contract was signed five years ago.'

'You must refuse him,' he said promptly.

'I cannot. It would break Father's heart, and, besides, Garret controls this area for Parliament; no one dare go against him.'

'I had thought a sister of Benedick Carthorne would have had more courage than that. Defy him. Tell him to do his worst.'

'But there is so much at stake.'

'The only thing at stake is your happiness, my sweet Alys. Disregard everything else.'

'You mean I am to be so selfish that I do not think of Father or Benedick or Prue and the other servants? Nor Waterlea Manor?' Her eyes filled with tears. 'I cannot, Lieutenant, I cannot.'

'You prefer to submit to tyranny?'

'Tyranny?'

'Yes, for that is what it is, the tyranny of a fanatical enemy, the tyranny of a selfish father over a young defenceless girl. But you are not defenceless, you have me, and together we will beat them all.'

'You?' she asked in surprise.

'Why not? I must do something to repay you and in the absence of your brother, I will help you to be rid of your unwelcome suitor.'

'How?'

'We must win this war and that will put an

end to the Roundhead's prospects. He will die along with Cromwell; if not in battle, then on the block with all other traitors. You will be free of him.'

'Oh, yes,' she said, caught up in his enthusiasm. 'But what must I do to help?'

'First, you must allow me to go out.' He smiled down at her, easily, confidently, as if he were accustomed to having his own way. 'I shall suffocate if I stay in this room a moment longer.'

'Someone will see you.'

'I promise to be careful. At the first sign of anyone coming, I will hide, though I had rather stand and fight. Fetch my clothes, my lovely Alys—let me go out.'

She smiled; his charming manner made it easy to give in to him. 'Very well, but you must stay in the walled garden and not go into the village.'

'Then you must go for me.'

'Why?'

'I need to know what forces are quartered in the area and where the ammunition and powder is stored.'

'The only troops in the area have been quartered here in the house, there is none in the village. As for ammunition, I know of none, except what is here to fire the saker and the demi-cannon.'

'I think there is more and I want you to find out for certain. It is important I take the information back to my commander.' He looked steadily into her eyes and saw her doubts mirrored there. 'Don't you think it would be better for your friends in the village if there is no blood shed when the Marquis of Newcastle comes?' he asked. 'You have it in your power to make sure they all live through this unharmed.'

'I don't know that I should,' she said. 'If Garret were to find out—'

'Don't know? Alys how can you say you do not know? You want the accursed Roundheads beaten, don't you?'

'Yes.'

'And the less blood spilled, the better, don't you agree?'

'Yes.'

'Then do as I ask. Find out how the village is to be defended. Do it for Benedick and our sovereign, if you will not do it for me.'

'Very well, I will try.'

'Good.' He laughed and bent to kiss her cheek. 'That is from Benedick. And this I do on my own behalf.' And he took her in his arms and put his lips to hers in a lingering kiss which left her blushing and breathless. 'And, Alys,' he murmured. 'There is something else the King needs as much as information.'

'More brave men like you and Benedick.'

He laughed. 'Yes, but something else. He needs money.'

'I have very little.'

'But you do have jewellery.' His voice took on a pleading note. 'Alys, I would not ask, but His Majesty is in dire need.'

'He shall have it,' she answered promptly. 'I tried to send it to him before, but Garret stopped it and gave it back to me.'

'Back to you! The man is a fool.' He smiled and stroked her hair back from her forehead and kissed her again. 'But that is his loss and His Majesty's gain. Where is it?'

'On the table.' He strode over to her jewel box and tried the lid, but, finding it locked, turned back to her with hand extended. She unclipped the key from her chatelaine and dropped it into his palm. 'Take it all, it is a small price to pay.'

He unlocked the box and looked down at the contents, then slowly put his hand in and fingered the pieces almost lovingly. 'I will take them when I leave, and thank you on behalf of the King.' He walked back to her, smiling. 'Now, Alys, my clothes.'

She fetched them herself and, while he was dressing, checked that there was no one about on the back stairs, nor in the yard. When he emerged, she helped him down the stairs, though he was quite capable of walking unaided. Together they went out of a side door, across the yard and into the walled garden.

'If I go to the village now,' she said, 'you will be good?'

He laughed. 'I am always good. Just be sure you are.'

She left him in the garden with its rows of vegetables and buzzing bee-skips and walked down the wide path which led from the house to the village road, picking up a basket from the kitchen on the way and saying she intended to buy fish from one of the fen men who daily sold his catch in the centre of the village.

How she was going to find out what the lieutenant wanted to know, she had no idea. There were no large buildings in the village, except the church. The church! That was where she had seen the recruits and Garret had been there too. As a Roundhead, he would care nothing for the sacrilege of using a church for military purposes; it had been done before.

Dr Sandy was at his prayers when she entered, but rose creakily from his knees when he heard her approach. 'Oh, Lady Alys, it is you, I had thought . . .'

She smiled. 'You thought I was one of those Puritan Roundheads who do not like the old ways?'

'They have no respect for God, my lady. It grieves my old heart . . .' He sighed. 'But there, Captain Hartswood is a fair man and he can turn a blind eye with the best of them.'

'Just so long as you, too, turn a blind eye, is that not so?'

120

He looked startled. 'What do you mean?'

She laughed and shrugged. 'Nothing, sir, nothing; except the soldiers seem to find great comfort in their religion. They come and go to church as frequently as if the place were a barracks.'

'Lady Alys, it is my duty to do all in my power to help my flock, whoever they may be. God works in mysterious ways.'

'Oh, indeed, very mysterious,' she said with a laugh.

'Why did you come here this morning?' he asked suspiciously.

'I, like you, need to pray.'

'Then do so, my child, and if I can offer any comfort . . .'

'I would rather pray alone, Reverend.'

He seemed surprised, but it was not for him to question the daughter of the lord of the manor, and he left, hobbling on rheumaticky legs to the sunshine outside.

As soon as he had gone, Alys began a systematic search of the church and it did not take long to find the muskets, ammunition and powder stacked in a small side chapel. There was a great deal of it, more than she would have thought necessary for the defence of a small out-of-the-way village. She had the information Lieutenant Forrester had asked for, but having it did not fill her with pleasure. She wished she did not know, wished she had never seen what she had seen. It made a spy of

121

her, and suddenly everything seemed far more serious, more sinister.

She went out into the sunshine and walked slowly back to the manor.

CHAPTER FIVE

The lieutenant was nowhere to be seen in the garden. She hurried up to her chamber, thinking that he might have returned there, but the room was empty. Her jewel box lay, open and empty, on the bed, on top of Benedick's discarded nightshirt, and his sword had gone from the wall next to the court cupboard where it had, until that morning, been leaning. Surely he would not have left without saying goodbye, or without the information he had asked for? She returned downstairs and searched the stable and barn. The outdoor servants who were working there looked up, but said nothing, and she dared not ask if any of them had seen a Royalist cavalry officer. In growing panic she ran up and down the old monks' cells, now crammed with enough stores and provisions to withstand a siege, and then in desperation set off across the grass to the chapel, and met him coming out.

'Lieutenant, I have been looking everywhere for you.'

'I've been in there.' He jerked his head back towards the building behind him. 'It is an interesting old place, full of dust and cobwebs. Don't you use it?'

'We no longer have our own chaplain and prefer to worship in the village church.'

'I found a little door behind a screen, leading down into a place like a cellar.'

In the days when it had been an abbey, there had been a crypt of sorts. Alys and her brother had explored it as children, but since then, no one, to her knowledge, had gone through the small oak door at the north corner of the chapel and down the twisting stone steps.

'It's the old crypt,' she said.

'It would make a good hiding place.'

'For what?'

He shrugged. 'Arms, ammunition, people.'

'It's too damp,' she said. 'And you promised to stay in the garden.'

He ignored her grumble. 'Now, tell me what you found out for me.'

'It's in the church, mountains of it.'

'Good, that is what I wanted to hear. I shall be rewarded for this, a captaincy at the very least. Now, one more thing—where is Cromwell concentrating his forces?'

'I do not know, but Prue said one of the soldiers told her that once they had recaptured Gainsborough, they were going to the relief of Hull.'

'Hull! That will fall to Newcastle without a fight. Why, even the governor, seeing his cause is lost, has changed sides and is dealing with the King.' He put his arm round her and hugged her to his side. 'Now I must leave.'

'Are you sure your wound is sufficiently healed?'

'It is well enough for me to ride.'

'Ride?' She had forgotten about his horse.

'Yes, where is my mount?'

'I turned it into one of Jan Van Hildt's meadows, I expect it is still there; we would have heard if someone had discovered it. Master Van Hildt has been busy on the other side of his domain, drying out his flooded fields.'

'I hope you are right, because otherwise I shall be obliged to take your mare.'

'Captain Hartswood is coming back for that.'

'And you would give her to him rather than me?' His eyes flashed with a hint of anger, which should have told her he could be ruthless if he were thwarted.

'No, of course not, but the mare's disappearance would be noticed and I would not want you to be discovered now.'

He smiled and took her hand. 'No, for there is much to do, and I must go.'

He did not sound as miserable about it as she felt, but then no one could feel as miserable as she did at that moment.

Everything seemed wrong; his use of her, his light-hearted selfishness, her betrayal of Garret, most of all her betrayal. Was that how wars were won and lost, not on the field of battle in glorious and honourable combat, but in the intrigue that went on behind the scenes? She hated it.

They were halfway across the grass and in full view of the courtyard when they heard horses on the path to the house, walking at a steady clop, as if they had nothing to fear.

Before they could retreat to cover, Garret rode over the drawbridge and in at the gate, followed by half a dozen battle-weary men. Some were slightly wounded, judging by the rough bandages they wore, and they slumped in their saddles, kept there by an innate sense of balance; almost all had the blank expressions and dull eyes of utter exhaustion. Only Garret seemed alert and bright-eyed. Beside him rode Sergeant Wally, leading Damian's white stallion.

Garret left the group and rode slowly towards them, his expression one of controlled fury. Damian grabbed her by the hand and dashed for the cover of the old abbey buildings, dragging her with him. Then he stopped and pulled her in front of him and drew his sword, facing the Roundhead.

'Don't resist, Damian, please,' she begged him. 'They are too many.'

'Lady Alys is right,' Garret said. 'Surrender

and you shall have quarter.'

'But I have the lady,' Damian said in a way which frightened Alys. 'Would you fight for her?'

Garret dismounted and drew his own sword. 'Would you forfeit your chance of mercy?'

'Oh, Damian.' Alys tried to twist towards him, but his arm about her kept her back against his chest. 'Don't fight him, he'll kill you.'

'Not while you stand between us, my dear.'

The two men stared at each other as one advanced and the other backed away; not for a moment did Garret's dark eyes give away the fact that his men had dismounted and were moving round behind the quarry. Suddenly Alys felt Damian's grip slacken as he was seized from behind. Garret, moving forward, shouted, 'Step away, my lady!'

She stumbled as she tried to obey. The sergeant rode up and picked her up bodily, setting her in front of him. 'You will be safer with me, my lady,' he said.

She twisted round to see what was happening, but Damian, seeing how impossible that situation was, had dropped his sword and surrendered. The weapon stuck into the soft earth, quivering with a life of its own, until Garret strode over and pulled it out.

'Take him away,' he ordered.

'What will happen to him?' Alys asked, as the sergeant lowered her to the ground in order to obey.

'He forfeited his right to quarter,' he said flatly. 'He must die.'

'Oh, no!' She ran to Garret and tugged on his arm. 'Please, please, don't kill him.'

'Why not? He is an enemy of the people, a delinquent. I would be a fool to let him live to fight again.'

She remained silent because there was nothing she could say which would not implicate both herself and Damian even further into intrigue; better to let Garret draw his own conclusions.

*   *   *

Garret's conclusions were drawn from the evidence of his own eyes and the tale Lettice had told him when she waylaid him on his return to the village. The Dutchman's wife had been on the upper platform of their barn, deploring the plundering of her husband's hay, when she had witnessed Alys's first encounter with the young Cavalier. Later she had fetched the horse and saddle into her own stable.

'There is no doubt of Lady Alys's allegiance,' she had told him, not half an hour before. 'I saw her run to him and put him on a

127

cart going to the manor. She must have kept him hidden up there, for I have not seen him leave. You are a fool to trust her.'

He did not want to believe her and wished he could have told her to mind her own affairs and leave the war to soldiers, but she had spoken in front of his men, and produced the white stallion and its saddle, and he had been obliged to thank her for the information and reward her by returning her pony. How that had galled him! And how triumphant she had been! He wondered why he had ever imagined her cared for her. Beside the fiery Alys, with her intense loyalty, Lettice was hard and scheming.

He was weary and dispirited from setbacks and disappointments, and so were his troops. The promised pay and supplies had not arrived; Westminster was more concerned with sending money to the Earl of Essex, who led the Parliamentary forces against the King in the south, than with the fragmented army of Lincolnshire and the eastern association. But that would have to change if the war was to be won; an army could not fight on an empty stomach nor without weapons and ammunition.

Thank heaven his own men had stayed firm and, encouraged by Cromwell's victory at Burleigh House, had marched with a will to North Scarle, where they had joined forces with troops from neighboring counties and routed the Royalists, before relieving Gainsborough with provisions and powder. But within hours of getting supplies to the town, the enemy had been reported only a mile away. They had gone out to meet them but, topping the rise of a steep hill, they had been greeted with the sight of the whole of Newcastle's horse and infantry, with flags flying, on its way to Gainsborough. They could do nothing but retire in good order and leave the Gainsborough garrison once more besieged.

Cromwell had withdrawn his infantry to Peterborough, as the Royalist advance continued deep into Lincolnshire. The Waterlea men, realising they were defending their own home ground, had contested every inch of the way, but had been forced inexorably back until, for some reason unknown to them, Newcastle stopped just short of the village. Given this small respite, Garret had brought them home to rest, gambling that they would be prepared to take up arms again when he received further orders. All but the few he had recruited in Cambridgeshire had dispersed to their homes in Waterlea and the surrounding villages. He had even allowed Aldous to go home to Grantham.

To return to find Alys aiding and abetting the enemy was almost more than he could stomach. She was looking up at him now, with her huge eyes filled with tears, and he was torn between venting his frustration on her and trying to comfort her.

'Now, my lady,' he said, his voice clipped with the effort of trying to be impersonal. 'Return to your father and leave the fighting of the war to those who know what they are about.'

'All I have done is shelter a wounded man and I would do that whichever side he favoured. Even you, Captain, if you asked it of me.' She gave a short laugh. 'But then you would never ask, would you? You would be too proud to admit you needed help from anyone, least of all me.'

'Yes, I am proud,' he said. 'Proud of my cause, proud of my men, and I will protect them as long as God gives me the strength. I will not have interference from you or anyone else who thinks war is nothing but a game in which no one is hurt.' He wanted to shock her, to make her see how important it was for her not to make herself conspicuous with acts which could be misinterpreted. 'Men are hurt and many of them are killed because they believe in the cause they fight for, and they have the right to expect their women to support them by staying at home and holding their tongues.'

'I am not one of your women,' she shouted. 'I will never be one of your women. Never! Do you hear? And I will not be told to hold my tongue! Punish me, if you like! Take me to prison too. Let everyone see what a tyrant you are when you can't have your own way.'

He was torn between slapping her and laughing at her spirit, and he wondered how much of her tirade was truly meant. He had laughingly told Aldous he would enjoy converting her, but he was beginning to wonder if he had any chance at all of succeeding. 'I have no wish to send you to prison, my lady,' he said evenly, 'but I want your word not to repeat the offence.'

'If anyone comes to my door needing succour, I shall give it,' she said. 'It is my Christian duty and I shall not ask for whom he fights.'

His men were watching the encounter with interest and he could not let her win. He turned, looking for a way out of his predicament, and was relieved to see Lord Carthorne, with his doublet awry and his hose wrinkled down into the tops of his bucket boots, hurrying out from the house to see what was happening. 'My lord,' Garret called. 'Will you take this erring child into the house and teach her not to meddle.'

'Child!' she shouted. 'I am no child to be thus ordered about. I have a free mind and a free spirit and you will not put either into shackles, though you take me and chain me to a prison wall!'

'I have no intention of doing that,' he said,

moving towards her and taking hold of her wrists. 'Your chains will be of your own choosing.'

'And if I choose to go with the King's lieutenant?' Her eyes flashed with a defiance she was far from feeling. His strength was evident in the way he held her, in the powerful breadth of his shoulders, in the set of his jaw; she was both terrified and elated.

'You will stay here in Waterlea and wait for my return,' he said. 'Then we will talk quietly and sensibly of the future. In the meantime, I leave your chastisement to your father.'

'Captain,' the sergeant protested, 'likely his lordship is guilty as she is.'

'Guilty of what?' Lord Carthorne asked breathlessly. 'What is afoot? I was taking a nap when Prue came running to me with tales of arrests.'

'The Lady Alys has been so ill advised as to shelter a delinquent,' Garret explained. 'I am sure you were not party to that.'

'Indeed not.' He turned to Alys. 'Alys, what have you been doing?'

'Lieutenant Forrester came to us for shelter after he was wounded at Burleigh House,' she said. 'Benedick told him to come. Would you have had me turn him away?'

'Why did you not tell me he was here?' He turned to Garret. 'I knew nothing of this, but, had I known, I would not have sent him away.'

'But you would have reported his

132

presence?'

'Yes. And I have no doubt that my daughter would have done so, if you had not caught the young man yourself.'

Garret did not dare ask Alys if this was so, knowing it was not, and that she would defy him in front of everyone.

'Enough time has been wasted,' he said brusquely. 'Take the prisoner away.'

'Come,' her father said, taking her firmly by the arm. 'The young man knew the risks he was taking by coming here.'

'Where else could he go?' she asked. 'He thought we were his friends and we have let him down. Now they are going to kill him.'

Lord Carthorne gave Garret a questioning look.

'I shall give him the usual choice—imprisonment for the duration of the war or fighting for our cause,' he answered. 'More I cannot do, not even to please my lady.' He looked down at her, smiling, hoping for some softening in her angry features, but she did not respond and he turned away, hating himself.

He ordered Damian to mount his own horse and then led the little cavalcade out over the drawbridge and back to the village. The men could rest in the church, but he could not; he had to make out a report and deliver the prisoner and, in doing so, would undoubtedly receive orders which would mean a further call to arms. He swore softly. Damn all prisoners! Damn this one, particularly. Did Alys know just how much trouble she had caused? He laughed aloud. He was under no illusions about her loyalty to that misguided King; if she knew she was making trouble, she would be glad. And yet he could not blame her. He admired her soft heart, her generous spirit and her loyalty; would that it were directed at him, instead of the young man who rode the white stallion ahead of him.

'You will ride with me to Peterborough,' he said to the sergeant. 'They can take charge of the prisoner there and, if fortune smiles on us, we will find the men's pay waiting for us.'

Alys stood helplessly watching them go, until her father tugged on her arm to draw her back to the house. 'Come, child, there is nothing you can do. The lieutenant is a soldier and he must take the consequences of being caught. War is like that.'

'He won't fight for Parliament, I know that.'

'Perhaps Benedick will be able to arrange an exchange of prisoners; it is often done.'

'But we don't know where Benedick is, it might be months before anything can be done.'

'Then we must be patient.'

But it was difficult to be patient when there was so little news. Running the domestic side of the manor and helping, as so many of the women were doing, with the outdoor work,

Alys found her hands busy while her mind had little to do but speculate. How was Damian being treated in gaol? Where was Benedick and what was Garret doing? Not, she told herself, that she had any interest in where the captain was or what hc did. She hoped she had succeeded in putting him off the idea of marriage, but was in no hurry for him to return and confirm this. Sometimes as she went about the village—on foot because there were no horses except an old nag left bchind for her father's use—she found herself wondering what life with him would be like, but, because she was determined not to find anything about him agreeable, she concluded he would be bound to make her miserable and in consequence would be miserable himself; she would be doing him a service in delaying the wedding just as long as she could. He could continue to take Lettice Van Hildt as a lover; they deserved each other, she told herself irritably.

The Van Hildts were a thorn in her father's side, and, because of that and the way they thought they could ride roughshod over the commoners, Alys could not think of them without feeling the anger rise in her throat.

The latest grumble was that without the labour to do the threshing, they were having to use women, boys and old men, and the work was not being done properly and swiftly enough.

'I haf to pay my fifths and twentieths,' Jan Van Hildt said, when she saw him carting his own corn on a haywain pulled by the one old horse Garret had left him with. 'No account is taken of de difficulties I haf. An' de vimmen let de cows into de corn and ruined it. Dey know not'ing of farming.'

Alys smiled. The women knew perfectly well what they were about; it was their way of sabotaging the Dutchman's efforts, carrying on where their menfolk had left off. 'They do their best, Master Van Hildt,' she said. 'And perhaps the men will be home soon.'

'Dey vill not,' he said gloomily. 'De vor vill last many years.'

'Why do you say that? Newcastle has taken nearly all Lincolnshire for the King and the eastern association cannot hold him back.'

'If dat is so, vy haf ve not seen de King's soldiers? Ve haf seen no one but a troop of men under Captain Hartswood. And this new flying army I haf heard of vill do more than fight in its own county, it vill go to the vest country. Ve vill be left undefended.'

News had filtered through to them that the eastern association, an army originally intended for the defence of the eastern counties, was to be joined by the troops of Lincolnshire and strengthened under the command of the Earl of Manchester, aided by Cromwell. The Earl had powers to impress men for military service, and he had been

136

riding through the counties, exhorting the local committees to raise the men and the taxes to pay and supply them.

'I had heard that many of the Roundhead soldiers had deserted,' she said.

'Cromwell haf been made a colonel and haf relieved Hull,' he went on. 'And de Earl of Manchester, who is major general, haf joined him and Sir Thomas Fairfax and von a victory at Vinceby. Dere is not'ing like a victory to make a man fight 'arder. De men vill not come back to finish de t'reshing, dey will go to more fights and I must work alone. I haf asked in the next shire for help, but dey haf no men eider. It vill be a yonder if I haf finished it before Christmas.'

She left him to his grumbling and, having bought fish and fowl from the trader who stood at the crossroads with his wares on a wooden board hung round his neck, she returned home.

She found her father in the small parlour, sitting at the table, which was scattered with papers and ledgers. He looked old and tired and that was something she had noticed more and more of late. The skin on his face was yellow and dry, like old parchment, and his hair, once so thick and dark, was white and tousled, as if it had not known a comb for several weeks. His hands, as he reached out to her, were thin and heavily veined and they shook as if he had the ague. Being a Royalist

137

in an area controlled by Parliament and commanded by a Roundhead who was also the son of his dearest friend was taking its toll. And his fierce love of his home made him compromise his commitment to the King's cause. He battled with himself daily, feeling himself disloyal, not only to his monarch, but to his son, who fought openly for Charles.

'The constable was here again,' he told her. 'The manor has been sequestered—we are here under sufferance.'

She took his hands in her own. 'So much for Garret Hartswood's promise to help us,' she said bitterly. 'I didn't believe he would, when he said it.'

'You are being unfair, because he did try,' her father said, with a heavy sigh. 'And we have him to thank that we are allowed to remain in residence.'

She stroked his forehead and bent to kiss him. 'The war will end soon and everything will be restored . . .'

'I wish I had your faith. I do not think Charles can beat Parliament and I am not at all sure he should.'

'Father—'

'At first I felt he had the right, that he was our King and nothing could take that away from him, and I suppose I still believe it, but should a King rule without the consent of the people?' He shook his head from side to side, perplexed by the problem. 'Perhaps I should try and find the money.'

'No, Father, they ask too much and the longer we hold out, the sooner the war will end in victory for the King.'

'I hold out no hope for a speedy end,' he said, leaning back in his chair and shutting his eyes. 'The constable has just been telling me of the Roundhead victory at Winceby and the retreat of the Marquis of Newcastle to York. I think it will be some time before we see a Royalist soldier in these parts again.'

She left her father reading his papers and went through the door at the back of the hall which led to the kitchen. Cook was making eel pie, one girl was churning butter, another was splitting reeds for rushlights, another was curing feathers for stuffing pillows and young Job, the steward's son, was preparing the mash for a new barrel of ale. She watched them for a moment, though she knew they did not need supervision, until the sound of horses crossing the drawbridge made her return to the hall and go to the window which looked out on to the courtyard.

Garret was riding across the drawbridge at the head of a troop of foot soldiers. The first column consisted of a dozen musketeers whose multitude of accoutrements rattled in noisy rhythm as they marched and advertised their coming. Behind them came twenty or so pikemen weighed down with armour, swords on their belts and sixteen-foot pikes in their hands. As soon as the last man was in the courtyard, the captain ordered them to stand down and then dismounted and made his way to the front door.

Alys went to rouse her sleeping father. 'Garret is back,' she said gently.

'What? Who?' He scrambled to his feet, still half asleep.

'Garret and a troop of Roundhead infantry,' she said.

He straightened his doublet and ran his hand over his ruffled hair, as the captain was shown into the room. Garret had taken off his pot helmet and shoulder belt with its sword and pistol, and, in divesting himself of the accoutrements of war, had somehow revealed more of the man, tall and strikingly handsome, not at all the popular conception of a Roundhead. Alys, looking at him, found her heart beating uncomfortably fast.

'Ah, my boy, come in and welcome,' his lordship said.

'I am not here for long, my lord,' he said, looking at Alys. 'I have been ordered to assemble my men and recruit more, then I must leave. I have given orders to those too wounded to return to the fight to set watches at all the vantage points and give warning if troops are sighted so that everyone can hurry within the safety of the manor. I hope that meets with your lordship's approval.'

'Of course, of course,' Lord Carthorne said.

140

'That has always been our custom.'

'And when will you be back again?' Alys queried.

'That I cannot say.' He smiled suddenly, understanding her. 'I am afraid the wedding will have to be postponed until then.'

'I shall be patient.'

Lord Carthorne smiled, believing the two young people had become reconciled. 'We must all be patient and bear our sorrows manfully. You have heard that the manor has been sequestered?'

'Yes, my lord, and I am sorry I could not prevent it. If Benedick were not fighting so openly for the King . . .'

'Benedick was your friend,' Alys said.

'He is still my friend.'

'But you would kill him if you met in battle?'

'I will try to avoid having to make the decision,' he said drily.

'How?'

He smiled. 'Your brother is with the King in Oxford—so long as he stays there, we are unlikely to meet. My troops are in Lincolnshire.'

'But for how long? I have heard talk of a national army, one that will march the length and breadth of the country at Parliament's command.'

'It will not happen immediately, there are too many other decisions to be made first.

How is such an army to be financed, equipped and supplied? It is difficult enough to persuade the county committees to raise taxes for the defence of their own areas without having to provide men and money for fighting outside them.'

'But it will have to come,' she said. 'Newark is not in Lincolnshire, but it is near enough for the Royalist garrison there to cause a great deal of trouble to the Parliamentary armies in the fens. I had heard that all the neighbouring counties were joining forces to capture it.'

'My lady is well informed.'

'But you will not pass this information on to anyone,' her father said, reminding her of Damian. 'We are in enough trouble as it is, and if it had not been for Garret we would not even have a roof over our heads.'

Alys felt her face colour and turned away from the men to poke at the fire, though it did not need it.

'I am grateful for your intervention, my boy,' his lordship went on. 'And so is Alys.'

'Yes,' she said, leaving the fire but not daring to look into Garret's eyes. 'If the fact that we can still enjoy our home is your doing, Captain, then I thank you.'

He moved to take her hand and lift it to his lips, looking at her with eyes full of humour. 'Goodbye, kitten,' he said softly. 'And may your claws be sheathed when we meet again.' Then he bade Lord Carthorne goodbye and strode to the door.

'You like him, don't you?' her father said.

'I . . . I do not know, he confuses me.'

Lord Carthorne smiled. 'But *I* know, my child. I have watched you together and I know. This marriage is right for you. It may have been thought of by two old men in their dotage, but it will be a good marriage, if you decide to make it so.'

'It takes two to make a good marriage,' she said.

'One will do for a start.' He closed his eyes. 'Now, leave me, I need to sleep a little more.'

She wrapped a sheepskin rug about his knees and went back to the hall. Garret had just buckled on his belt and had his helmet in his hand. They looked at each other silently for several seconds, then he smiled and took his leave.

Alys rode out early the next morning on her father's mount, though she would never have admitted that she hoped to catch a glimpse of Garret before he left. She wished she could understand him, she wished she knew what was going on in his head. He had kissed her more than once in a way which had sent her senses reeling, and he had called her kitten, but those moments of tenderness had passed and he had become his usual cold self. He had contracted to marry her and yet he did not really want to. She told herself she did not want it either.

The sun was barely up and the sky was a glorious suffusion of pale mauve light and pink-edged clouds, layer upon layer from the low-lying horizon to something approaching a second horizon high in the bowl of heaven, now turning from grey to palest blue. It contrasted oddly with the scene on the ground on either side of the high road above the village.

The fields were full of the paraphernalia of war: cannon mounted on field carriages, mortars and their pieces loaded on to carts, tumbrels full of iron roundshot, caseshot, boxes of musket balls, barrels of powder. There were wagons for food and utensils, and row upon row of tents, one of which flew a standard which Alys supposed belonged to the field commander. Through the flapping canvas of one wagon Alys saw the bottles and jars and the shining implements of the chirurgeon hung in readiness. And everywhere there were men and horses. The horses —from huge carthorses to tiny half-grown ponies— stood tethered, patiently waiting to be harnessed or saddled, while the men— gunners, musketeers, dragoons, pikemen and cavalrymen—went about the business of preparing for battle. The ground around them had been churned into a quagmire of mud which had frozen into iron-hard ruts and made moving the heavy vehicles doubly difficult.

She rode past them and on into the village where she saw Garret supervising the carting of the arms and ammunition from the church to a fenland lighter on the New Drain. His men worked with a will, though why they should do so when everyone knew they might not be paid for weeks on end, she did not know. Perhaps it had something to do with the way he treated them. He was certainly not soft, because she had seen him ordering the punishment of one of the troopers who had been looting, but neither was he harsh. And he did not ask anything of his men that he was not prepared to do himself.

Her curiosity overcame her determination not to speak to him. 'Where is the fighting now, Captain?'

'It is all around us,' he said non-committally.

'Then do we not need the arms and ammunition here?'

'It has a more important destination.'

'And where is that?'

He smiled. 'I suggest you ask no questions and then you will not be misunderstood.'

'You do not trust me, do you?'

'Should I?' he asked mildly. 'Would you not pass the information on to your delinquent friends?'

She had not considered that; her enquiry had not been motivated by the idea of spying, and if it had, who was there to tell? 'If I did, it

145

would only be to bring about an earlier end to the war,' she said, refusing to explain herself.

'Or to make widows of the women in the village,' he snapped. 'Most of my troops are your neighbours, men you have known all your life, men who trust the Carthorne name. Please remember that.'

He turned from her to shout at one of the men who was handling a powder keg carelessly, and did not see her leave. If only he had the time he might have been able to explain to her why he did what he did, why it was so important for Parliament to win the struggle against the tyranny of a King who thought he could rule without an elected legislature. He wished Charles no physical harm, any more than the other Roundhead commanders did, but he had to be beaten, and beaten quickly. It was important for the coming operation that every pike and musket, every ounce of powder, every cannon ball, should be gathered up in an effort to free Sir Thomas Fairfax and his cavalry who were bottled up in Hull. It would be a dangerous undertaking through Royalist-held country and he wished he had her good wishes to take with him. He wondered if telling her he had allowed Lieutenant Forrester to escape would soften her attitude, but he could never admit that, not to her, not to anyone, while the conflict continued. The young man had paid dearly for his freedom and the money had allowed him to make up the men's arrears of pay and recruit more. He judged it was worth it.

Now, paid and clothed, the men were ready for action and he must put his personal wishes to one side and concentrate on the war; the sooner it was won, the sooner he could return home for good and settle down as a married man. If only Alys were more amenable to the idea!

Waterlea, isolated as it was, had so far escaped being fought over, but if this latest move were unsuccessful it would not be long before its inhabitants were hurled into the fray. Any Parliamentary forces left in the vicinity when the enemy came would defend the small fortress and the saker and cannon would be put to good use. If the Royalists reached the village first, they would take advantage of the guns to repel attempts to retake it. Either way there would be deaths and bloodshed and the innocent would suffer along with the guilty. Offering up a fervent prayer that it would never happen, he ordered Aldous to take the troop to the rendezvous with Cromwell, while he boarded the lighter, with the sergeant, to accompany the arms and powder to its destination just short of Lincoln.

As he picked up the long pole to quant the vessel out into the New Drain, he caught sight of Alys, with her back to him, riding along the bank top towards the manor. The hood of her cloak was thrown back and her light gold hair, shimmering in the autumn sun, lifted and fell as she rode. 'God keep her safe,' he murmured. 'Keep them all safe.'

*   *   *

Alys followed the conduct of the struggle as carefully as any strategist; she questioned every visitor, bought unnecessary items from itinerant traders in order to loosen their tongues, and seized and read the London newspapers before her father could lay his hands on them; their news was often weeks old, but taken together they gave her a good idea of how the war was progressing.

On leap year day, a Parliamentary force besieged Newark, but it was not a united army and as usual there were arguments among the various commanders, which resulted in nothing very positive being done to take the town. The delay gave Prince Rupert time to assemble a relief column, and three weeks after the siege began, he appeared at the rear of the besiegers and forced them to surrender. The victory heralded a second phase of Royalist dominance over the county.

Alys had always thought of the Cavaliers as being gentlemen, honourable men, as Benedick was, men who respected another man's property and were courteous to women; it was the Roundheads who were supposed to

148

be uncouth, grasping and merciless. Seeing the Royalist foragers from her bedchamber window, raiding the homes of the villagers and carrying away food and drink the people could ill spare, she began to realise how well they deserved the name of Cavalier. Did they loot to keep alive or for the sheer pleasure of it? It made her think of Damian and she remembered his behaviour when he had been caught and the way he had used her to shield himself from Garret's sword. His kisses and soft words had been meant to blind her to his real motives and she wondered if he would have allowed her to be hurt, if Garret had not been so careful of her. She was unsure, unsure even of her own feelings, and she had been right when she had told her father she was confused. She was very confused.

Lord Carthorne was becoming more and more frail and hardly ventured beyond the walls surrounding his home. His armchair had been brought from the hall to the smaller, less draughty parlour and placed close to the fire. He often sat there, wearing a velvet dressing gown and a nightcap with earflaps, with his feet resting on a cushioned stool with more cushions at his back and head. He looked old and weak, though his eyes had a life the rest of his body lacked. Alys helped him to rise each morning and helped him to bed each night, and in between she fetched and carried for him and listened to tales of his youth and his constant cry that things would never be the same again.

'The house used to be full of people,' he would say wistfully. 'Neighbours, friends, cousins would come to visit and we would have whole roasted pigs, venison and peacocks. There would be pies and puddings and huge cheeses and all the sack and mead you could drink, besides wines from France and Italy. We had fine gold plate and delicate Venetian glass, and tapestries and rugs worth hundreds of pounds hanging on the walls and decorating our beds.' Every time he spoke of it—and that was nearly every day—he heaved a regretful sigh and added, 'Gone, all gone. And for what? Because King and Parliament could not agree and fell to squabbling like children. They should have their heads knocked together.'

She smiled at the mental picture that suggestion created and said, '*Your* head would be on the block if you tried that, Father; better to lie low and hope for better times to come.'

'Not for me,' he said. 'I am almost at journey's end.'

'Father, I will not have you talk like that.'

'You will marry Garret, won't you? It is for your own good.'

'I have given you my promise, Father, but my word is not enough; Garret must return and honour the contract.'

'He will. You have only to be patient. The

news is good.'

She did not need to read newspapers to know that the Earl of Manchester and his eastern association army had rescued the Parliamentary troops in Lincolnshire because it had happened all around them and sometimes, when the wind was in the right direction, they could even hear the heavy guns. The Earl marched into Stamford towards the end of April and drove the Cavaliers from Grimsthorpe and Sleaford, before pushing forward to retake Lincoln and ending, once again, the Royalist occupation of the county.

'The men will come home now,' Lord Carthorne said. 'They will be here in time for the haymaking.'

'No, Father, Dr Sandy told me the Earl's orders are to link up with Sir Thomas Fairfax and his northern army who are besieging York.'

'Then what will happen here? Are we to be undefended from those marauding fellows in Newark?'

'The Earl of Manchester has left a regiment in Lincoln and ordered new infantry and cavalry to be raised for the defence of the county.'

'Where is he going to find more men? Will he rob cradles? And what do we do in the meantime?'

'What we always have, Father. We go on

with our life as normally as possible.'

'Normal? Nothing will ever be normal again . . .' And he was off on his favourite topic, which she knew by heart. It left her mind free to wander, but its wandering always returned to the same theme—Garret and his promise to talk about their future. He had given his word to her father, as she had, but he had given it reluctantly and it was possible that, in time, he would find a reason for not going on with the marriage; she had made it very clear that was what she wanted herself. When Garret did not return after the battle at Lincoln, she knew he had gone with the army to distant battlefields, and she could not help wondering if he was glad to go.

Lord Carthorne's predictions proved correct, and as soon as the main Parliamentary forces had left the county the Newark Royalists resumed their plundering. While they were in control, very little news reached the villages and, although many of the women were indifferent to the tide of war, they were all anxious for tidings of their menfolk. With all the able-bodied men gone from Waterlea, it was left to the women to do work traditionally done by their menfolk, looking after the few cattle they had managed to hide in the fen when the scavenging armies of both sides paid their calls, fishing for eels and working in the osier and reed beds.

Alys, with her skirt pulled up between her

legs and fastened into her waist at the front and her hair pushed into a wide-brimmed sun-bonnet, was out in the fields helping with the haymaking one July day, when a horseman galloped along the road into the village, shouting 'Victory! Victory!' Alys flung her scythe on the bank by the ditch and scrambled up on to the road, with everyone else. They caught up with him outside the church where he had stopped to nail a notice on the door.

'What news?' they asked breathlessly.

'Parliament has won a great victory at Marston Moor. Prince Rupert's forces have been scattered and we have Cromwell to thank for that—he turned the tide of battle when all seemed lost.'

'Is the war won, then?'

'I don't know about that,' the harbinger said. 'The King is still master of the south.'

'Ne'er mind the south. What we want to know is when will our men be home?'

He did not know and would not even hazard a guess, and they returned to the hayfield hardly wiser than before.

Alys was in an outhouse, helping salt down a newly slaughtered pig, when the arrival of a stranger with his arm in a sling brought the next report. The sleeves of her brown bodice were pushed up above her elbows and the huge white apron she wore was splattered with blood. She did not stop to take it off, but hastily washed and dried her bloodied hands and ran to the courtyard where he stood surrounded by eager servants.

'The King himself has led an army into Cornwall and defeated the Earl of Essex,' he said, confirming that the war had not yet been won. 'And Manchester failed to stop him returning safely to Oxford.'

Alys's thoughts flew to Garret and then to Benedick and the worry, never far from her mind, that they would meet in battle filled her with alarm. It was what she had come to dread most because they would have to put aside their former relationship and fight as sworn enemies.

She questioned the wounded man closely, but could extract no more information. Reluctantly she bade the servants give him food and a bed for the night and returned to her work.

When autumn came and the cows were brought into the barn, a handful of men drifted back. Some had been wounded, others had decided that homes and families were more important than fighting and had deserted. They brought tales of distant sieges and long marches, of heroism and cowardice; of Garret there was no sign.

The weather was certainly not suitable for fighting battles; it was the wettest autumn Alys could remember. The summer grounds at Waterlea were inundated much earlier than usual, and the water was high in the dykes.

Underfoot the earth was soft; a pool of water was left in every footprint wherever she walked. If the ground was so wet so early, it did not bode well for the newly drained fields. When the water topped the banks, they would flood again and nothing could be done about them until the spring, but the fen people had lived with annual floods all their lives and they simply brought out their stilts and boats and carried on.

Alys and Prue were returning home from church one Sunday in late October when they chanced upon Hannah Martin, hurrying up to the manor. 'The Lincolnshire men have been sent home,' she told them. 'Ingram has seen them.'

The overnight rain had slackened to a fine drizzle which hung in the air and shrouded the fens in mist, so that they could hardly see the path ahead of them. Prue had not wanted to attend the service, complaining that the damp air was enough to bring them both down with the ague, but Alys had insisted and, clad in heavy cloaks with fur-lined hoods and with pattens on their shoes, they had ventured out. Now she was glad that they had; news—any news—was like meat and drink to her. 'Where are they now?' she asked eagerly.

'Outside Crowland. According to Ingram, they have it under siege, but it can't hold out. The town is surrounded by floodwater and cut off from supplies. When the Royalist garrison

155

surrenders, our men will come home.'

'And Captain Hartswood? Is he with them?'

'I do not know, my lady—my man had no chance to speak to any of them. He did say not to try and go there.'

Crowland was their nearest market town. Because of the difficulty of travelling over flooded terrain, no one had tried to go in recent weeks, but Hannah knew that some would attempt it by boat as soon as food stocks fell low.

They thanked her and continued on their way, holding their cloaks closely about them as they headed into the wind. Was Garret really only twenty miles away? If he came home, did it mean a wedding? He had said they would talk of the future, but she had not been able to tell whether he meant talk of marriage or talk of postponement. But could he put it off, when he had given his word to her father? And how could she bring herself to marry an enemy?

CHAPTER SIX

It was not Garret's idea of fighting a war, sitting in a boat watching and waiting, and taking pot shots at anyone who ventured out on the water to catch eels. They were starving out the innocent townspeople of Crowland, many of whom he knew as friends and neighbours, along with the enemy forces which held the town. 'Give me a battlefield any day,' he said to Aldous. 'I'd as lief have the hard ground beneath me and both sides drawn up in battle array with horses and heavy guns and lines of musketeers and pikemen. At least you can see your enemy and there are no innocent women and children involved.'

'Everyone becomes involved in a war such as this is,' Aldous said. 'And if the enemy uses women and children as pawns in the game, then we have no choice but to make war on them too.'

Garret knew he was indirectly referring to Alys and the Cavalier lieutenant. It had amounted to more than simply giving succour to a wounded man; she had betrayed a trust. She and her father had been left to enjoy their home on the implicit condition that they did nothing to help the Royalists. Lord Carthorne understood that, so why had Alys flouted it?

For over a year, his anger had been like a flame in his gut, and it fed on the memories which haunted him. He had nurtured it with thoughts of revenge, and he had promised himself that neither his love of his dead father nor his respect for Lord Carthorne would stop him from sending her to her just punishment. It was war and she had, by her own actions, become a warrior. It made no difference that she was a woman; her weapons were just as lethal as musket and pike, and their effect just as devastating.

They had been taken by surprise as the fen lighter, loaded with arms and ammunition, glided up the river towards Lincoln. He had been standing at the prow, using the quant pole to keep it away from the reeds, when the firing had started. Before he could do anything to retaliate, the attackers had hit one of the powder kegs and he had seen the vessel's owner blown into a thousand pieces, before he had felt himself being hurtled over the side and the breath being sucked from his body, as if a mule had kicked all his ribs in. He had surfaced some way from the sinking vessel and, gasping for air, had trodden water and looked back. Half a dozen Royalists had stood, with smoking muskets, on the river bank, surveying their handiwork. It was only when he had seen Damian Forrester among them that he had realised how they had learned about the boat and its cargo. The young man had been laughing aloud and shouting, 'That is how I serve those who cross me. Do you hear me, ghost of Garret Hartswood? Waterlea Manor will be mine. The Lady Alys will be mine. The victory will be mine. She wanted you to die and I have granted her wish. May your soul rot in Purgatory.'

'And may you survive long enough for my vengeance,' Garret had muttered, ducking beneath the water and silently swimming to the other shore. He surfaced once or twice to make sure of his direction and then hauled himself out among a clump of reeds, where he had lain panting and bleeding from a wound to his shoulder, until the cold air forced him to move. A few yards along the bank, he had found Sergeant Wally, covered in blood and so badly burned that he was almost unrecognisable, but he was alive. In spite of his own wound, he had dragged him to an abandoned cottage by the side of a fen. He could do little except bind the man's wounds and give him water and try to quieten his shrieks because the Royalists were still in the vicinity. The sergeant had lived for two agonising days before death came to release him and in that time Garret's rage had festered like the wound in his shoulder. He cursed the day he had set Damian Forrester free. How he could have fooled himself into thinking either he or Alys would be grateful, he did not know.

She had looked at him, with those wide blue eyes which had so captivated him when she had been a child and which had been one of the reasons he had been persuaded to agree to the marriage, and he had been fool enough to trust her. Now he knew those eyes were part of her woman's armoury; they disguised a cold, calculating heart and she used them to lay a man open as quickly and cleanly as a butcher's cleaver. No more, he had told himself, as he fought his way back from the brink of death, no more being soft with her.

His fermenting anger had given him the strength and courage to fight with renewed fury when he had joined Lord Willoughby's troops and helped to clear the Lindsey coast of its Royalist garrisons. He had discovered that his own troops were wintering in Boston, but he had not been in the mood for idleness; he had deliberately set out to find the fiercest fighting and had been with the forces which retook Gainsborough. His rage had been still burning, though in the absence of anything tangible to fasten it on it had been growing cooler, when they had driven the Royalists from Lincolnshire. He had not wanted to return to Waterlea and Alys, knowing that to do so would revive his fury and that somehow he could not face that. Instead he had tried to volunteer for service in the north, where the Scots had been persuaded to come in on Parliament's side and had crossed the border to harass the Royalist's northern army. He had been refused and been ordered to rejoin his old company, under the Earl of Manchester, for the fight at Marston Moor, which he had survived unscathed. The Earl had refused to march to the west country to the aid of Essex and had sent his army back to Lincolnshire and the eastern counties. And here they were, the Waterlea men, sitting in rowing boats, within twenty miles of home, and every one of them, with the possible exception of Garret himself, anxious to lift the siege and return to their loved ones.

*   *   *

On the day Crowland finally surrendered, Alys decided to enlist the help of Simon to row the boat, and set off into the fen with a dozen eel traps. Because the villagers needed to be extra careful with food stocks, they had to use the bounty of the fen to best advantage, and catching eels was one way; the cook at the manor was famed for her eel pie.

The weather was fine but very cold, and sounds carried clearly on the still air as they moved out on to the water. They could hear Ingram Martin's dog barking and the distant boom of a bittern and, close at hand, the croak of a frog in the bank, all normal peaceful noises. They had been out about an hour, punting their way among the reed beds and dropping the traps, when they heard the sound of horses galloping along the high road. Alys stood up, rocking the boat and making Simon cry out for her to have a care, but she could not see the riders.

'Back!' she ordered Simon, thinking immediately of Garret. 'Quick as you can!'

As soon as the boat had grounded, she

scrambled out and ran towards the manor, her inexplicable eagerness to see him lending wings to her feet.

She arrived at the end of the path to the manor, just in time to see the riders cross the drawbridge ahead of her, and she knew at once that Garret was not with them. They were not even Roundheads, but Royalists, the sort that had plagued them through the summer months. She could hear them yelling as they rode into the courtyard. Alys ran the faster, knowing their sudden appearance would alarm her father and the old servants left behind in the house.

Hurrying across the drawbridge and in at the gate, she could hear them shouting. 'Who is at home? Out with you! We need refreshment.'

They were answered by a pistol shot from one of the windows. It felled one of the riders and so incensed his companions that they let off a fusillade of musket balls, followed by another shot from the house. The whole courtyard seemed to be a writhing mass of men and horses, made indistinct by gunsmoke.

Alys picked up her skirts and ran forward. It was no good going to the front door where the soldiers were milling about and demanding entrance; she changed her direction and ran round the side and in at the kitchen door. There were servants cowering under the table and more in the hall which led to the front of the house. John was there, shouting orders while he pushed powder down the muzzle of a musket. A length of lighted matchcord lay on a chair nearby, ready to fire it.

'Where is Lord Carthorne?' she asked him.

'In the great hall.'

She ran past him and into the hall as more shots were fired from outside. Her father, who was kneeling on the floor beside the window reloading his pistol, looked up as she entered. His cap had fallen from his head and he looked wild and years younger than he had done of late; it was almost as if he were enjoying himself.

'Father, why did you fire on them?' she asked. 'They are Royalists.'

'Are they?' he said mildly, as if the fact had no relevance. 'They are too noisy by far, and no one makes demands on the Carthornes with impunity.' He turned back to the window and raised himself to see over its sill to fire.

'Father, don't!'

The sharp sound of her voice caught his attention at last. She was not sure afterwards whether he turned towards her before he was hit or as a result of it, but the weapon left his hand and spun crazily across the floor as he fell.

'Father!' She ran to kneel beside him. There was blood oozing from a hole in his doublet. She cradled his head in her lap, shouting for the steward. 'John! Cease firing and come here, his lordship has been hit.' And then, as the attackers resumed their shouting and hammering on the front door, added. 'Tell someone to let those men in before we are all killed.'

She did not know how she remained so calm, but someone had to take the lead and there was no one else to do it. The colour had drained from her father's face and he was bleeding profusely. She held him, talking soothingly to him until Prue arrived with her unguents and bandages and a pain-killing medicine, and pushed her to one side so that she could attend to his wounds. The hall was crowded with soldiers and servants and no one seemed to know what they should be doing.

'Where is your officer?' she asked one of the men.

'He will be here later.'

'Why did you fire on the house? This family has always supported the King.'

He laughed. 'Then you have a strange way of showing it. We asked for admittance, nothing more, and we were fired on. You must blame the old man.'

'He was confused by the manner of your arrival.'

She turned back to her father, as Prue rose from her knees and said quietly, 'He has gone, my lady.'

'Gone?' It was a moment before she

understood what was being said to her, then, as the strength left her legs, she sank down beside her father and cradled his head on her lap. 'It isn't true, it can't be true, he has just lost his senses, that's all.' She pushed his hair from his forehead, stroked his cheeks and murmured, 'Father, oh Father . . .' But his brave spirit had left his tired old body and there was no one there to answer her. She dropped her head down to his and sobbed.

She was unaware of the silence which had come over the crowded room, or the sudden wailing as the servants realised what had happened, or the dragoons, gathering in a corner uncertain whether to continue their demands for food and shelter or to retire and leave the family to their grieving. Not until a heavy vehicle drew into the courtyard and stopped did she remember where she was sufficiently to turn tear-filled eyes towards the door to see who had arrived.

'What has happened here?' Damian Forrester's voice was loud in the quiet which had descended on the room at his entrance.

'The old man fired on us before we could identify ourselves,' one of the soldiers told him. 'We thought he was an enemy . . .' His voice tailed off as Damian went over to where Alys sat on the floor beside her father's body.

'Is he dead?'

She nodded, unable to speak.

'I am sorry, Alys—my men were told to

treat you all with respect.'

'They are *your* men?'

'Yes, I am their captain.' He paused, watching her rocking herself beside her father's dead body. 'I am as grieved as you are, but it was an accident.'

'Accident!' she shrieked. 'Accident! Respect, you say! They had little of that, shouting and laughing and banging on the door. No wonder Father thought they were the enemy.' It was better to be angry, better than crying helplessly. 'And if you are their officer, then it is your fault.'

'I was not even here.'

'Then you should have been. You should have been leading them and making sure they obeyed you.'

'I am sorry,' he said again, bending to take her arm and help her to rise. 'I am sorry. If I could undo what has been done, I would.' His voice softened. 'Leave him now, my dear, leave him to others. Come away.'

She pulled herself away from him and scrambled to her feet unaided. 'Go away! Take yourself and your murderous band away from here.'

'I am afraid I cannot, we need quarters . . .'

She did not stay to hear what else he had to say, but pushed past him and fled to her room, refusing to come out until the time of her father's funeral two days later.

She found it hard to accept his death; he

166

had been such a caring father, such a good man. Life without him was going to be difficult enough without the added burden of having Damian and his troops quartered at the manor. She learned that the reason he had not been with his men when they arrived was because he had so much loot—he called it supplies—he needed a cart to carry it all, and he had not trusted anyone else to drive it. The contents of the cart had been transferred to the old crypt and more added to it, as his dragoons ranged over the countryside picking it clean. Watching him and listening to him, Alys began to have doubts; she was no longer sure of the wider issues, but here, at Waterlea, she knew she did not want the Cavaliers occupying her home and village. She longed for peace with every fibre of her being.

The troops made free with all the rooms except her bedchamber and she wondered how long it would be before Damian invaded that. He seemed to think that she cared for him, that his earlier kisses had meant something to her, and his arrogance infuriated her. She needed support and comfort and, though he made a token offer of it, she knew he was insincere. If Garret were to arrive now, she told herself, she would throw herself on his neck and admit she had been wrong about him.

'The Waterlea men are not far away,' she told Damian, hoping to persuade him to leave.

167

'Do you think I care about a handful of ignorant villagers? Without their captain they will be only too pleased to surrender.'

'Without their captain?' she queried. 'Do you mean Garret?'

'Yes. I told you I would rid you of him, did I not? He is dead.'

'Dead?' Alys sat down heavily on the nearest stool as the strength left her legs. Her voice was a whisper, barely audible above the noise in the courtyard of off-duty soldiers relieving their boredom with drinking and singing and firing their muskets to frighten the servants.

'Do you want to know how he died?' Damian asked. 'He let me go free, which was very foolish of him, because I knew about the arms store in the village, did I not? I did as I said I would; I reported the matter to my superiors in Newark, who were considerate enough to promote me and allow me to lead the raid against the vessel. It and its cargo were blown to the heavens and everyone on board went with it. That, my lady, is how Garret Hartswood died.'

Alys felt numb with shock. His description of what had happened was graphically blunt and all the more shocking because of that. She remembered Garret as she had last seen him, standing with a quant pole in his hand, ready to help the owner of the vessel propel it into midstream. She found herself imagining the

168

horror of the explosion and saw in her mind's eye, the fragments of the boat and the bodies flying into the air, the debris floating on the water, and the fire, soon extinguished, as what was left of the lighter went down. Her actions had struck a blow for the King's cause, but she could not pretend to be glad. It was all very well to take sides in a war, to help those you favoured, but when it came so close to home, when you had met and spoken to the enemy, it was very different. She had wished Garret dead and said so, but now she felt bereft, not only racked by guilt and shame, but with the full realisation that she had loved him all along, that her confusion had been her pride battling with her desire. Fate had been doubly cruel to her; it had taken a beloved father and the man she loved and wanted to marry, almost in one blow.

Damian thought her tears were all for her father, and she did nothing to disabuse him of the idea.

'Do not grieve, my lovely Alys,' he said when he found her one morning just before Christmas sitting in the window seat of the great hall gazing out on to the courtyard with a faraway look in her eye. 'Your father would not have wanted you to mourn so.'

She did not know how he did it, but his blue doublet with its slashed sleeves was immaculate and the lace on his collar, cuffs and boot hose was pristine white; his manservant must be continually at work on his clothes, she decided. He smiled and walked over to sit beside her and take her hand in his.

'How do you know what he would have wanted?' she said. 'You knew nothing about him.'

'Benedick often spoke of him and I met him once when he visited your brother at Cambridge. He treated me kindly.'

' 'Tis a pity you did not think of that when you sent your men to terrify him.'

'I have said I am sorry. Am I to be punished for that forever?'

'You have not been punished at all.'

'You punish me by being so unforgiving. Now, put it behind you, Alys, and let us talk of the future, *our* future.'

'Future?' she repeated dully.

'Yes. Benedick is now Lord Carthorne and, if I ask it, he will marry you to me. We will live here with him and be happy for the rest of our lives.'

It was a moment before she understood what he was saying, and then she was so taken aback all she could reply was, 'My brother will not make marriage contracts for me; he will let me choose a husband for myself.'

'Good.' He stroked the back of her hand idly as he spoke. His self-confidence was infuriating, but, then, she told herself, why should he not be confident?

'Benedick does not yet know of our father's

death,' she said, deciding it would not be wise to argue with him. 'I have no idea where to send the news. Do you know where he is?'

'As far as I know, he is still with the King.'

'Could you find him and persuade him to come home?'

'That might be difficult.' He paused. 'Not only because the King needs him but because I must remain here to prevent the Lincolnshire men reaching their homes and regrouping.'

'Have you not done enough without shedding the blood of simple honest men who have no quarrel with you?'

'They enlisted for Parliament and that is quarrel enough.'

'Most of them were impressed, they had no choice.'

'And some are professional soldiers,' he said angrily. 'And those honest men you spoke of follow willingly. I am surprised at you, my lady, you who profess to be a loyal subject of Charles.'

'I am,' she said. 'But I have known the Waterlea men all my life and I do not want to see them hurt.'

'You are too soft, but then you are a woman and a very beautiful one too.' He smiled and lowered his lips to hers. She felt nothing except revulsion; how could she possibly have preferred him to Garret? When he released her, she stood up with a show of reluctance and forced herself to smile. 'I must speak to Cook about the dinner. Please excuse me.'

'Very well. We will talk again tomorrow.'

She did not go to the kitchen, but went to the small sitting-room where a fire burned brightly in the grate, dispersing the December gloom, and where Prue was busy mending.

'If the men come home, they will be met by force,' Alys told her, sitting down and picking up a half-finished tapestry. 'And then heaven knows what will happen to their families and homes. We must warn them.'

'How many times have you been told not to meddle in men's business?' Prue, who had always been outspoken, was filled with alarm at the thought of any further involvement in the war. 'You would be best advised to put up with the inconvenience of having soldiers quartered here and wait patiently for them to leave, which they will do as soon as there is no more plunder to be had.'

'This is different. This time I am thinking only of the Waterlea men.' Alys saw no inconsistency in her behaviour, although it was not lost on Prue. 'I am going to see Hannah. Goodman Martin will know where to find them.'

'That would be very unwise, my lady. If Captain Forrester should hear of it—'

'I can deal with Damian. He imagines I love him.'

'He must be blind then, for you have

behaved very coolly towards him.'

'He puts that down to grief. If you do not want to accompany me, then I shall take Anne or go alone.'

'My lady—'

'I do not want to hear another word, Prue. And after I have spoken to Goodman Martin, I shall go to Oxford to see Benedick. He should know what has happened here.'

Prue sighed and went off to find their cloaks and pattens and then followed her to the cottage beside the mere. They would catch a fever or a chill or something equally dire, she forecast, as they tramped over the boggy ground in pouring rain and then waited for over an hour while Hannah went to find her husband, who was out fishing.

By the time they returned home, Alys had to admit she was chilled to the bone and, indeed, she could not stop shivering. She did not protest when Prue insisted she strip off all her clothes and go to bed with a dose of medicine.

'You had best forget about going out again, until the weather improves,' Prue said, as she watched her drain the glass.

'Do armies march only when the sun shines?' she asked, already drowsy. 'I mean to start out for Oxford in the morning.'

But Prue knew differently. Under the influence of the drug, Alys slept late into the next day and, when she finally awoke, the rain had stopped and the sun was shining. Annoyed that she had been allowed to stay abed so late, she sprang up and ran to the window. The manor and the higher parts of the village were standing on a tiny island; all around it was water, acres and acres of it, stretching as far as the eye could see, from the mere on one side to the high road on the other. In the middle the Van Hildts' home stood on its half-acre of high ground, and above it hung a pall of smoke.

It was Ingram Martin's doing, of course, though why he should have chosen that moment to resume his sabotage of the drainage, Alys did not know. She was frustrated because she had been prevented from leaving, and angry with Prue for drugging her into sleeping through it all.

'Did no one try to stop him?' she demanded, when she found her maid in the kitchen. Most of the servants were gathered there, totting up the provisions they had stored and trying to estimate how long they would last, given that the Royalist troops would be with them until the floodwater receded or until someone could reach them by boat.

'I expect Goodman Martin thought it was an opportunity not to be missed,' John answered. 'The water was high from the rain and there was a big tide in the Wash which rose higher than usual up the rivers. He had only to breach the banks in a few places.'

'It was senseless,' Alys said.

'Perhaps.' He smiled. 'But Captain Forrester is in a rage because he knows the Waterlea men are coming home and he and his men are trapped here.'

'But do our men know they are here?'

'The flag,' someone said suddenly. 'We are flying a Royalist flag.'

'Our own men will fire on us,' wailed Anne, throwing her apron over her head and bursting into tears.

'Either that or starve us out,' John said. 'We must be careful with our provisions.'

'I do not believe they will do that,' Prue said. 'The men know we have good supplies of food because they helped to gather it in, and they know about the saker and the demi-cannon and will not risk an assault.'

'Perhaps not,' said Alys, conceding that her maid was probably right. 'But there is smoke over the Van Hildts' farm. What caused that?'

Prue looked from Alys to John and back again before speaking. 'That was Ingram, too.'

'But why?'

'Master Van Hildt would not honour the settlement,' Prue went on. 'He refused to restore the summer fields to the villagers, even though the year was up and he had not established his legal title. Goodman Martin was so angry, he raised a band of men and women—mostly women, o' course—and sent

175

half to breach the banks, while the other half marched against the Van Hildts' house, threatening to tear it down. Master Van Hildt went out and took a pitchfork to one of them, injuring him badly. They sent for me to tend the injured man. I saw the flames before I ever got there.'

'They set fire to the house?' Alys was appalled.

'No, the barn. Mistress Van Hildt went mad with rage, shouting something about her mare, then the Dutchman ran into the inferno to fetch out his beasts. They heard him shrieking, but they could not save him before the roof collapsed on top of him.'

'You mean he is dead?'

'Yes, my lady.'

'But this is dreadful,' Alys said, feeling very sorry for Lettice in spite of their disagreements. 'Ingram Martin cannot go unpunished.'

'Who is there to punish him, my lady?' John asked. 'Your father is dead, Captain Hartswood is dead and Master Benedick is miles away. As for Captain Forrester . . .' Not wishing, out of deference to the Carthorne family, to be disloyal to the Royalist cause, he did not voice his contempt of that young man.

Alys was the only member of the Carthorne family left in Waterlea; it was up to her to put aside her personal grief and do what had to be done. 'John, go down to the village and fetch

176

everyone up here, all of them, including Mistress Van Hildt. We can shelter in the crypt if we have to.' She paused and looked about her. 'Simon, go and see if you can find a boat and bring it up to the moat. Do not let Captain Forrester or any of his men see you go. When it is dark, we must send someone to contact our men and tell them we are prepared.'

'I will go,' Simon said, grinning from ear to ear. 'I can find them.'

Alys left them to carry out her orders and went up to her bedchamber, where she put on several underskirts, one above the other, and topped them with a heavy brocade overdress and a warm, full-length coat. Her hair she tucked into a coif and tied a tall-crowned hat on top of it with a silk scarf. Thus clad, she crept from the house without being seen and rowed the boat Simon had found across the flooded fields to the cottage on the edge of the mere, though what she would do and say when she reached it, she did not know. First of all she had to establish the facts; Prue's account might not have been totally accurate.

She found Hannah tying up the ferry, as if she had just returned from crossing to the other side. She had wrapped a shawl over her shoulders with the corners tucked into the waistband of the apron she wore, and she had another covering her head, but Alys knew she must be feeling the bitterness of the weather.

She greeted Alys and finished tying up the boat with hands blue with cold, then she led the way back to the cottage. The ground floor was several inches deep in freezing water, but Hannah was used to floods and had lifted everything from the floor on to tables and cupboards.

'I am sorry to see you have been inundated too,' Alys said. 'Come up to the manor until the water goes down; you cannot live here like this.'

'Thank you, my lady.' The woman's voice revealed how tired and dispirited she was.

'Where is Goodman Martin?'

Hannah shrugged. 'I do not know.'

'I heard about Master Van Hildt's barn, Hannah. Why did he do it? Why? Ingram must have known such a thing could not be overlooked or treated lightly, not even in wartime. Did he think that because there was no justice in Waterlea since his lordship's . . .?' She faltered, but took hold of herself quickly. 'Did he think my father's death meant that he would escape without punishment?'

'Ingram meant only to frighten the Dutchman into honouring the settlement. After all, that did give the villagers the right to seize the land if he did not establish his claim come Michaelmas, and Michaelmas is long past.'

'It did not give him the right to break the banks and flood it, did it?'

178

'The land has always been flooded in winter, you know that. That was how God created it and that is how it should stay.'

'But that is no excuse for killing Master Van Hildt.'

'He did not die by the hand of the Waterlea people, my lady; it was his own wife.'

'His wife?' Alys found that almost impossible to believe, but she could not imagine Hannah would lie. 'Are you accusing Mistress Van Hildt of murder?'

'I don't know about murder, my lady, but I do know the barn was not fired by any of the commoners and she made him go into it when it was well ablaze. He would not go at first, but she kept shrieking and yelling about her horse and the cattle, and when he hesitated, she pushed him in and then stood back while the barn burned.'

Alys leaned heavily against the table, cluttered as it was with shoes, pattens, fire irons, pots and pans. 'I can't believe she would deliberately do anything like that. She was just overwrought.'

'If she was, I saw no signs of it. She did not shed a tear.'

'Sometimes,' Alys said softly, 'grief is too deep for tears.'

'I saw what I saw,' Hannah said stubbornly. 'My husband is innocent of anything but wanting to bargain with the Dutchman, and he has no one to defend him but me. But I see it is useless to ask you to believe me.'

Alys put out a hand and touched the woman's arm. 'Justice will be done, Hannah. Come with me back to the manor.'

Hannah agreed reluctantly. 'Just until Ingram comes back,' she said.

For the first time since the war had begun, the manor was full of people. Old men, women and children were crowded into the great hall, rubbing shoulders with the soldiers and the parson who had, in her absence, taken advantage of his captive congregation to preach a sermon against trying to beat the elements.

'This is how it was in the old days,' he said, when Alys and Hannah arrived. 'In winter we were always cut off, but we had no trouble surviving. God has provided us with fish and fowl in plenty and there is enough fodder to keep the cows alive until the land drains again. We have milk and, if my memory serves me, his lordship always kept a good cellar. Let us give thanks.'

'I do not give thanks,' Lettice said. She would have preferred to remain in her own home even though the ground floor had been inundated, but her food store had been soaked and everything ruined and none of her servants was prepared to stay with her. Reluctantly she had agreed to accept Alys's hospitality. 'I have nothing for which I need to give thanks.'

Alys took off her hat and heavy cloak and handed them to Prue. 'I am sorry at your loss, Mistress Van Hildt,' she said, going over to where Lettice sat by the fire. 'If there is anything I can do——'

'You! You are useless and so was your father. If he had listened to my husband, that man Martin would have been safely locked up, my land would not have been ruined and my husband would not be dead. I insist the constable arrest him.' Lettice reminded Alys more than ever of a cat, a cat with cold green eyes. 'You think you can trample on me, you and your friends in the fens, wild, all of you, wild and lawless.'

'Lawless?'

'Yes, lawless. I shall expect swift action against the commoners, or your lack of enthusiasm will be reported to the Privy Council and no amount of compromise will help you keep Waterlea Manor.'

'It seems to me that the kettle is calling the pot black,' Alys said, knowing that if she kept cool she would gain the upper hand; Lettice was too agitated to think clearly. 'It seems to me that pushing a husband into the middle of an inferno to rescue an animal is nothing short of murder.'

'You have been listening to the ravings of a mad woman,' Lettice went on, giving Hannah a look of withering scorn. 'Hannah Martin wants you to believe that in order to save her

181

husband. If she persists in her folly, I shall denounce her and you along with her and when Garret comes back he will deal with the rabble and he will devise a suitable punishment for you which will give him greater satisfaction than handing you over to the law.'

Lettice obviously had not heard of Garret's death. 'Mistress Van Hildt,' Alys began. 'I think you should know—'

Lettice was determined to have her say and ignored the interruption. 'You will stay here only so long as it pleases him and you will not be able to complain if he finds his pleasure elsewhere; that will be your punishment.' She laughed and the sound echoed round the great hall like the cackling of a hen and then she noticed the stricken look on Alys's face. 'You love him! Oh, that will make his revenge doubly sweet, for he cannot abide you. You did not know we have been lovers for years, did you? After he has tired of you and sent you to the block, he will marry me, you will see. Garret will have the whole estate as payment for his services to the cause and I shall be mistress of it.' She stopped in triumph.

'Mistress Van Hildt,' Alys said quietly. 'I think you should know that Captain Hartswood is dead.'

'Dead?' Lettice's look of triumph faded. 'Garret is dead?'

'I am afraid so.'

'I do not believe it.'

'Then ask Captain Forrester, for he was the one who killed him.' Alys turned, seeking out Damian in the crowded hall. 'Where is the captain?' she asked.

They heard the shatter of glass, coarse laughter and then the foundations of the house shook as the saker was fired. There was more ribald laughter and Alys wondered what they were firing at to cause them such amusement. Could it be the Waterlea men? She did not think so, because there had been no call to arms, no sign of preparations to withstand an attack. She looked towards the door as Damian came in. 'What did you hit?' she asked.

He grinned. 'Oh, one of those wind machines that tips the water off the fields.'

Lettice gave a shout of anger and dashed out of the room to go upstairs and look from an upper window. Alys allowed herself a wry smile; without the help of that contraption, she would find it next to impossible to drain her fields again.

*   *   *

The sound of the saker shot echoed across the flooded fields. 'Have they seen us?' Aldous asked.

Garret shrugged. 'Who's to tell.'

'What do you see?'

Garret lowered his perspective glass and picked up the oars again. 'Nothing, there is no sign of movement.'

'And the flags?'

'Royalist. What else did you expect?' He spoke bitterly. Alys was running true to form and, in spite of Lord Carthorne's apparent change of heart over the war, she was still an out and out Royalist.

'Can we storm it?'

'No—as soon as we row into open water, they will be able to see us easily and pick us off like flies before we can get within musket range.'

'We could go back and fetch a cannon of our own and bombard the village,' Aldous suggested.

'And run the risk of killing or injuring our own women and children? The men would never stand for that.'

He pulled on the oars to return to where his men waited, tired and restless and anxious to be home. 'The men are used to moving about in floods,' he said. 'We will go in after dark and evacuate the villagers, then storm the manor.'

'And what about Lord Carthorne and Lady Alys?'

Garret was thoughtful. Which mattered most—protecting Lord Carthorne and his rebellious daughter or his loyalty to his men, who looked to him to get them safely home? He looked up as the boat grounded on the spot where the road on which they had been marching disappeared beneath the water. One of the men held the bow steady while Garret and his lieutenant climbed out. They were all looking towards him, cheerful and loyal to a man. 'They must take their chances,' he said, answering Aldous's question. 'After all, they are harbouring enemy troops.'

Some hours later, Garret pulled the boat into a clump of reeds, tied it up and clambered over the side into the icy water, followed by Aldous. They waded along what had once been a dry path and clambered out on to the village road, thankful that there was no moon and the night was very dark.

'There are no sentries,' he whispered. 'That's a blessing.'

'It's too quiet,' Aldous said. 'There should be some signs of life. None of the cottages has a light. And that big house—'

'That's mine.' Garret crept forward, though he thought the squelching of the water in his boots made a noise loud enough to wake the dead. He let himself into the flooded ground floor and it did not take many minutes to be sure that the house was deserted. So was the cottage which stood close by, and the next and the next.

'Where are they all?' Aldous asked, as Garret stood in the middle of the road, looking towards the manor, rising from the surrounding fen like a fairy-tale castle, ablaze with light.

'Up there,' he said, nodding. 'It has always been a place of shelter in times of trouble, I should have remembered that.'

'But do they know there is trouble coming? After all, they are used to being surrounded with water, it does not frighten them.'

'No, but the prospect of being in the firing line might.'

'Then we shall have to change our plans.'

'Yes. Go back and tell the men. Row them over a boatload at a time and muster them at the bottom of the road to the manor. Keep them out of sight and for God's sake keep them quiet. When you hear my signal, attack over the drawbridge.'

'Will it be down?'

'I am going to make sure it is. Now go as swiftly as you can.' He did not wait to see if Aldous obeyed, but turned back into Eagleholm and changed into dry clothes before hurrying along the only unflooded road in the village towards the lights of Waterlea Manor and Alys Carthorne.

CHAPTER SEVEN

It was a long day in which nothing stirred on the water except a few ducks and a heron or two, and nothing was heard except the gentle lap of wavelets against the broken banks and the occasional quack of a wild duck. Inside the manor the close confinement of Royalist soldiers, who feared an attack, and villagers whose loyalties were, because of Garret, mainly to Parliament, made for a tense atmosphere. It was made worse by Lettice, who alternated between periods of brooding silence and noisy outbursts of anger, directed at anyone who crossed her path. She was bitter and vengeful and Alys began to wonder if the woman had deliberately engineered the death of her husband in order to be free to marry Garret. To lose both husband and lover was a terrible irony if she had.

Something had to be done to ease the tension and stop her guests quarrelling among themselves. 'Let us have some music,' Alys suggested. 'And dancing. It will be like the old days.'

While the men pushed the heavy table against the wall, Prue fetched Alys's recorder and John brought out his guitar and in no time the air was filled with the sound of music.

Damian took Alys's instrument from her

and handed it to Anne. 'You play,' he commanded. 'I want to dance with your mistress.' Then he took Alys by the hand and led her on to the floor.

This was greeted with applause and then more people followed suit until the floor was crowded with young and old and, for the first time for weeks, the manor was filled with the sound of music and laughter.

They had been dancing for several minutes and Alys was circling slowly round Damian, when she noticed something over his shoulder which made her stumble. There was a movement behind the screen which divided the great hall from the front door; a shadow which moved swiftly out of sight as, her circling done, Damian took his turn to move round her. She craned her neck, trying to make out who or what it was, but that end of the hall remained in darkness.

'You are not paying attention, my lady,' her partner said. 'That is the second time you have missed the step.'

'What? Oh, yes, I am sorry.'

'What ails you?'

'Nothing, nothing at all. I think I should go and see if there is enough food.'

The shadow had resolved itself into a man, a tall broad-shouldered man in a plain brown leather coat with an orange sash. Was it a ghost come to haunt her? A wraith without substance or warmth? Her hand went to her mouth to stifle her cry.

'Of course there is enough, you worry too much.'

'I think I should go and make sure.'

'Alys, you are dancing with me. If you insist on running off, I shall think you find my company not to your liking.'

She was trembling and afraid of giving herself and Garret away, but she had to find some way of going to him and finding out if he was alone or supported by troops. 'It isn't that,' she said. 'But I must look after my guests.'

The music came to an end at last and he smiled slowly, before tucking her hand under his elbow and leading her towards the screen. 'Now we will go and see about the refreshments together.'

She hung back. 'No, Damian, you are right, I do worry too much. Let us join the galliard.'

He turned sharply to look into her face. 'Something is wrong. What is it?'

'Nothing, nothing at all.' They were very near the screen now and she did not see how she could do any more to prevent him from seeing the man who hid there. 'I simply want to please you.'

He laughed and drew her into the shadows. 'You do please me, my lovely Alys, but I want more. I want much, much more.' He pulled her into his arms and kissed her, lingering with his lips on hers, until she had no breath left. 'Oh, there is so much more I want and you can give me. I will do as you ask and go and find Benedick, because the sooner he comes home, the sooner we can be married. Will that please you?'

Before she could reply, she heard the clatter of a sword being flung to the ground and he was pulled forcibly from her and dealt a blow which put him on the floor. Garret stood over him, waiting for him to get to his feet so that he could punch him again, but Damian, feigning more hurt than he had really suffered, reached out and grabbed both Garret's ankles, bringing him down.

'Garret!' Alys shrieked and rushed forward, but she could do nothing but watch helplessly, with her knees turning to jelly, while they dealt blow for blow and first one, then the other, rolled on top. Everyone crowded round as the two men struggled, but no one made a move to try and separate them.

'Stop them, someone! Stop them!' Alys cried, only half aware that Lettice had pushed her way to the front and was standing beside her. 'Stop them before they kill each other!'

John appeared with an old pike he had pulled off the wall, intending to try and come between them, but before he could so two of Damian's men arrived, and dragged his adversary clear of him.

Garret looked pale and drawn, with dark shadows beneath his eyes, but the eyes themselves, dark points of brown velvet reflecting the lamplight, had more life than the rest of his features, which seemed to be hewn from rock. He wore no headgear and his hair tumbled to his shoulders in soft waves. His doublet had been torn at the shoulder but the white cuffs and falling collar of his shirt were so clean and fresh that Alys knew he must have recently changed his clothes.

She could do nothing but stand and gaze at him, while a whole range of conflicting emotions chased each other across her face—disbelief at the evidence of her own eyes; an overwhelming relief when she realised her eyes did not deceive her and he was alive; joy that he smiled; pain, because deep down, she had not wanted to hurt him, and his look was more of hurt than anger. But he was angry, she could tell by the set of his shoulders, the determined jut of his chin, his clenched fists, and it was not just because he had allowed himself to be captured.

Damian scrambled to his feet, wiping blood from his mouth, and turned towards his men, who were trying to control the still struggling Garret. 'I left you on guard,' he snapped at them. 'How did he manage to pass you?' They did not answer and he turned to the Roundhead captain. 'Where are your men?'

'I have none. I am alone.'

'Why, Garret?' Alys asked, trying to sound calm when all the time her heart was pounding and she wanted to sing and dance and kiss him over and over again for the sheer joy of seeing him alive. 'Why come alone? Did you not know the manor was occupied?'

He looked directly at her and there seemed to be an accusation in his brown eyes. He had seen her dancing with Damian and being kissed by him and she wanted to cry out, to explain that she had not wanted it.

'Would you have me risk good Waterlea men to take this den of delinquents?'

'It is not a den of delinquents. The men have been quartered here, that does not mean—'

'It means what it has always meant, that you cannot be trusted.'

'No, she certainly cannot,' Lettice put in, moving over to put her hand on his arm in a possessive gesture. 'You know she will stab you in the back, the minute you turn it on her. She took the Royalists in willingly and allowed them to bring all their plunder here. She has been party to robbing the people and she cannot gainsay it.'

Damian was watching Alys with some amusement, as if daring her to deny Lettice's accusations, but she could not, while he had the upper hand. She could help Garret best by staying cool and waiting to see what Damian did with him; precipitate action might make matters worse. Surely Garret knew that? She looked up at him, trying to convey a message in her eyes that would reassure him, but although he met her gaze he gave no indication that he understood.

'She told Ingram Martin to flood the fields,' Lettice went on. 'I saw her go to the cottage myself. She did it to stop you returning.'

It was too much. 'I did nothing of the kind,' Alys said. 'I—'

'You went to see that law-breaker,' Damian turned on her. 'For what reason?'

Alys was in a cleft stick; she could not appease one without antagonising the other, and she looked from one to the other, trying to find a way out of her dilemma. 'I went to fetch Hannah. Her home was flooded too, you know.'

It was all the two men could do to hold Garret, who had begun struggling again, and Damian realised that he had more important things to do than worry what Alys had been up to. 'Search the whole place!' he ordered, as more of his men arrived from outside. 'Search every inch. If he could get in unseen, then so could others.'

'He did not cross the drawbridge, I give you my word,' a sergeant said.

Damian turned to Alys. 'Is there another way?'

'Not that I know of.'

'You would tell me if you knew?'

'Certainly I would. Your men must have been neglecting their duty.'

'Take him to the crypt and lock him up!' Damian ordered, pointing to the Roundhead captain. 'Then pull up the drawbridge. We will have no more coming in over that tonight.'

As they hurried to obey Alys looked at Garret, a question in her eyes, but, if he understood it, he gave no indication that he did. Did he have men with him and had they already crossed the moat? Or would lifting the drawbridge cut them off on the wrong side? Why did he not understand what she was trying to do? If Lettice had not been there with her malicious accusations, would it have been easier to convince him? She doubted it because of what had happened to the lighter; he would never forgive her for that.

They marched him away and she bent, without thinking, to pick up his sword. Why had he not used it on Damian? Why had he simply used his fists? She glanced around her; everyone was talking in huddled groups and all Damian's men had gone off on the search. She hid the sword at the back of the sideboard behind a stack of plates; he might need it later and perhaps if she helped him to escape he would be convinced of her fidelity.

There was a great deal of shouting going on outside and then the sound of musket fire, and more shouting, and then Aldous ran into the hall, his bloodied sword in one hand and a pistol in the other. He looked round the crowded room until his eye found Alys.

'Where have they taken him?'

'To the crypt. Lieutenant, have you—?'

He did not wait for her to finish, but dashed from the room, shouting to someone else to follow him.

He had hardly gone before Damian returned, with a pistol in his back held by one of the Waterlea men.

'Joshua!' screamed his wife, and ran towards him, but she stopped short of embracing him and diverting him from his task. 'Thank God you are safe.'

'And the others?' one of the other women asked. 'Are the others here?'

Joshua grinned. 'Aye.' He prodded Damian in the back and jerked his head towards the only armchair in the room, the one traditionally occupied by the head of the household and, since Lord Carthorne's death, left vacant. 'Sit down there.'

Damian moved over and sat down, putting his hands on its polished wooden arms and smiling easily. 'I have often wondered what it would be like to sit in this chair,' he said. 'It fits me well, don't you think?'

'Be silent!' Joshua snapped and then turned to Alys, 'My lady, I need something to bind him up.'

Alys sent somcone to fetch the cord from her bed curtains and when it was brought to him, he handed the pistol to Alys. 'Point this at him, my lady, and if he moves so much as a finger, shoot him.'

'No!' Lettice cried, running forward. 'You must be mad to give her a weapon—she will turn it on you and set him free.'

But Alys already had the gun, though she did not know if she would have the courage to fire it. She stood watching the man tie the prisoner securely to the chair, but her mind was on Garret and what had happened. She wanted to go and find him, but until Damian had been safely tied she could not leave the hall, and, judging by the noises coming from the rest of the house, it was not yet safe to do so. There was musket fire and the clash of swords, besides a great deal of running about the corridors, doors banging and shouting, though the babble of conversation in the great hall drowned the words.

A sound, sharper than the rest and close at hand, made her spin round in alarm. She was still holding the pistol and she saw Garret recoil very slightly before she realised she was pointing it at him. 'If you please, my lady,' he said, moving forward and taking it from her unresisting fingers. 'I will take charge of this.'

She wanted to fling herself into his arms, but his attitude precluded that. He was a military commander directing a military operation and human frailty, either his own or hers, had no part in that. She dropped her hands to her sides and waited in desperation for him to notice her misery, to speak softly to

196

her, to give her a chance to explain about Damian.

Lettice had no such inhibitions; she ran to him and took his hand. 'Oh, Garret, how glad we are to see you! Have you beaten those scoundrel Cavaliers?'

He smiled at her and it was like a knife-thrust in Alys's heart. 'They were but few in number.'

'And you did it all alone. How brave of you.'

'Not brave at all,' he said, answering her but looking directly at Alys, as if speaking to her. 'It was very foolish of me to attempt to take the captain on by myself.'

'But you had help,' Alys said. 'Your men were behind you.'

He laughed, as the Waterlea men crowded into the room and embraced loved ones they had not seen for nearly a year. 'At the time, they were nowhere near.'

'You mean they were not waiting outside? I thought—'

'You thought I had arranged a little diversion to give them time to take the manor? No, my lady, I acted alone, out of temper, because I had captured the King's man once before and could have killed him then, but instead I released him and was repaid with treachery. That was a great mistake.'

'And you are making a bigger one now,' Damian said from his chair. 'You Roundheads cannot win the war and, more than that, *you* cannot win the lady.'

Alys did not want Garret to listen; to Damian and she put herself between the two men, though there was nothing Damian could have done, except talk. But his tongue was more dangerous than his sword and she was afraid of it. 'If your men were not with you,' she said, facing Garret, 'where were they?'

'On the other side of the moat, with the drawbridge up.'

'How did they get in?' Damian put in.

'There is a secret tunnel from the old chapel.'

'You said there was no other way,' Damian accused Alys. 'You showed it to him.'

'I could not have done; I did not know it was there.'

'I was unaware of it myself,' Garret said. 'I came in over the wall near the gate.'

'I showed them,' Simon put in gleefully. 'I knew it was there. I did like you said, my lady, I found Goodman Martin and we went together to look for the captain's men, but when we found them the captain was not with them. Lieutenant Stone said he had come to the manor alone.'

'Oh, Garret,' Alys said. 'How very foolish of you.'

'Yes, foolish,' he said. 'In my foolishness I imagined you would be prepared to aid the village men, if not me. I thought if I could speak to you alone, you would help me to overcome the guards on the drawbridge and make sure it stayed down for my men, seeing that they are the husbands, brothers and sons of people you have known all your life, people who have served the Carthorne family faithfully for generations. I thought that whatever you thought of me, you would help them. I realised how wrong I was as soon as I saw what was happening here. It was like a scene at court, laughing and dancing and making merry when all around you is hardship and bloodshed. And as for that . . .' He indicated Damian. 'He is not worth your kisses, my lady.'

'You are jealous,' Damian said.

Garret treated him to a look of scorn. 'Take him away! Take him away and shoot him.'

'No!' Alys cried. 'Garret, please don't do that. I don't want anyone killed.'

'What you want is no longer any concern of mine,' he said. 'I shall do what *I* want, and *I* wish him in hell.'

'No! No! Please don't,' Alys begged him, running to Garret and catching hold of his arm. 'Let him live. He was going to find Benedick and tell him of Father's death. I wanted him to do that. If you had not come, he would have gone as soon as the floods receded. Let him go. Please, let him go.'

He shrugged her off. 'I was very sorry to learn of your father's death, my lady,' he said.

'He was a good friend to me, in spite of his Royalist views. I would have done almost anything to please him.'

'He would have wanted you to spare Captain Forrester,' she said, noting that he said, 'would have done' as if it no longer applied. The wedding, she was sure, would not now take place, but instead of being glad she was heartbroken.

'Would he?' He smiled. 'We have no way of knowing that. And besides, if what I have heard is correct, Damian Forrester was not blameless in the matter of his lordship's death.'

'It was an accident,' she said. 'Father was confused and fired first. Please, Garret—'

He looked at Joshua, who still stood beside his prisoner. 'I told you to take him away and shoot him.'

'Yes, sir.'

Damian was released from the chair and his hands bound behind him with the cord. 'Am I to die like a coward with my hands tied?' he asked. 'I am an officer of the King's army. At least give me the satisfaction of fighting for my life.'

'Man to man?' Garret seemed to be amused by the prospect, for he was smiling.

'No!' shrieked Alys. 'I will not have it. Garret, what have I to do, to convince you that he cannot harm you or your men?'

'Convince me?' he mused. 'Why do you feel

the need, unless it is to save your lover at all costs? Is that it?'

'No.' It was as if she and Garret were the only people in the room; she had forgotten everyone else in her anxiety to make him understand. 'He is my brother's friend, just as you are.'

He looked round at the assembled company, all agog, some with mouths agape, listening and taking it all in, to be brought out later and retold and commented on and embroidered until the tale bore little resemblance to the truth. 'Take him and lock him in the crypt,' he ordered. 'He would have had me spend a cold night there—we shall see if he enjoys his own punishment. Tomorrow, I will decide what is to be done with him.' He turned to Alys. 'As for you, my lady, I think a few private words are called for. We will go in the parlour.'

He took her arm and led her through the door, with Lettice calling after him, 'Do not trust her, Garret, she will turn on you again if you do.'

'Is that so?' he asked Alys when the door had been shut on them. 'Will you turn on me again?'

'I never did before.' Now they were alone, she was shaking. Too much had happened too quickly and her mind was in a whirl. 'I sent Ingram Martin to warn your men of how things stood here. I was told you were dead;

how was I to know you were alive and would take it into your head to come up here alone and take Damian on single-handed?'

'Yes, how were you to know? If you had, you would, perhaps, have been more discreet about letting him kiss you where all could see. I am not blind, Alys.'

'Yes, you are,' she cried. 'Indeed you are, if you thought I was enjoying that.'

'Why let him do it, then?'

'Because I had seen you and I . . .' She looked up into his eyes, but he did not seem to want to believe her. 'Oh, what is the good of talking to you? And why should I anyway? You care nothing for me; it is your pride that is hurt.'

'Yes, a man must have his pride.' He paused before adding slowly, almost gently, 'I cannot let you win, Alys.'

'Punish me, then, but do not kill out of pride and pretend it is for me.'

He threw back his fine head and laughed. 'Oh, Alys, how little you know me. But I must think of a way of doing it which everyone will understand.'

Alys was suddenly reminded of the conversation she had had with Lettice about punishment, and she held her breath, wondering what he was about to suggest. If he thought to punish her by marrying her . . . She smiled.

'What amuses you?'

'Nothing. The best punishment would be to marry me, don't you think?'

'That is not a subject to be treated lightly.'

'No, indeed not. And you should know my feelings on the matter.'

'Yes, you have not been backward in making them known.' He paused, reached out for her hand, then changed his mind and let his arm drop to his side. 'What would you do to save that wretched Cavalier?'

'You mean you will let him go?' Her eagerness was not lost on him, though he did not understand the reason for it. She did not want the shedding of Damian's blood—anyone's blood—to come between them, now or ever; nothing must come between them.

'The price is high,' he said.

'Name it.'

'Marriage.'

'To Damian?' She was horrified.

'No, I am sorry to disappoint you, but, if you remember, we made a promise to your father. I, for one, do not break promises. Marry me at once, and I will release Damian Forrester as a wedding gift to my bride, on condition he goes directly to Oxford and acquaints your brother of his inheritance and then leaves the country. Is it agreed?'

'That is my punishment?'

'Yes.' He was smiling, but she could not tell if it was because he was pleased or simply that he was amused by the irony of it. 'It will be a

203

lifelong one.'

'But won't you also be punishing yourself?'

'I am a soldier; I shall be away from home much of the time, so do not worry your head on my account.'

It was cold and calculating and she told herself she hated him for it. Lettice Van Hildt had been right; he did know how to punish her. 'If I refuse?'

'Captain Forrester will be shot tomorrow in front of your eyes, and all his men along with him.'

'Have you no heart?' she stormed. 'How can you contemplate such a thing?'

He did not know how he could even say it, let alone do it. He did not want to kill the man any more than he had wanted it before; his death served no useful purpose in the war and it would be disastrous for his relationship with Alys, frail as it was. If only she would defy him and tell him to do his worst, he would know that she cared nothing for the Cavalier. It would also mean she was not prepared to pay the high price he asked of her. One day the war would come to an end, though there was no sign of it yet, and he would return to Eagleholm as a private citizen and that would be soon enough to return to the subject of marriage. Why could she not see what he was trying to do? Why did she have to be so contrary all the time? Defy me, he pleaded silently, refuse me, for both our sakes.

'Well?' he asked, as they stood looking at each other with a gulf as deep as the ocean between them. 'I am waiting for your answer.'

'I am thinking of something my father said, the day you left for the war. He said our marriage would be a good marriage, if we decided to make it so.' She looked up at him with eyes bright with tears. 'He was a good and wise man and he loved me. I wonder if he would think the same if he could see us now?'

'Alys . . .' He took a step towards her, intending to comfort her, but she pushed past him to go to the door.

'I, too, made a promise to my father and his memory is very dear to me,' she said, with her hand on the latch. 'And for that reason my answer is yes.'

She did not wait for him to reply but rushed from the room, and he did not know for whom she shed the tears.

* * *

The news that there was to be a wedding was greeted with cries of pleasure and congratulation from everyone except the sour-faced Lettice. Prue, ignoring the despairing look of her mistress, offered up a prayer of thanksgiving that she had finally come to her senses.

'When is it to be?' asked John, beaming at them both.

'Immediately.' Garret spoke for both of them because he seemed to be the one who was more in command of the situation. Alys stood beside him with her hand in his and a fixed smile on her face which made it ache. 'Why delay?' he added, looking down at her in a passable imitation of a loving bridegroom. If only it were real, how happy she would be. 'We have the parson and the congregation already with us and it is about time I took my lady in hand, if only to protect her from her own folly. Never again will it be doubted whose side she is on—she will be on mine.'

Amid the general laughter, he bent his head to whisper to Alys, 'Come, my dear, marriage to me will not be so terrible. I am not an ogre and I will not beat you.' His lips touched her ear and the sensation the touch gave her spread right to her toes and set her whole body tingling, and she hated herself for it. 'Nor will I humiliate you.'

'Thank you.'

'But you must do the same for me. You must do nothing to weaken my position with my men or the good people of the village, who look up to me, especially now your father is gone.' He lifted her hand to his lips and smiled down at her, adding loudly enough to be heard by those nearest, 'How does the day after tomorrow suit you, my love?'

'It suits me well enough.'

'Be more enthusiastic than that,' he hissed,

wishing he had never thought of bargaining with her. It would not work, she was wooden and unresponsive and he did not see how he could change things.

She smiled and forced a light laugh. 'I meant that I would it were sooner.'

'I am afraid we could not be ready earlier, sweetheart. The manor has to be set to rights; there is furniture up-turned and windows broken and if our friends from the village are to stay here the rooms have to be made ready. We can hardly send them back to flooded homes. And as for the chapel, it is covered in dust and cobwebs. Dr Sandy will not wish to perform a marriage ceremony there until it has been cleaned.'

'It won't take long if we all give a hand,' Prue said.

'And did you not say you intended to dress as befits the daughter of a lord of the realm?' Garret went on, reminding Alys of her own earlier defiance. She had been so sure of herself then, so determined to upset his plans, but it was she who had been upset, she who was being made to eat her own words.

'Leave that to us, Sir Garret,' Prue said. 'I promise you she will look beautiful.'

'She looks that now,' he said. 'To me she is the most beautiful woman in this land or any other.'

'A toast!' called John. 'A toast to the betrothed couple, and another to his late lordship and another to Benedick, Lord Carthorne, who would be here if he could.'

'Amen to that,' chorused several voices.

'And an end to war,' shouted Joshua, standing with his arm round his wife and grinning from ear to ear.

'Aye, to that too,' they said fervently, as glasses, silver goblets, tumblers and pewter pots were handed round and charged. 'Peace. Peace between King and Parliament, peace between all men and women.'

'I drink to that,' Garret said, holding up his glass and drinking deeply. 'And just to show how peaceful I feel, and to please my bride, I will let the prisoners go.'

'Let them go?' echoed Aldous, who was standing near Garret and Alys, a little aloof from the others.

'Yes, my friend.' Garret smiled and put his hand on the shoulder of his lieutenant. 'I know you do not approve, but I mean to send them to Oxford—under escort, of course-with a message for Lord Carthorne. If he comes home, he will be greeted as an old friend and all enmity between us banished. It is Lady Alys's wish and I want to grant all her wishes.'

They cheered, they drank and sang songs and danced and forgot the war, forgot their flooded homes and the events of earlier that night. Everyone was happy and at peace with everyone else, everyone, that was, except Alys. She knew she loved Garret with an intensity that hurt and she wanted to be married to him more than anything she had ever wanted, but not like this, not with this terrible barrier between them, so that everything they said was like a double-edged sword which cut both ways. She did not know if she could go through with it, and a wicked voice inside her kept telling her she need not, because once Damian had left she could change her mind and there would be little Garret could do about it. But another voice said, if she did that, there would be no hope for her at all; she would be damned for breaking a vow to a dying man and damned by Garret as unworthy of anyone's love. Long before the revelry died down, she pleaded tiredness and went up to her bedchamber.

'What ails you, my chick?' Prue asked, as she helped her out of her skirts and petticoats. 'You are not sickening, are you?'

'No, but it has been such an exhausting day.'

'It has indeed, and tomorrow will be busier because we have all the preparations to make: gowns, cooking, cleaning. We shall have to get out what is left of the plate, and chance the wrath of Lieutenant Stone. We shall say we forgot it when he asked for our contribution, or that we did not know his lordship had so much.' She laughed, taking a brush to Alys's hair. 'What a fortunate thing it was that Sir Garret recovered your jewels for you.'

'My jewels.' She looked up at her maid with anguish on her face. 'Oh, Prue, I gave them to Damian for the King.'

The brush stopped moving as Prue digested this piece of information. Then she shrugged and continued with her task. 'No matter, most of the Parliamentarians are Puritan or Presbyterian, they do not hold with jewels and decoration. We shall have to make a Puritan bride of you.'

'Oh, no,' wailed Alys. 'Garret is not Puritan, he is an Independent, like Cromwell. Besides, I said I would dress as befits the daughter of a lord and that means yards of rich material and lace and jewels and silk slippers and—'

'All vanity,' said Prue.

'Not vanity, but pride,' Alys said. 'If I dress plainly, it will be one more battle he has won.'

'Is that what marriage is to be for you, child, one battle after another? And do you count success by the number you win?' She gave an extra hard tug at the girl's hair, making her squeal. 'Leave things like that to King and Parliament and see if you can make your life with your husband a smooth passage for both of you. It is your duty, when he is troubled by events outside, to make his home a haven of peace, not another battleground.'

'You do not understand,' Alys cried. 'You do not understand how I feel.'

'Oh, yes, I do. I understand you very well. I
210

have watched you grow from a baby and been proud to see you becoming more beautiful every day, and more caring of the needs of others, so that you earned the love of all around you. Now you also need to earn their respect. As a child, you were a delight; as a woman, you are still a child. It is time you grew up.'

'And you have no right to speak to me like that.'

'Indeed I have, and even if I had not, I would have done so because, without mother and father to guide you, there is no one else. If you want to keep that man of yours, you will heed me, otherwise—'

'Otherwise what?'

'He will turn to someone else and you will lose him.'

'Prue, if he does that, I will die.' She allowed herself to be led to the bed. 'What I do not know and will never understand is why he wanted to marry me in the first place.'

'Don't you know?'

'No.'

'Child, he loves you and you are blind not to see it.'

'That I do not believe.'

'Whether you believe it or not, you will remember your promise to your father and go to your wedding with a smile.' Prue tucked the covers round her mistress. 'Sleep now and all will be well, you will see.' She closed the bed curtains and crept softly from the room.

Alys woke next morning when Prue bustled in carrying what appeared to be a huge mound of shining cloth. 'See, my lady, see what I have found.' She shook the bundle out and Alys gasped, because it was a magnificent gown of heavy brocade, embroidered all over in flowers of gold and silver thread, with a single pearl at the centre of each. The sleeves ended in a froth of gold lace and the neck was cut square and low. 'It is a mite old-fashioned,' the maid went on. 'But it is so beautiful.'

'Where did you find it?'

'In the chest in his lordship's bedchamber; it was the gown your mother was married in. I remember that day as if it were yesterday. She was beautiful, just as you are, but not so wilful. Her demeanour was loving and obedient, and she was pleased to accept the bridegroom her parents found for her.'

'Enough of the lecture,' Alys said, scrambling out of bed to begin her toilette and try it on. 'I shall wear it, and astound the whole company, including the groom.' She sighed as Prue slipped it over her head and helped to fasten its tiny silver buttons. ' 'Tis a pity about the jewels.'

'I have a single strand of pearls, my lady, which your dear mother gave me as a present when I left her service to look after you. You are welcome to wear it.'

*   *   *

Alys saw little of Garret that day because he was occupied for most of it in the village. Before he could give a thought to his own preparations for the wedding, he set about looking after the needs of the villagers. He inspected their homes to assess the flood damage and made a tour of the flooded fields in a boat and decided which could most easily be drained. If everyone could be persuaded to help, Lettice Van Hildt's ground could be dry again by sowing time the following spring. He had the men make an inventory of all their arms, ammunition and supplies; there was still a war to be waged and he suspected the Royalist raids would be resumed as soon as the water had left the roads. After that, he went to Eagleholm. The floods had subsided a little so that the ground floor was covered in mud and weeds, but no longer awash. He set his servants to cleaning up, but realised it would not be sensible to bring his bride home after the ceremony, which was what he had planned—a new start in a new home. They would have to spend their first few nights as husband and wife at the manor. He did not like the idea because it would look as though he were occupying it as a conqueror, but he could see no help for it.

He returned to the manor and was busy with the demi-cannon when Aldous came to tell him that the prisoners and their escort were ready to leave for Oxford. 'But before they go, there is something you should see in the crypt,' he added.

Garret finished his inspection of the gun and followed his lieutenant down the twisting stairs and into the dark cellar, where he struck a flint and lit a torch in a wall bracket. The light flickered on to broken furniture, motheaten tapestries and bent pewter pots, nothing of any value.

'This is where we housed the prisoners,' he said. 'When they were taken out, I decided to look round, more out of curiosity than anything else.' He took the torch down and picked his way over the rubble to a small door at the end of the cavern, which he pulled open. The room beyond it was packed with furniture, tapestry, gold, silver, pictures.

'I questioned the one-eyed fellow,' Aldous went on. 'He told me the Royalist lieutenant brought it here a little at a time.'

'It was never meant for the King, I'll wager,' Garret said. 'The lieutenant was using his authority to store up wealth for himself.'

'Do you think Lady Alys knew of it?'

'I should like to think she did not,' he said, idly picking up a small velvet bag, pulling open its drawstring and tipping its contents on to a tapestry flung over a table. He found himself looking, once again, at Alys's jewels. 'But I am afraid she might have.'

214

'What are you going to do?'

'Confiscate everything and send it to the commissioners, who will undoubtedly put it to good use.' He returned the gems to the bag. 'All but these. These I will return to their owner.' He put the bag back in its hiding place and followed Aldous from the crypt.

Not until he had dispatched Damian, and those of his men who were not prepared to change sides, to Oxford under escort, did he give a thought to his own preparation for the coming nuptials.

CHAPTER EIGHT

It had been impossible to restore the chapel to anything like its old splendour because it had been stripped of anything which could remotely be called decorative; the gold and silver had long since been donated to the King's cause, and the altar rail dismantled, but the floors had been scrubbed, the pews dusted and the windows polished, so that its tranquil simplicity was all the more moving. The whole village was there to witness Garret Hartswood take Alys Carthorne to be his wife, and Alys, moving slowly down the aisle on John's arm, was conscious of the gaze of a hundred pairs of eyes. The pearl-encrusted gown, with the many petticoats she had beneath it to make it

215

stand out, felt heavy after the country clothes she had been dressed in of late, and she began to wonder if she had been wrong to wear it. After all, this was not a love-match, no great celebration was called for, and she might be doing exactly what he had asked her not to do, which was to humiliate and embarrass him. But he deserved that, she told herself rebelliously, he had blackmailed her into the marriage and she was going to show him that, though she had agreed to it, he would not have things all his own way.

She was halfway to the altar before she had the courage to lift her head and look towards the groom. He was standing waiting for her, in satin burgundy breeches and a velvet doublet with a double row of silver buttons. His wrists and boot hose frothed with lace and he wore his beautiful sword in a chased leather scabbard. A shaft of sunlight from the high window lit his hair, curling on his shoulders. He was smiling at her. This was not the Puritan she had expected, this was not even the soldier she had come to know; this man was magnificent. Her heart gave a great lurch and her knees would have buckled if she had not been holding John's arm.

She reached Garret's side and he took her hand and together they faced Dr Sandy. She listened and responded in a dream, a dream in which the man beside her made his responses in a loud clear voice and squeezed her hand

216

reassuringly in his, and smiled.

He was still smiling half an hour later when they emerged into the open to a chorus of cheers, and ran, hand in hand, across the sward to the manor and into the great hall, followed by the villagers.

'Kiss the bride!' someone shouted. 'Do you have to be shown how to do it?'

'That I do not,' he said, taking Alys into his arms.

She would wake up soon, she thought, she would wake up and find this beautiful man gone and in his place the gruff soldier who had married her to punish her. The sweet kisses would turn sour, the smiles would turn to scowls; this was only for the benefit of the onlookers. But, even believing that, she could not help returning his passion with passion of her own, so that she forgot everyone else in the room, and melted into his arms. Let me have just one day when everything is right, she prayed, let me have this one day and one night to hold on to.

'Alys, my sweet Alys,' he whispered. 'No more quarrelling, eh? There is such a fire inside me, I can hardly contain my impatience.'

She looked up at him and laughed. 'Husband, it will not do to leave the company yet awhile. We must have the rout first.'

'Then the sooner you order the servants to bring in the roasted pig and all the other

217

delicacies I heard were being prepared, the better.' He clapped his hands and beckoned to John, then turned to the assembled company. 'Friends, forget about the war and its shortages on this special day; eat and drink your fill.'

An army of servants, many of them men returned from the campaign, trooped in carrying the food, and set it on the long oak table. Garret and Alys sat at the head and everyone, from the steward to the lowest pot-boy, ranged themselves down its length, while the jollity continued. Alys, who could think of nothing but the man beside her and the wedding night to come, could not eat. Her untouched food was taken away and the next course brought, but it was given the same treatment as the first.

'Are you not hungry, little wife?'

'No.'

'You are not afraid, are you?'

She looked up sharply. 'Of the punishment you have in store for me?'

He smiled. 'I seem to remember telling you your chains would be of your own choosing, and you have chosen.' He pointed at her plate. 'Eat. I insist.'

She forced some of the food down. When he was satisfied she could eat no more, he stood up and held out his hand for her. 'Come,' he said. 'I have something to show you.'

Instead of taking her up the stairs to the chamber which had been prepared for them, he took a torch from a bracket and led her back to the chapel and then down to the crypt. Silently he preceded her down the steps and across to the door at the far end. Throwing it open, he ushered her inside. For one terrifying moment, she thought he was going to lock her in, but then he held the torch high so that its flickering flame revealed the stacked treasures. She gasped. 'Where has it all come from?'

'From the homes of your neighbours, rich and poor, from this village and the next, from Grantham and Crowland. It was brought here by your Royalist friend.'

'For the King?'

'That may have been what he said, but it is loot, pure and simple. The young man was lining his own nest. That was why he stayed here, not because he was ordered to, but because he felt safe here. Waterlea is isolated and he knew he would have a welcome from the mistress of the manor.'

'Garret, I did not welcome him.'

'It is because I want to believe you that I have sent a letter with his escort to the King, explaining how he behaved here. It will be for his Majesty to punish him and I don't doubt that he will do it.'

'And these things?' She pointed to the store.

'Will go to the commissioners for the defence of the county.' He paused. 'Except these.' He picked up the velvet bag. 'These I will restore once again to their owner.' He tipped the contents out as he spoke. They lay on the tapestry, gleaming in the light of the torch.

'My jewels!'

'Yes. Are you going to tell me for a second time that they were stolen?'

'No,' she said softly. 'I gave them to Damian for the King.'

'Then they *were* stolen, for Charles was never meant to have them.'

'I find that hard to believe. Damian was loyal and brave—'

He laughed. 'You do not understand men, do you, my lady, but then how can you be expected to, when you have had no one to instruct you?' He put the jewels back in the bag and gave them to her. 'Here, my lady, take more care of them in future. Now, we will speak of that insufferable Cavalier no more.' He tucked her hand in the crook of his arm and they walked slowly back to thc house.

They passed the great hall where there was music and dancing, but they did not stop with their guests, who smiled indulgently at their impatience to be alone together. Garret, with his arm lightly round her, took her up the stairs and along the gallery to their bedchamber. He pushed the door open and drew her in, slamming it behind him with his foot. Then, without taking his eyes from her, he reached behind him and shot the bolt home. It had a finality about it, a shutting out of the past, a signal that there was no going back, but she was hardly aware of it as he picked her up and carried her to the bed, where he sat down, with her still in his arms.

'Little wife,' he whispered, burying his head in her neck and kissing her throat. 'No more talk. Tonight is for other things, for making up for lost time, for making new discoveries.' He laid her back on the bed and began slowly undressing her, uncovering one breast, then the other, exploring her body with gentle hands, until she felt she would burst for love of him. This man, this wonderful, beautiful man, was her husband and she loved him with a passion which was not to be denied. She reached out and began unbuttoning his shirt.

*   *   *

When she opened her eyes next morning, she thought it had all been a dream. The winter sun was shining in at the window and the birds were singing, but Garret was not beside her. She sighed and turned over, wishing she had not woken, because in her dream the ecstasy of their union had been complete. It had made one being of them, indivisible, eternal.

She sat up as Prue came bustling in with

water for her to wash. Her maid was smiling broadly. 'Come, my lady, Sir Garret has been up betimes and you lay abed like a sloth.'

'Sir Garret? I thought I had dreamed him.'

'He is no dream, my chick, he is very substantial, and in fine good humour. He had his breakfast and rode out to Eagleholm, saying he would be back in an hour, so up with you and be ready for him.'

She had not dreamed the passion of their lovemaking; it had been real, and she prayed it would go on and on through all their lives. She wanted that more than anything she had ever wanted—to be loved and cherished by Garret, just as she loved him with every fibre of her being. She scrambled from her bed and washed, while Prue sorted through her gowns and clicked her tongue disapprovingly. 'You have been going about like a peasant,' she said, tumbling skirts and bodices on the floor. 'There is nothing here that befits a lady of rank. You will shame him.'

'There is a blue silk with lace a-plenty in the chest. Fetch that out.'

If it had not been for Prue, Alys would have been careless of her appearance, so anxious was she to be with Garret again, but her maid insisted she dress with care and spent longer than usual on her hair, so that Garret had already returned by the time she went downstairs.

He sat and watched with indulgent

amusement as she ate frumenty and cold tongue. 'It is good to be home,' he said. 'But Eagleholm is in a sad state. It was never more than the home of a single man, but now the floods have damaged everything on the ground floor and it is hardly fit to live in.'

'We can stay here until it is set to rights,' she said, wondering why she suddenly felt shy of him. She supposed it was because they had always been fighting before. 'It will be time enough to move in when Benedick comes back and takes over the manor.'

He did not immediately answer and she stopped to look up at him. He was gazing at her with a thoughtful expression, as if undecided whether to speak his mind. 'Alys, about Benedick . . .'

She became alarmed. 'You have heard something of him? What is it? Is he well? He hasn't been wounded?'

'I have heard nothing,' he said hastily. 'But I must talk to you about him.' He reached across the table and took her hand. 'You know, if your brother remains loyal to Charles until the end, it will go ill with him. He must be warned.'

'You expect him to desert His Majesty, just because things are not going well?'

'The King's cause is lost, Alys. Benedick should think of saving himself.'

'Benedick would not do that, he is too brave and honourable.'

He sighed. 'If you are right, he will share the King's punishment, whatever that may be.'

'You cannot punish a King, Garret.'

'We have to. If he does not pay for bringing the country to war and shedding the blood of thousands of his subjects, our struggle will have been for naught.'

'He could say the same of you.'

'But he is being beaten and I, for one, give thanks to God for that.'

'He could be allowed to go to France.'

'He must be prevented from doing that at all costs,' he said grimly.

'Why? What harm can he do in exile?'

'He could try to raise a new army and set us in conflict with Europe. Unless he is thoroughly beaten and admits his defeat, there will always be the possibility that he might return and then the bloodshed would go on.' He lifted her hand and turned it palm up before lifting it to his lips. She wanted to kiss him and cry out to him to stop talking of the war, but she desisted because what he was saying seemed important, and he had not yet reached the point of it all. He was looking into her eyes as if searching for a sign that she understood. 'Do you know where Benedick is, Alys?'

'No, but I imagine he is at Oxford with the King.'

'But if the King is defeated and his army scattered, what then?'

'I am sure he will stay close to His Majesty.'

'And if that happened and you heard from him or discovered where he was, you would tell me?'

She looked at him in dismay, unable to believe he could ask that of her. 'No,' she said slowly. 'I do not think I would.'

'I cannot believe that you mean that.'

'And I cannot believe you would ask it of me. If the shoe were on the other foot, if Benedick were the conqueror and you were in hiding, would you expect me to tell him where you were?'

'That would be different.'

'Why? I see no difference.'

'Alys, you are my wife and you have vowed before God to obey me.'

'That is unfair!' she cried, snatching her hand from his.

'I am thinking only of Benedick's safety. He will lose everything if he does not leave the King. I ask only for the chance to talk to him and persuade him to renounce his loyalty to Charles. If he does it now, we may yet save him.'

'Do you truly want to save him?' She was angry, because he could not, or would not, understand the dilemma she was in, and she did not care that her temper had got the better of her.

'Have I not just said so?' He stood up and came round to stand beside her and she lost what little advantage she had while he remained seated and had her hand in his. She had to do something to regain it. She jumped to her feet, knocking over her stool; neither stooped to right it.

'It is more likely that you want to hand Benedick over to that bloodthirsty rabble in Parliament,' she stormed. 'If my brother is caught and punished by death, you no longer need me to gain control of Waterlea, do you? As soon as I have obeyed you, as a dutiful wife, and told you what you want to know, you could have the marriage annulled. Why don't you do it now? If you don't, then I will.'

'Is that what you want?' He paused and she saw what might have been a look of pain cross his face, except that he was too angry to feel such a thing. 'An annulment? So soon after the nuptials?'

She stopped suddenly and stared at him. Her cheeks flamed as she remembered the passion of the night before and her complete abandonment to his lovemaking. The marriage had been consummated and she had been fool enough to think he had done it because he loved her! 'You tricked me!' she shouted. 'You tricked me! And if you think I would ever betray my brother to your vindictiveness, then I will tell you now, I will never do it. Never!'

'Very well,' he said. 'You have made it clear where your loyalties lie, and, so that you may know that possession of Waterlea Manor is of little importance to me, I will return to Eagleholm and leave you to enjoy it alone. When you realise your folly, you may come to me there, but rest assured I will not come to you.'

She felt a trickle of ice down her back as the look in his brown eyes hardened, but she could not back down; he asked too much. 'What do you mean?' Her voice was a whisper of apprehension.

'Simply this, my lady: that I, as a soldier and, in the absence of your brother, also a justice, have many duties, some of which will keep me from you. There is no need for anyone to know that our marriage was still-born, unless you are unwise enough to spread it abroad.'

'People will guess,' she said miserably.

'Not if you play your part. Until Lord Carthorne returns and takes a wife, you are needed here at the manor, and I suggest you continue to live here until that time.'

'We live apart?' Her legs felt weak and her insides turned to water, as she realised the implication of what he was saying. Lettice Van Hildt had been right; he had wanted only to punish her. And how he had succeeded!

'There is a great deal of work to be done at Eagleholm,' he went on in an even voice which gave away nothing of his own feelings. 'I must oversee the repair of the banks and the

227

draining of the fields again, and it will be easier if I live in the village.'

'But we might just as well not be married.'

'And is that not what you have wanted all along, my lady? I forced you into it, but you have the last word, after all; we might just as well not be married. Now I bid you good-day.'

She did not move until she heard the front door bang and the sound of a horse's hooves, then she ran to the window and knelt on the seat to watch him ride out over the drawbridge and down the path into Waterlea. She stayed there long after the sound of his horse had died away, gazing with unseeing eyes on the flood-filled fields and clear skies of a December day; a quiet scene at odds with the turmoil in her heart, while the tears chased each other down her cheeks and tasted salt on her lips.

*   *   *

The villagers went back to their homes a few days later, returning to spend Christmas Day at the manor at Alys's invitation. Although Garret joined them and laughed and joked, along with everyone else, he carefully avoided being alone with her. In the early weeks of the new year of 1645, he went frequently to Westminster, where those who wanted a negotiated peace with the King were at loggerheads with those who wanted the war pursued to his final defeat. The Earl of Manchester, who headed the army of the eastern association, leaned towards the former and harsh words were being said about his generalship by Oliver Cromwell, who was of the opinion that the King must be defeated decisively, so that he could never again defy the elected leaders of the people. Garret, who liked and admired both men, did not want to become involved in the argument but, after much soul-searching, he decided to throw in his lot with Cromwell and the New Model Army.

'Sir Thomas Fairfax is to be overall commander,' Garret told Aldous, after one visit to London. 'But he has left the post of lieutenant-general vacant. I think he means to have Oliver fill it.'

'How can he, when Cromwell must return to Westminster and his parliamentary duties?' Aldous said, knowing that the newly passed self-denying ordinance precluded members of Parliament from holding rank in the army.

'A way will be found, you'll see.'

While Garret waited for orders, he worked tirelessly to help repair the banks of the drains. Few of the village men would help him, being more afraid of Ingram Martin than they were of him, and he did not have the heart to force them to do it. Lettice was constantly at his side, directing his efforts and bringing food and drink out to him. Alys knew

229

this, but there was nothing she could do about it; she and Garret were as distant as ever and there seemed to be no hope of a reconciliation, not while he insisted on sleeping at Eagleholm.

But she could not live an isolated existence; the village was too close and she had to go to market and to church and she had to hold her head up for her own pride's sake. She continued to befriend those who needed it, but the return of the men meant that she was no longer needed in the fields, and Garret had taken over the duties of justice and lord of the manor.

It was unfair; those duties properly belonged to Benedick, but because her brother was faithful to the last he had forfeited everything. Did he know that? Did he know that if he returned home there would be no welcome for him, except perhaps within the four walls of the manor, and she was not even sure of that. Garret was respected, even by her own servants, and most had long ago decided that it was more comfortable being on the winning side.

She found a certain solace, during the earliest months of the year, in rowing out alone on to the fen. Here, far from the usual haunts of man, the peace was disturbed only by birds and fish and otters playing on the mudbanks. She would lean on her oars and contemplate her universe, a universe of low horizons and wide skies, of murmuring reeds and the tiny call of the willow warbler and the godwit, the croak of the frog and the raucous cry of gulls coming inland in search of food. She put down eel traps so that she could not be accused of idling, and she took her father's fowling piece, but she never used it. She could not kill the lovely birds, who gave her so much pleasure.

Sometimes she met Hannah Martin, either in a boat or on the path, and they would pass the time in conversation. Hannah would tell her about her life on the edge of the fen, where the water was king, and show her the best places to sink her eels traps. Sometimes they spoke of Ingram and his war against the drainers.

'My husband likes to be alone,' Hannah said one day as they sat facing each other in Alys's rowing boat. Both had fishing lines over the side, though neither was paying much attention to them. 'For him the fen is all the company he wants. To him, it is beautiful.'

'So it is.'

'Some don't think so. Some say it is an evil place. They are afraid of it because they do not understand it, and what you are afraid of, you destroy.'

'But there are very strong arguments in favour of drainage, Hannah.'

'We know that. Ingram is not against all drainage; some of it is good, but he believes it is the people who live here should say what is to be drained and what left to nature, not foreigners.' Hannah pulled in her line and deftly rebaited its hook.

'My husband is not a foreigner and I believe he has arranged an extension of the settlement,' Alys said. She rarely mentioned Garret, but when she did she found the word 'husband' sticking on her tongue, as if she had no right to say it.

'For another year, my lady, and that favours the Dutchman's widow. We are sorry that he has taken a stand for her, because we would not like to go against him. He was good with my sons when they were children and it was he who saw how clever my James was, and paid for him to go to school. Matthew is at Lincoln's Inn now and doing well. We are indebted to Sir Garret, which is why Ingram agreed to show Lieutenant Stone the secret way in to the manor, but gratitude will not stop him from attacking the banks again if he should be so minded. Sir Garret is wasting his time, my lady.'

'Are you saying that Ingram will not abide by the agreement?'

Hannah threw her line out again and smiled. 'Ingram agreed on Sir Garret's promise to withdraw the warrant for his arrest, but that's not to say the men will stand by and let Mistress Van Hildt dry out more fields than she already has.'

'Do you think she means to do that?'

'I would not be surprised.' Hannah drew in her line, pulled off the struggling fish impaled on the hook and threw it into the bottom of the boat. 'But she did try to persuade Sir Garret that she deserved special treatment. She said she did not believe the villagers would leave her in peace to cultivate her land, so he has agreed to bring in troopers from outside to watch over the work and see that there is no trouble.' She paused. 'But has he not told you this himself, my lady?'

Alys coloured. Hannah knew, as every villager did, that she and Garret lived in separate houses, but she was preserving the myth that it was only because Garret was needed at Eagleholm and, until Benedick returned, someone had to manage the manor. She made herself busy with her own line. 'He has been too much occupied.'

Hannah accepted her answer without comment. She pulled in another fish and looked at the two very small roach Alys had managed to hook. 'Your luck is out today, my lady.'

'It seems to be.' Alys knew it was not so much ill-luck as lack of attention which was responsible for her poor catch. Her mind had been on Garret, who, she mused with a wry smile, might, by his delaying tactics, be able to accomplish what her father had not—the acquiescence of the villagers in a scheme to

233

allow the drainage work to continue. In time, they might even become convinced of the benefits of turning summer grounds into all the year round dry fields.

'My lady.' Hannah spoke diffidently, as if half afraid to continue. 'When do you expect Lord Carthorne to return?'

Alys sighed. 'I do not know. Sir Garret sent a message by Captain Forrester telling him of our father's death, but I have no way of knowing if he received it. Why did you ask?'

'My lady, the Waterlea people are behind Sir Garret and must therefore give their allegiance to Parliament's cause.'

'I understand,' Alys said.

'Yes, but will Lord Carthorne understand it?'

'He does not yet know of it.'

'But should he come home, my lady . . .' She left the sentence unfinished.

Alys looked at her sharply. 'You mean he would have no support from the people? You would betray him?'

'Better he did not come home, my lady.'

Alys picked up the oars and began to row furiously. How dared he? How dared he plot and scheme and turn the good people of Waterlea against those they had always looked up to and revered? It was enough to make her father turn in his grave. And to use Hannah Martin as his courier was the meanest trick of all. Apart from Prue, Hannah was the one person she trusted above all other, and it seemed that even she was against her.

'Have a care, my lady! You will have us in the water.' And when Alys did not reply, she added, 'You are going too close to Devil's Hole, let me take an oar.'

Alys looked across the calm surface of the water towards a spot where a trick of the light made it look as if the water were running against the current, until it gathered itself into a pool and then swirled downwards as if being poured through a funnel. It was said the hole was bottomless and led directly into hell. There had been several drownings when unwary people had been caught up in it, and the local people avoided going within a hundred yards, even in a boat. Alys relinquished one of the oars and together they rowed back to the landing stage near the Martins' cottage.

'I am sorry if I have angered you,' Hannah said, as they tied up the craft.

'I am not angry with you, Hannah, and I am sorry if I frightened you.' She bent down and picked up the two small fish from the bottom of the boat and laughed suddenly. 'We shall need a miracle to make these feed everyone at the manor.'

*   *   *

She was reminded of that remark late that

afternoon, when she heard the clatter of horses in the courtyard and, looking out of her bedchamber window, saw three dust-stained, travel-weary riders dismounting at the door. Her first thought was that here were more mouths to feed, and only then did she wonder who they might be, but by that time John had gone to the door and she heard his cries of welcome which sent her rushing pell-mell down the stairs and into the hall.

'Benedick!' She ran to embrace him. 'Oh, how good it is to see you safe.'

It was only when he held her at arm's length to look at her that she saw how gaunt he looked. His eyes were sunken into hollow cheeks and he was thin as a lathe. His clothes, a dark blue doublet and black breeches, were muddy and stained and the lace on his sleeves was torn. Even his usually ready smile seemed an effort. 'We have a welcome here at all events.'

He turned her to face his companions. Benedick's personal servant she knew, but the other was a girl of perhaps her own age, tired as they all were, but beautiful none the less.

Benedick took the girl's hand and drew her forward. She was much shorter than Alys and had a pale piquant face with finely drawn brows above wide grey eyes. Her hair was almost silver, unlike Alys's which was the gold of ripening corn; it gave her an ethereal quality despite the roundness of her belly.

'Alys, this is my wife, Amy.'

Alys could not disguise her surprise, but then she laughed and embraced the girl, who smiled shyly, and said, 'I am sorry to be such a shock to you, sister—I may call you sister?'

'Of course.' Alys recovered quickly. 'And it is no shock but a very pleasant surprise. Now, come into the small chamber, it is more private than the great hall and we can talk.' She began to usher them away, worrying about how many of the servants had seen them arrive. 'John.' She beckoned to the steward. 'Make what arrangements you can for our guests, but tell no one who they are.'

'But his lordship cannot be kept a secret in his own home, my lady. I have no doubt his horse has already been recognised.'

'You may tell the servants I have arrived and brought my lady with me,' Benedick said.

Alys knew that as soon as Garret heard about her brother's arrival he would be on the doorstep, because he believed the way to Charles was through Benedick. It would also be the end of any hope of reconciliation with him; he would never believe she had not known he was coming, nor understood that she could not turn him or his wife away.

While the servants did their best to prepare a meal fit for their new lord, the travellers were taken to their bedchambers so that they could wash and change, and Benedick was soon happily sorting through his old wardrobe to find something to wear. Amy had a small basket with her containing a change of clothes and Alys instructed Prue to help her.

When all had rested, they returned to the parlour where the table had been laid for three. There was a leg of mutton and several kinds of fish because others in the household had had better luck than she had; there was spiced beef and salsify and beans. And, for the sweet of tooth, there was custard and flummery and baked apples. Benedick ate heartily and even Amy seemed to have a good appetite, but Alys could not swallow a morsel; she was too on edge, listening for the sounds of heavy feet and loud voices demanding the surrender of the King's faithful follower.

Only when the table had been cleared and the servants dismissed did Alys feel free to talk openly to Benedick and his wife. 'You have no idea how pleased I am to see you,' she said. 'I had a dread that you would be killed or wounded and the relief it gives me to know you are all in one piece is beyond telling, but you cannot have been in battle all the time, or you would not have had time to take a wife.' She smiled at Amy to reassure her she was welcome. 'Tell me all about it.'

Benedick reached out and took his wife's hand. 'Amy was a ward of court and lady-in-waiting to the Queen, who, when she saw the way things were going with us, heartily approved the match. We were married last year, in Oxford.' He sighed and leaned back in his chair. 'It is good to be home.'

'His Majesty was pleased to provide me with a dowry,' Amy said. 'Not a very large one, because he is in straitened circumstances himself, but it was kind of him to give me one at all.'

Benedick chuckled. 'I would have taken you without a groat and you know it.'

Amy smiled contentedly. 'And what was even better, the King told Benedick that he was releasing him from his service and ordered him to stay at home with me. He *ordered* him and would not listen to Benedick's arguments.'

'Oh, I am relieved to hear that,' Alys said, offering up a prayer of thanks.

'He is a wonderful man.'

'Benedick?'

Amy laughed. 'He is too, but I meant the King. To be so selfless and so sensitive to the problems of his followers.'

Alys smiled; she knew Garret would not agree with that and she was not at all sure she agreed herself.

'So Benedick has decided to settle down as a peaceful citizen,' Amy went on, then added, her eyes shining with happiness, 'As you may have noticed, I have a special reason to want that now, and it is one of the reasons he agreed to stay at home. I am with child.'

'Oh, Amy, I am so pleased for you.' Alys

hugged her sister-in-law, then, remembering her conversation with Hannah, turned to her brother. 'But, Benedick, I must tell you the people of Waterlea are for Parliament, every one of them.'

'How can that be? They have always followed the lord of the manor.'

'So much has happened since you left, brother, I hardly know where to begin. Garret sent Damian to Oxford under guard; did you see him?'

'Yes, he told me of our father's death.'

'Did he tell you it was his fault?'

'No, he did not. How did it happen?'

She told him briefly, watching his face carefully to see how he would take the news, but he was too exhausted to react in any way but to accept the hand of fate; there was nothing he could do to change it. In the years of war he had seen too much tragedy, too many lives wasted, too many wounded men left to die or drag themselves home as best they could, to rave about the injustice of his father's death. War was unjust. 'Garret gave him his life and we were married immediately afterwards.'

'You married a Roundhead?' Amy was aghast.

'You were contracted to do so,' Benedick said, with a smile. 'But when I last saw you you were determined that it would never happen.'

'I wish that it had not,' she said quietly.

'Where is he, then, this husband of yours? Away fighting battles?'

'No, he is in Waterlea.'

At last his face showed signs of animation as he leaned forward in his seat. 'You mean he will be coming home at any minute?'

'His home is Eagleholm,' she said quietly. 'He lives there and I live here.' She noticed the raised eyebrow and smiled. 'Without father, someone had to manage the running of the manor.'

'And a fine job you have made of it, little sister, but I am home now and you are free to go to your husband.'

'I do not understand,' Amy said. 'Are we not safe here?'

'Of course we are,' Benedick reassured her. 'Garret is an old friend first and an adversary only second.'

'I wish I could be sure of that,' Alys said. 'He asked me to tell him if you came home or I learned where you were.'

'You would never do that, would you?' Amy cried, reaching across to clasp Benedick's hand, almost as if to reassure him that she would protect him. It was a touching gesture because she was so small and so young and he had filled out in the years he had been away from home, so that, although thin, he was tall and broad. 'You would not betray your own brother?'

'The news of your arrival cannot be kept

241

secret in such a small village as this,' Alys said. 'And as soon as Garret learns of it, he will arrest Benedick.' She paused. 'He told me that if you stayed with the King until the very end, you would share his fate.'

'And what has he in mind for that?' He seemed unconcerned.

'I don't know,' she said miserably. 'All I know is that it is not safe for you to stay here, not unless you give yourself up and ask for quarter. I believe he will protect you if you do.'

'Where else can we go?' asked Amy. 'I am exhausted with travelling. I thought, once we came here . . .'

Alys put out a hand to touch the girl's arm. 'Of course you must stay here, my dear Amy. The manor has been sequestered but Father found the money to compound and we have been allowed to remain in residence. You are Lady Carthorne now; Waterlea Manor is your home and when the war is won you will be its mistress.'

'I will not stay without my husband. Where he goes, there will I go.'

'You are tired, my love,' Benedick said, rising and drawing her to her feet. 'We will sleep now and tomorrow we will decide what is to be done.'

They bade Alys good night and went to their bedchamber, and a few moments later Alys climbed the stairs to her own room. She sent Prue away when she came to help her and then sat in the window seat clasping her knees to her chin and gazing out on to the moonlit countryside.

Her reign as mistress of the manor was at an end, and, although she knew Amy would invite her to stay as long as she liked, it would not be the same thing. But it was not that which taxed her brain most through that long sleepless night, but what to do about Benedick. Could she do anything at all?

By the time dawn streaked the eastern horizon with red, she had made a decision. She washed and dressed in a grey cotton dress with a plain white collar, then she sat down and wrote a letter. When that was done, she sent for Prue and gave her careful instructions, before looking round the bedchamber for the last time. Then she crept silently along to Benedick's room. She pushed the letter under his door and stole away, like a thief in the night.

CHAPTER NINE

The stables were full again since Garret's return and even Alys's own mare was in her usual stall. She woke the stableboy who was sleeping, as was his habit, among his charges and, still rubbing sleep from his eyes, he

243

saddled Beauty for her without a murmur; it was not his place to comment on the early rising of his mistress.

The sun was well up by the time she rode into the village and her mind was on what she was going to say to Garret, so that she did not immediately see him riding in leisurely fashion along the fen path towards the village road. He wore a plain brown coat and breeches and had a sporting gun slung on his back. On the pommel of his saddle hung two newly shot ducks. Coming up on to the road ahead of her and seeing her first, he reined in and allowed her to come up to him.

'Alys, what are you doing out so early?'

He had evidently not heard the news of Benedick's arrival. She smiled and gripped the reins to stop herself shaking. 'You said I had to come to you, husband, and it seems you meant it, for you have certainly not been anywhere near the manor in search of me. I was on my way to you.' She smiled suddenly at the irony, as she added, 'But, as you have met me halfway; that, perhaps, is fair.'

He turned his horse to ride beside her. 'Then let us go home, by all means,' he said.

They rode side by side in silence through the village, past the church and along the lane which led to Eagleholm. To the early rising villagers they met, Garret called a cheery, 'Good-day,' and received a tug of the forelock or a bob of skirts in reply. Children, sent out of doors to play, crowded round them, chattering and laughing. He smiled and teased and stooped to ruffle their curls and rode on. Alys smiled automatically when they included her in their greetings, but her mind was on how she was going to eat humble pie and make it convincing.

At the gate of Eagleholm, he dismounted and helped her down, shouting for his groom to take the horses. 'Have you eaten breakfast?' he asked as he escorted her indoors.

She shook her head.

'Then that is what we shall do first. After an hour or two on the fen with Goodman Martin, I have a good appetite.'

The cook had been on the look out for him and, as soon as she heard his voice, picked up a plate of sizzling hot bacon and carried it into the small room in which he usually dined.

'Lay another place,' Garret ordered her. 'Her ladyship is come to join me.'

Alys looked on as he was obeyed and more servants appeared, bringing frumenty and coddled eggs. It was no good protesting she was not hungry, they were determined to show themselves willing to please her. Not until the meal was finished and the remains had been whipped away, did Garret sit back and regard her quizzically, waiting for her to begin. She decided to plunge straight in. 'Garret, Benedick is back.'

'Is he now?'

'He has brought a wife with him.'

He smiled slowly. 'Oh, I see, my Lady Alys's nose has been put out of joint by the arrival of the new mistress.'

'Not at all. Amy is a sweet girl and I took to her at once, but—'

'But there is no room for two mistresses at the manor.'

'It is her right to be there.'

'As it is your right to reside here. Is that what you are saying?'

'You said I could come to you.'

'It was not your homelessness I had in mind.'

'I am not homeless; no one has said I must leave the manor and no one would.'

'Then why?'

'You are my husband.'

'Indeed I am.' He smiled, treading eggs. 'But what I cannot understand is your change of heart, if it is a change of heart.'

'My heart is where it has always been.'

'A riddle,' he said, laughing. 'I enjoy a good riddle.' He reached across the table and took her hand. 'Do you truly want to live here at Eagleholm?'

'Yes.'

'As my wife?' The bantering tone had gone. She knew what he meant. 'Yes.'

He stood up, still holding her hand, and drew her to her feet. 'And what conditions would you have me agree to?'

Don't make me say it, don't make me beg, she pleaded silently, looking into his eyes. At last she said, 'I make no conditions.'

He smiled wryly, knowing what she wanted without pressing her. As far as he was able to accomplish it, he would see her brother safe; he would have done it anyway. If there were any deeper reason for her sudden arrival, questioning her would not reveal it and, just for the moment, he would savour the pleasure of having her with him. He bent his head to kiss her and was surprised by the warmth of her response. He would never under-stand her, never in a thousand years; her sharp tongue and apparent deviousness disappeared as soon as their lips met. She was soft and yielding and roused a fire in him which engulfed his good sense. He held her hard against him, while his mouth explored hers. He lifted his head at last, but he did not let go of her. 'Alys . . .'

She laughed, pulling herself from him and putting the table between them. 'Tut, tut, husband, so early in the day?'

'What has the time of day got to do with it?' He was laughing too. 'You have kept me waiting too long as it is.' His hand shot out across the table and grasped her wrist. 'Come, my little fire-eater, we must install you as mistress of Eagleholm and decide which bedchamber shall be yours. I think the large one at the front; it has a big bed with curtains thick enough for privacy.'

She could no more ignore their physical desire for each other than he could; the reason behind her move was thrust aside as she allowed him to pretend to show her the bedchamber and demonstrate the softness of its feather mattress.

*　　*　　*

It was much later in the day before Alys even thought about what might be happening at Waterlea Manor but she could not go back in order to find out. She must wait patiently for Prue to come and, because she was all too aware that she had used Garret disgracefully, she made every effort to please him. When they were together and he was in a cheerful frame of mind, she could almost forget that he did not love her for her own sake.

The instructions she had given Prue had been that if she did not return by midday it meant that Garret had accepted her back and she would be staying at Eagleholm, and Prue was then to pack all her personal belongings and bring them to her. She did not think it would take her maid more than an hour or two to obey, but it was late in the afternoon before she saw the cart rumbling along the village road towards the house, and by that time Garret had gone out to the drainage works.

'No doubt Benedick will be interesting himself in village affairs now he is home,' he had said. 'But until I have spoken to him, I had best carry on. I do not think there will be trouble, but I gave my word that I would protect the workers.'

'You are not going to see Benedick?' She had tried to make her voice light, as if it was of no consequence whether he went to the manor or not.

'Not today, little wife, I do not feel like making bargains today. Tomorrow is soon enough.'

When Prue arrived with the cart, Alys realised that she had not come alone; sitting up beside the driver was Amy. She ran out to welcome her and bring her indoors.

While Prue supervised the unloading of her belongings, Alys led her guest to the parlour and ordered wine and cakes to be brought to them. 'I am so pleased to see you,' she said. 'But where is Benedick?'

Amy smiled. 'He has spent the day catching up on what has been happening on his domain. He made a tour of the house and spoke of alterations and improvements, and he has been hours and hours with John and the farm manager, so I decided to come and visit you.'

'Was Benedick angry with me for leaving so suddenly?'

'No, I think he understood, but, Alys, you should not have left on my account. We could have lived together very contentedly, you and I—there was no need to leave.'

'But this is my home, Amy, this is where I belong.'

Amy looked around her as if afraid to speak, and Alys laughed. 'My husband is out, you need have no fear of speaking freely.'

'How can you be married to a Roundhead?' Amy asked, almost in a whisper. 'Surely, you do not support Parliament?'

'My father arranged the match, long before the war,' Alys said, as if that answered the question. 'Come, now you shall have a tour of my home and later, perhaps, you will meet Garret.'

'Did you mind very much? About marrying a Roundhead, I mean?'

'I did at first, but I have come to accept it.'

'Oh, how terrible to be forced into a loveless marriage.'

Alys did not want to talk about it, because she could not put her emotions into words which made any kind of sense. 'My husband is a good man,' she said, then, to cover her embarrassment, went quickly to the long window at the head of the stairs. 'Come and look at the view. Have you been in fen country before?'

'No.' Amy joined her at the window. 'How desolate it looks. There are no trees, no shadows, except the clouds on the water. Does anything live out there?'

'Oh, yes, it is full of life. And now some of the land has been drained and grows crops. See!' She pointed along the line of the fen towards Lettice Van Hildt's fields where a large dairy herd grew fat on peat-fed pasture. 'And those outhouses need never again be inundated.' It was easier to talk about impersonal things, to explain about the drainage and how the villagers felt about it, to laugh and tell her about the people, and about Dr Sandy who managed to change sides whenever he thought it expedient and square his conscience while he did it. They chatted happily together until Benedick arrived to fetch his wife, and, almost at the same time, Garret came home.

It had to happen sooner or later and Alys supposed it was better over and done with, and the air cleared. The two men greeted each other amiably, while Amy looked on with an expression which was half fear, half curiosity, which amused Alys. It was almost as if she had expected Garret to be something less than human. To find that the first Roundhead she had ever spoken to was not only well-proportioned but exceedingly handsome and well-mannered took her completely by surprise.

'My lady,' Garret said, bowing. 'I am pleased to meet you.' Then he laughed and

251

added, 'I hope you will be able to keep my wife out of mischief, for she has a great tendency to meddle in the affairs of men. Is that not so, Benedick, my friend?'

Benedick laughed. 'Father often said she should have been born a boy.'

Garret gave her a meaningful look and said, 'I am very glad she was not.' Then added, 'I think, as you are here, Benedick, it would be as well to straighten one or two things out between us. The ladies can amuse themselves while we talk in the library.' The two women watched as he ushered Benedick from the room, saying, 'Did you know I had installed a library? It is far from complete; I have been too occupied to think of buying books . . .'

'Oh, dear,' Amy said. 'What will happen?'

'Nothing,' Alys said, sounding more confident than she felt.

What the two men said to each other Alys did not know, but they emerged in good humour and Benedick took Amy back to the manor. It appeared that Garret had agreed to leave them there unmolested, though what conditions he had imposed she did not know, though she guessed that some of his leniency, if not all, was due to the fact that Amy was with child.

Alys was grateful on their behalf and settled down to life with Garret at Eagleholm. It was an uneventful sort of existence, as long as they did or said nothing to disturb the equilibrium.

They never tired of each other in bed, but Alys wanted something more, something indefinable, a meeting of minds, a fusion of spirits. She wanted Garret's love, and it seemed that was denied her, for he never spoke of it. Watching Amy grow bigger and more contented, she wondered if a child might be the answer. She was surprised that she had not yet conceived, but Prue, who knew most things, told her there was plenty of time and God had his reasons for withholding that blessing for the moment.

Early in April, Simon was sent down from the manor with a message that Prue was needed. It could only mean that the birth was imminent and Alys helped her maid to put together a few things she might need and went with her to see what she could do to help.

It was not an easy labour, because Amy was so slight, and the baby had come before its time, and if it had not been for Prue's competence both might have been lost, but, twelve hours after Prue took over as midwife, Amy had a son. Benedick, allowed back into the room after hours of pacing the boards outside it, crept on tiptoe to the bed and stood grinning down at his wife and the little bundle she held. Alys quietly left the room.

Her eyes were dimmed by tears, and yet she could not explain why she wept. Amy was as well and happy as anyone could be, and Benedick looked thoroughly pleased with himself, so why cry? Could it be because of her own childlessness? Was it that important to her? Or was it simply that she envied the little family their love?

She knew Garret still believed she had married him to save Damian and had gone to him at Eagleholm to protect her brother, and somehow the opportunity had never come, the time had never been right, to tell him differently. There was nothing between them but a physical passion on his part which she was sure he was afterwards ashamed of, and an inability on her part to speak of her own love for him. A marriage based on that was doomed.

Garret had been out when she left, but on returning and being told where she was he hurried to the manor to offer his congratulations.

'So Waterlea has an heir,' he said when Benedick had thrust a glass of wine in his hand to wet the baby's head. 'What have you named him?'

'Harry,' the proud father said. 'Harry followed by Charles.'

Garret raised his glass. 'To Harry Carthorne, may he live and prosper.'

'It will be your turn next, my friend,' Benedick said, after joining the toast.

Alys looked at Garret, afraid he would take offence, but he smiled and said, 'You forget, I spent much time away at the war; my marriage did not really begin until you came home.' He lifted his glass and looked at Alys through its amber liquid. 'Besides, it takes two—perhaps you should be addressing your remarks to my lady.'

Alys blushed crimson and flounced from the room, murmuring something about returning to Amy. Did Garret believe she was barren? Was that one more thing he could hold against her? And did she really want a child just to gratify his wish for an heir? The answer, she had to admit, was yes. . .

*　　　*　　　*

In Waterlea, that spring, the drains were full to overflowing, but most of the villagers, faced with more rain than usual, had been glad to have the water off their land and had grudgingly conceded that the drainage had done some good; by the end of May most of the repair work was done. But that did not mean they wanted the work extended and they watched with keen interest as the drainers tried to add height to the existing banks. Hannah told Alys that if Lettice Van Hildt used the heavy rainfall as an excuse to extend the drainage and add more land to that she already held, they would be ready for her.

It was because of this that Garret took seriously his promise to protect the workmen Lettice employed to keep her fields dry. It did not make Alys feel any better about the Dutchman's widow, who used every excuse she could think of to send for Garret and demand his help.

To compensate the Waterlea men who had served with him, Garret gave them their arrears of pay from his own resources and allowed them to live at home, provided they stood ready to obey a new call to arms if they were needed. Alys wished he would, like his men, be content to stay at home.

'Do you have to go away so often?' she asked him one day when he was gulping his breakfast in order to be early on the road to London. 'Is there no one else who can do whatever it is you are doing?'

'Why, little wife, do you miss me when I am gone?'

'About as much as you miss me,' she retorted, unable to tell if he were teasing.

He sighed heavily. 'I am afraid duty comes before pleasure, my dear, and I have to attend the army council.' He came and stood facing her, taking her shoulders in his hands and looking down into her eyes. 'Rest assured, I shall return as soon as I can. I promised Benedick we should go fishing together; he has a new line he wants to try out.'

It was a very unsatisfactory answer, but one she had to accept. She relieved her loneliness by visiting Amy and Benedick.

Harry was growing plump and rosy-cheeked

and Alys watched his progress with an ache in her heart.

'Do you not think he grows more like Benedick every day?' Amy asked for the hundredth time. 'He is going to be strong and brave like his father.' She bent to kiss the downy hair on the top of his head. 'Alys, you have no idea how much happiness he brings to us. If anything should happen to him or to Benedick, I think I should die . . .'

'What nonsense is this?' Alys asked sharply. 'Why should anything happen to him?'

'I am too happy—no one should be as happy as I am and not be punished for it.'

'Rubbish! I never heard such silly talk in all my life. You deserve your happiness, so be thankful and enjoy it.'

'You deserve to be happy too, and yet I know you are not. Alys, what is wrong?'

'Nothing, my dear sister, nothing at all. Perhaps I am in a mood because Garret is away from home again.'

'And you love him very much?'

Alys smiled; it was impossible to be angry with Amy. 'Yes.'

'But he does not know it?'

'I . . . No, I suppose not.'

'What do you mean, suppose not? Have you never told him so?'

'No.'

'Then do so, do so at once. How can you be happy if you never speak of your love?'

257

'I do not think it is something he wants to hear.'

'Now you are the one who is talking nonsense. Tell him, tell him the minute he returns.'

Alys rode home in reflective mood. It was good advice, but she did not know if she had the courage to carry it through and risk a rebuff. As things were they lived in a kind of harmony, like two shipwrecked people sharing the same log; the smallest disturbance of the water could upset the balance and pitch them both into the depths. Making demands, which was what declaring her love would amount to, could be an act of self-destruction. And yet they could not go on as they were; her own yearning made her restless and sharp-tempered and miserable.

When she dismounted at the stable door, she saw Garret's horse already there and, leaving Beauty with a groom, she hurried eagerly into the house through the kitchen to greet him, but any idea she had of following Amy's advice immediately was cut short when she heard Lettice Van Hildt's voice in the parlour.

'But I did it for us, Garret, my dear, so that we could be together.' She gave a cracked laugh. 'And then you went and spoiled it by marrying that empty-headed Royalist rebel, when you could have had her executed or thrown into gaol. That was madness, Garret, my sweet.'

He sounded weary. 'Yes, perhaps it was.'

'Leave her and come to Westminster with me. Help me plead my case and confirm my title to the land, then I can sell it and we can go away together. I hate this place; it is dank and drear and full of pestilence. I only stayed because of you.'

'Go to the Lords if you must, but if you say a single word to implicate Ingram Martin in your husband's death, I shall be forced to uncover the truth.'

'And in so doing, you will have to reveal your own implication with me and the whole world will know of it. How will my lady take that, do you think?'

Alys, whose head was buzzing with Garret's admission that he regretted marrying her, did not hear his reply, but the next minute Lettice came out of the room and, seeing Alys, gave a derisory laugh. 'Good-day, Lady Hartswood, I am so sorry you were out when I called, but no matter, your husband has entertained me most royally.'

'If he has made you welcome, then there is no need for me to do so,' Alys said sharply, as Garret followed Lettice into the hall.

'Mistress Van Hildt is just leaving,' he said, clapping his hands for a servant to show the visitor out. 'She came to ask for my help in a legal matter.'

As soon as she had gone, Garret turned to

259

Alys. 'I have to return to London immediately.'

'On that woman's account?' Alys was determined to keep calm, though her head was swimming and her heart was pounding.

'Yes. Mistress Van Hildt is taking her case to the Lords. She wants the settlement overthrown before the villagers insist on her relinquishing the land. I must go with her.'

'Why? It seems to me she is more than capable of turning the heads of their lordships without your help.'

'If you had been at home when she came, you would have heard the discussion; as it is, I have no time to explain it now.'

'You do not need to explain your actions to me, Garret Hartswood, I am merely your wife.'

'And a damned shrewish one at that. Now, if you will excuse me.'

She sank into a chair as he left the room. There was no point in trying to detain him. He was certainly in no mood to hear her protestations of love; and after what she had overheard she could never make them. She heard him giving orders to the coachman, before hurrying up to their chamber and directing his personal servant to pack a change of clothes. Then he returned to where she sat.

He stooped and took her hands. 'Alys, come, bid me farewell with a smile.'

'I am to be pleased that you are leaving once again? It is either Parliament's business or the army's business, or the drainers' business, that keeps you from home. I begin to wonder what the truth of it is.'

'It will all come to an end, my dear, if we have patience. Now, I must go.' He bent to put a kiss lightly on the top of her head, just as if nothing dreadful had taken place. Oh, how could he be so blind? Why could he not see that her whole life had been shattered?

'Oh, Prue,' she said, when the sound of the departing coach had faded into the distance. 'I am very afraid. I think he might be gone for good.'

*　　　*　　　*

Lettice came back a week later without Garret. Alys could not bring herself to go and ask her where he was, but she knew Ingram Martin had also gone to the hearing, so she set off for the cottage on the edge of the fen. She learned from Hannah that Ingram had no sooner returned than he had gone out again, presumably to report the outcome of the proceedings to his fellow commoners, but Hannah told her that the Lords had upheld Garret's agreement and extended it until the end of the war, so that as far as Lettice was concerned the journey had not only been a waste of time, but had made matters worse. 'I

261

knew Sir Garret would help us again,' she said.

'You mean, he did not go to speak on Mistress Van Hildt's behalf?'

'No, only to see we were treated fairly.'

'Then why has he not come home?' It was a foolish question to ask; she knew why.

'I believe he has been detained by Cromwell—there is talk of a new offensive.'

The thought that Garret would rather go to war and risk losing his life than live with her was a terrible blow, and Alys could think of nothing else as she made her way home. If only she had behaved differently right from the start, if only they had not been on opposing sides in the war, if only . . . if only . . .

She looked up as she approached Eagleholm; it was her home and Garret's and she could have been so happy there, if fate had not conspired against them. She dismounted at the gate and called to the groom to take Beauty, then she walked slowly towards the house. Garret was standing at the window as if he had been watching for her.

She started forwards, then made herself walk calmly in at the door and along the hall to the parlour, where she hesitated a moment with her hand on the latch to steady herself before going in. He was wearing his sword in a shoulder belt over the red coat of the New Model Army with the insignia of a colonel, and his hair had been cut so that it barely reached his shoulders. She stopped just inside the door, unsure of how to greet him.

He turned and came towards her. 'I came back to say goodbye; I may be away some time.'

'You are going to fight?' Her hands were trembling because he was standing so near and because his brown eyes were looking so intently into her own. 'Must you go?'

'Alys, I am a soldier, I must obey my orders. I have been too long at home as it is. While I have been enjoying the peace of Waterlea, our troops have been fighting in the west country and the King and Prince Rupert have moved north and sacked Leicester. Cromwell has been reappointed and ordered to bring Charles to battle. I go to join him.'

'And the Waterlea men are going with you?' She could not speak of her own misery; it was too deep to express and he would not understand. That he might be killed worried her; that he did not love her and welcomed the opportunity to follow Lieutenant-General Cromwell into battle terrified her.

'Yes.'

'Must you take them from their homes?'

'If I do not, they will be taken by the press men, and they would rather have the devil they know.' He smiled. 'I will do my best for them, Alys.'

'I know you will. When do you go?'

'Today. At once.'

'So soon?' She would not let him see her cry, but if he did not leave soon she could no longer prevent it.

'I am afraid so.' He paused, then went on, 'Alys, when I come home, we will talk about this marriage of ours. Please think about it while I am gone, and if you wish to bring it to an end, then I will agree.'

'Is that what you wish?' she asked in a whisper. Why did he have to mention it now, just when he was going away?

'Things cannot go on as they are, can they?'

'No.'

'And, Alys, if I do not return—'

'Don't say that, please don't say that.' She turned away so that he could not see her face.

'Does it matter?' he asked. 'Would you not sooner be rid of me?'

'No! No! I would not wish anyone dead, least of all you.'

He took her chin in his hand and turned her head towards him. 'Do you mean that?'

'Of course I do.'

He looked down into her eyes, as if unsure whether to believe her, as if the truth would be written in them. And he thought he saw it sparkling there. 'Alys.' He bent his head to kiss her lips, very gently, making no demands, and then he brushed away the tears which she could no longer hide.

Before he could say any more, Aldous came striding noisily into the hall, with his spurs jingling and his overlong sword banging against his leg. 'The men are ready, Colonel, and the horses champing at the bit. We need to catch as much daylight as we can.'

Garret opened his mouth to reprimand him, but changed his mind and, putting the palm of Alys's hand to his lips, he murmured, 'Goodbye, little wife,' then turned and followed his lieutenant out of the house.

'God keep you safe,' she murmured as she went to the door and watched him mount his huge horse and lead his company towards the high road and distant battles.

* * *

Garret ached for love of her, a love he could not express except in their physical union, and he knew that was not enough. If he had been a scholar or a poet, instead of a blunt soldier, he might have been able to find the right words, but as it was whatever he said was misinterpreted. Their marriage had been ill-conceived from the start. How could a marriage based on coercion succeed? Why had he ever hoped that it would? And yet, when he had told her he was leaving, she had wept. She was so obviously unhappy, and if it was his presence that made her so, then perhaps it was for the best. And if he died honourably in battle, she would be free of him. He made a deliberate effort to put his problems behind him because he knew a man who worried too much about what was going on at home could not make a good soldier. His men depended on him and he could not fail them.

He had left Waterlea on Thursday the eleventh of June and on the fourteenth he took part in the fight of Naseby. Cromwell was commanding one flank and it was, in Garret's opinion, due to his generalship and control of the cavalry that the engagement was a decisive victory for the New Model Army. The prisoners they took told them that the King's army was well scattered, although Charles believed it was nothing more than a setback and that the west country was still loyal to him. He had, according to the prisoners, gone to recruit a new army. Garret wrote home to Alys.

We must pursue him there. We have suffered some casualties: Joshua has been wounded by a musket ball in the arm and is on his way home; David Green fell over a tree stump and broke his nose, but will fight on, and James Turner has a sabre cut which will keep him from the fight until it mends. As for the rest, all are well and thinking of those they love. God keep you all until we return.

Your husband, G.

Alys, who had been worrying and waiting, hungry for news of him, read the letter over and over again. It could certainly not be called a love-letter, but it did show that he was thinking of her and that, for the time being, had to satisfy.

'I wish he were safely home,' she said to Prue, 'and nothing ahead of us but a peaceful existence in Waterlea.' All she had to sustain her in her hope that matters could be put right between them was that one gentle kiss and the endearment 'little wife'. It was little enough but she clung to it, as if letting go meant that she would drown in the deep waters of despair.

'Have patience, my chick, and put your faith in God.' Prue had watched the dawn of a new maturity in her young charge, a maturity which had been forced upon her by circumstance, but she hoped the woman who emerged would be better able to deal with the problems which would beset her when the men came home, for she was under no illusions that there would still be problems.

It was late October before Alys heard from Garret again and by then Langport and Bridgwater had fallen to the new army, derisively called thc 'New Noddle' by the Royalists, who were nevertheless made to learn that it was no laughing matter. On the tenth of September, the Parliamentary troops had stormed the outer defences of Bristol in spite of fierce resistance. Sir Thomas Fairfax had offered Prince Rupert terms and he had accepted and surrendered the town, advising His Majesty to sue for peace. Garret wrote:

> By all accounts, the King was furious with his nephew for giving in. He has relieved him of all command and ordered him overseas. I think he will rue that decision; the Prince is one of his ablest and most loyal commanders. Benjamin Gotobed died of his wounds two days after the battle for Bristol and I desire you to comfort his widow as best you can. Now Charles has set off to relieve Chester and I suppose we must follow. We must pursue him to the end.

It seemed that the war was lost for King Charles and Alys felt more than a twinge of sorrow on his Majesty's behalf, even though he had kept his followers at his side longer than was fair on them and, in so doing, had lengthened the war by many months, causing the deaths of so many good men on both sides. It did not occur to her that she was slowly coming round to her husband's way of thinking; her old loyalties were dying hard, but they *were* dying.

It would not be an easy task to break the dreadful news to Liz Gotobed of her husband's death and Alys was afraid she would not know what to do if she became hysterical, but it must be done. Alys tied a shawl about her shoulders, for the autumn air was chill, and went to the stables to saddle her mare, then rode slowly into the village.

After the initial shock the woman seemed to draw on some hidden strength, a faith that supported her through every adversity. Once the first flood of weeping had subsided, she sniffed and said, 'Thank 'e for coming to tell me, my lady, but no need to stay. I have me boys and I will do well enow.'

Alys left the cottage, but she did not feel like going home. She did what she always did when she wanted to be alone; she went out on the fen with her fishing line and eel traps and did not return until dusk.

She was in a calmer frame of mind, but still thinking of what might be happening in the west country when she dismounted at the stables and called for the boy to take the mare. Only then did she realise that there was a new horse there. She let out a squeal of pleasure and dashed into the house, where she stopped in confusion. Garret had heard her arrive and was coming out of the parlour to meet her. He had removed his coat and his shirt was open at the neck, as if he had been in the house some time and had made himself comfortable.

They stood and stared at each other, while she struggled with her emotions. Her hopes and dreams had been centred round this moment; she had rehearsed it in her mind so often and always it was a joyous occasion because she chose to ignore the harsh words and ill-considered actions which divided them. Would he do so too? Looking at him now, though he was smiling, she could not tell.

'Well, wife, is there no welcome for the returning soldier?'

'Yes, yes, of course.'

'Then come here.'

He was going to make her go to him. But someone had to surrender pride. She walked towards him slowly as if each step was a step in the dark. If only he would move towards her, making the gesture of meeting her halfway. Inside she was shaking like an aspen, outside she was stiff and afraid, resisting the impulse to fling herself into his arms. The old Alys would have done that; the new, mature version was determined to remain cool. She was very close to him now and his eyes were regarding her intently.

'Alys . . .' The word was whispered, but it was enough. She ran into his arms.

He held her against him for a moment, while she fought the tears, and then he bent his head to kiss her, gently at first, but then hungrily, as a man would who had been away from the woman he loved for almost six months.

'When did you arrive?' she asked when he

allowed her to draw breath.

He laughed. 'I have been here nigh on two hours, but as no one knew where you had gone I could not come and find you.'

'I was out on the fen. Have you come home alone?'

'No, my men are with me, all who survived, that is. Did you speak to Trooper Gotobed's widow?'

'Yes, today, as soon as I received your letter. Have you been given food?'

'Yes, I have been well looked after while my wife has been communing with fish and fowl.'

She was not sure whether this was meant as a criticism, but he was smiling and she decided not to comment, but called for a servant to order wine.

She watched as he made himself comfortable in the armchair and sat looking up at her with his head to one side as if it helped him to see her the better. 'You have grown even more beautiful. But what of your temper, little wife, what of that?'

'I will give you a taste of it,' she said sharply, 'if you do not satisfy my curiosity. Are you home for good?'

'That depends on that devious monarch.'

'Where is he now?'

'Our intelligence says he is marching to join his allies in Scotland. It is one of the reasons I was sent north again.'

'Does Benedick know of this?'

'It is no secret, so if he has not heard he will soon learn of it. Why do you ask?'

'He will be very downcast by the news. I hope . . .'

'You hope that he does not take it into his head to do something desperate on behalf of the King, is that what you were about to say? I hope so too.'

A maidservant brought in a tray containing a flask and two silver goblets. Alys motioned her to set it on the table. 'No, I am sure he would not be so foolish,' she said, pouring wine and handing him one of the goblets.

He held it up to her in salute. 'Your health and happiness, my lady.' Then he swallowed it at a gulp.

She coloured, but stared him out. For the first time she noticed how tired he was. He had washed and changed his clothes while he had been waiting for her, but nothing could disguise his hollow cheeks and the dark rings of fatigue round his eyes.

'You are exhausted,' she said. 'I will have a bed made up for you. We can talk tomorrow.'

He looked at her sharply, then smiled. 'I am indeed tired, but not so tired I need to be put to bed like a sulking child. I will say when I want to sleep and where.' He stood up and held out his hand. Slowly she slipped her hand in his and together they climbed the stairs.

CHAPTER TEN

Alys's fears about Benedick were increased a thousandfold two weeks later when Amy arrived, late one afternoon, in a great panic. She had not even stopped to put on a cloak, although the afternoon air was freezing. 'Benedick has gone!' she cried, rushing into the parlour without waiting to be announced. 'Oh, Alys, what am I to do? I tried to stop him, but he would not listen. Oh, Alys, he gave Garret his solemn vow not to go to war again.'

'Then this must be kept from Garret. It is fortunate that he is at one of his interminable army council meetings.' She paused and added, 'Do sit down, Amy, and calm yourself. It is not the end of the world.'

Amy was too agitated to obey. She paced the room from hearth to window and back again, while Alys wondered what she could do to help. 'I know Benedick is loyal and brave,' Amy went on. 'He does not have to prove it to me or anyone, but he is risking everything, everything; if not his life, then our home, our future, everything . . .'

'What do you mean?'

'It was part of the bargain he struck with Garret when he came home. You know the manor had been sequestered?'

'Yes, but Father paid the composition to keep it.'

'Yes, but what he paid was only a fraction of what the commissioners demanded. Because Garret spoke on his behalf and said his lordship was a true patriot in spite of what he called Benedick's misguided allegiance, they allowed him to stay and gave him two years to find the balance.'

'I did not know this,' Alys said. 'And Father had no resources above what he had already given and the income from the land. How could he pay?'

'He died with it still unpaid, but then Garret gave Benedick back your dowry—'

'He did what?'

'He said he did not need or want it, and Benedick put it with my dowry and paid the fine for the manor. In return he promised not to go to war against Parliament again.' She ignored Alys's look of astonishment and went on, 'Oh, Alys, we must stop him.'

Alys had no time to dwell on Garret's reasons for what he had done. She stooped and drew the girl to her feet. 'Hush now, and tell me, where has Benedick gone?'

'To Heronlea, by the fen path. He left about an hour ago. Oh, I knew I was too happy, I knew something like this would happen. Fetch him back, Alys, please fetch him back.'

'I will do what I can. Now calm yourself.

274

Did you come alone?'

'Simon brought me on the cart.'

'Then he can take you back. Stay there and wait for me, do you hear?'

'Yes.' Now that Alys appeared to have taken charge, Amy was calmer.

'And it would be best if you said nothing of what has happened to anyone. If I can only persuade him to come home, no one need ever know he was implicated.'

Alys dared not spend any more time comforting her sister-in-law, if she was to catch up with her brother. She gave her into Prue's capable hands, grabbed a cloak from a downstairs aumbry, and went to saddle up Beauty. In less than five minutes she was riding through the village towards the fen path.

As soon as she had left the huddle of village buildings behind her, she put her horse to a gallop and made for the fen path to Ingram Martin's cottage. Once on that, she was forced to reduce her pace to a walk because of its narrowness. As she reined in at the ferry crossing, Ingram came out to her.

'Did my brother pass this way?'

'Aye, my lady, over an hour since.'

'Do you know where he was going?'

'Aye, my lady. You will find him at Master Clark's.' He paused. 'Do you think it wise to follow him, my lady? The meeting is supposed to be a deathly secret and if you was to be seen . . .'

He obviously knew something was afoot but whether he approved of it or not she did not know. It would be better not to ask. He had punted her over and she was on the path on the other side of the mere before she began to think about what she would say to her brother when she caught up with him. She did not think it would be wise to remind him of his promise to Garret, a promise extracted under duress. She would have to appeal to his love of his wife and son, but then Amy had already done that and it seemed to have had no effect.

The village of Heronlea had a small church and a group of very poor cottages, set round the farmstead of Master Clark. It was almost dark when she arrived, but the barn to the side of the farm was lit by flares and she could hear a babble of conversation. She dismounted, left her mare tethered to a post and crept forward on foot.

She moved cautiously towards the half-open door, undecided whether to approach openly and demand to see her brother, or to listen to what was happening and try to speak to him alone. She was unaware that she was not the only one out there in the dark.

The barn was crowded with men, and it was not just the villagers, for some of them listening to the speaker were, like Benedick, dressed as gentlemen. The man addressing them was standing on a table and wore a grey velvet doublet and a great quantity of lace about the wrists and throat. He had a small pointed beard and his hat was set at a rakish angle, so that its feather brushed his cheek as he spoke. He held the attention of his listeners so completely that Alys was able to squeeze into the barn without being seen.

'We must praise God that Newark is still loyal,' he said. 'His Majesty is resting there, while he decides what to do. His army in Scotland has been destroyed and he cannot continue with his march north. He is in dire straits for men and money. His Majesty must return to Oxford and we must raise a new army. We have right on our side and God will surely give us victory over the accursed Roundhead.'

Alys could not stifle her cry of dismay. Amy had been right, and if Garret found out what was happening, as, in the end, he must, Benedick would forfeit his life. She suddenly became aware that she had been spotted and a sea of hostile faces was turned towards her. 'A woman!' they shouted. 'There is a spy in our midst!'

Benedick drew his sword and pushed his way through to her. 'Alys, what, in God's name, are you doing here?' he demanded, sheathing his sword.

'Benedick,' she said. 'Amy is distraught with worry about you. How can you go back to war when you have such a lovely wife and son to

277

think of?'

'I also have my duty to do.'

'She is married to old Ironside's right-hand man!' someone shouted. 'She must die!'

'No!' Benedick stood in front of her as if to protect her. 'The marriage was arranged when she was still a child,' he said. 'She is a loyal subject of His Majesty. She will never betray him or you. I give you my oath on it.' He looked meaningfully at Alys, as if defying her to contradict him.

'Is that right?' they cried. 'You swear never to reveal what you have seen and heard today?'

'I will say nothing,' she said.

'Swear!'

'Go on,' Benedick urged her. 'I cannot save you if you do not.'

'I swear,' she whispered, praying that Garret would never find out.

'Not even to your husband?' one of the men asked. 'Not even when you are alone?'

'I will not speak of what I have seen, I give my word.'

They seemed satisfied and Benedick took her arm and escorted her back outside. 'Come, sister, go back home, while I extricate myself from your folly,' he said. 'You have shaken their faith in me and I doubt if they will trust me again.'

'Then I am pleased,' she snapped. 'Perhaps now you will think of your wife and son and the vow you made to Garret.'

'Oh, it is Garret you are thinking of, is it? I am glad those fellows in there did not hear you say that, or we would both be in chains. Go and tell Amy that I will be home as soon as may be and she is not to worry.'

'Benedick, I'm sorry, Amy was so distraught . . .'

He smiled and kissed her cheek. 'How Garret puts up with you, I do not know. Why can't you behave like other women and stay at home and mind the house? How did you come?'

'On Beauty. She is tethered by the path.'

'Then go, and mind the way in the dark.'

She did not need the warning. The path was narrow and the night cloudy so that the moon shone only fitfully to light her way. But her mare was sure-footed and she knew she could rely on her. She untied her and mounted and then, hearing a sound behind her, turned in the saddle. Someone was following her; they had changed their minds about letting her go. She dug her heels into Beauty's flank, but the path was too treacherous for her to outrun whoever it was and he had the more powerful horse.

'I don't know what your brother was thinking of to send you off into the night alone,' said a voice she recognised.

She turned as he drew level with her. 'Damian Forrester. I did not know you were with Benedick.'

'I was not. Like you, I had my reasons for wanting to know the King's plans. Now my curiosity has been satisfied, I can escort you home.'

'I am perfectly safe.'

'Of course you are, for I shall be with you.'

She did not like the tone of his voice, nor the way he was smiling at her; like the cat that had got the cream, she thought, and wondered what devious plan he had in mind for her now. She was absolutely sure he was not accompanying her out of gallantry. 'I do not need an escort, Captain.'

'Oh, but you do, and it pleases me to furnish it.'

She tried to make Beauty go faster, but the animal had more sense than she had and refused to increase her pace. Damian tried to draw alongside her on the narrow path and she kicked into the mare's flank and made her go.

'Come back, you fool!' Damian shouted, following.

Beauty faltered and Alys slipped sideways from the saddle. She was not hurt, but it meant that while she scrambled to her feet, he was able to come up to her and dismount beside her.

'Why are you trying to run away from me?'

'I would rather be alone.'

'How can you say that? I know you only

married the Roundhead to save me, just as I endured capture and imprisonment for you.'

'For me?' She laughed nervously. 'You never did anything for me, I know that. You plundered and stole and deceived your King, when he trusted you.'

'And, thanks to Garret Hartswood, I am in disgrace and he no longer trusts me. That devilish Roundhead ruined my life, do you know that?'

'He gave you your life.' She tried to remount but he grabbed her arm.

'And he made sure the King knew what I had done. I will have my revenge for that.'

'Let me go!'

'Oh, no, my dear, because you are part of my revenge.' He pulled her towards him and held her chin in his hand, forcing her to look at him. 'You will be mine, this night; then we will go together and tell that pestilential husband of yours that we are going away together, that you love me and always have.'

'He won't believe it.' She did not think it wise to tell him that Garret was away from home.

'Oh, yes, he will, because it will be the truth and you will not be able to deny it. And before we go we will make him a parting gift; we will tell him where he can find the King. That should compensate for his loss of you, don't you think? His Roundhead cause has always meant more to him than his wife.'

She wrenched herself away from him, made a mad dash for her mare and threw herself on her back. In her anxiety to escape, she did not watch the path and poor Beauty, sensing the panic of her mistress, rushed hock-deep through freezing water, trying and failing to keep to the path. It took all Alys's concentration to find firm ground and by that time Damian had caught up with her again.

'Now we will ride comfortably together until we reach Waterlea,' he said, taking her bridle from her nerveless fingers.

When they reached the crossing, the flat-bottomed ferry was on their side of the water and there was no sign of Ingram. Damian led the horses on board and signalled for her to follow. There was no point in refusing; she had to gain the other side, if only because it was nearer habitation and help.

Her mare was very restless and inclined to prance, rocking the unstable craft as he poled them out into midstream. Alys stood close to her, stroking her neck and murmuring softly. 'I know you are just as cold and frightened as I am, Beauty, but we shall soon be home.'

Suddenly the animal gave a snort of terror and kicked out at Damian's mount. The ferry rocked crazily and Damian turned on her. 'Can't you keep that beast still?'

'I am trying.'

'Here, you take the pole.'

He turned and grabbed the mare's reins.

Beauty reared up and the next moment Alys felt her legs go from under her as the platform tilted, and she found herself groping empty air as she tried to find something to hold on to. She heard a shout and then there was nothing but thrashing horses and freezing water and her heavy cloak was dragging her down and down.

* * *

Garret, who had been out searching for her, carried her cold wet body home in his arms, refusing all help. Ingram had gone on ahead to warn everyone, but it was too late to help her, too late to help him. He might live for a hundred years, but her death would be on his conscience until the end of it. If only he had arrived a few minutes sooner, she could have been saved. If he had paid more attention to Benedick, she need never have gone out; if he had not stayed arguing with Lettice, because he did not want to believe that Alys was, once again, dealing with his enemies, he might have been in time. He stumbled along, bending his face to put his cheek against the cold face of his beloved and wished he could die too.

There was a crowd at his gate, but they were a blur of unrecognisable faces, as he pushed past them with his burden. Prue was standing, ashen-faced, on the doorstep.

'Bring her in, sir, bring her in to her own

room.'

He turned on the step, feeling he ought to say something to the people there, but unable to find the words. Lettice's face loomed up at him in the pool of light from the open door. 'Did I not tell you?' she crowed. 'Did I not tell you she could not be trusted. It is God's punishment and you are free of the witch.'

In a dream he heard his own croaking voice say, 'Witches do not drown.'

Prue took his arm and propelled him indoors. 'Come, sir, if we are to save her, we must hurry.'

'Save her?' Did the woman not know it was too late for that?

He climbed the stairs and laid her on the huge bed, the only place where they had truly been happy. Prue got to work at once, stripping off her mistress's wet clothes and turning her on her face. Then she began pummelling her back, harder and harder.

'Stop it! Stop that!' Garret shouted, trying to pull her off. 'Leave her in peace. Leave me to my grief.'

Prue signalled to the steward and that worthy gentleman enlisted the help of other servants and lifted Garret bodily from the room. 'Get him out of those wet clothes before he freezes to death, and then give him plenty to drink,' she shouted after them, though she did not stop working. People had been known to come back from the dead and

284

if it was at all possible she would do it. No one would take her chick from her without a fight.

Almost an hour later, she went down to the library where Garret sat slumped in his chair in his dressing gown with an empty brandy bottle beside him. He was not drunk, though he had tipped the whole lot down his throat in an effort to find oblivion. The servant was almost as wet as he had been; her clothes were stained with a mixture of water and vomit and she looked exhausted, but there was a gleam of triumph in her eyes.

'She sleeps,' she said.

It was a moment or two before he could comprehend what she was saying, then he shook his head, as if to clear it. 'She is alive?'

'She is, but only just. I pray God that we can keep her so.'

He dashed up to the bedchamber, where Alys had been put into a clean nightgown and was tucked up into as many blankets and skins as could be piled on her. He tiptoed gently over to her and sat down carefully on the edge of the bed, leaning over to kiss the white lips which were cold as marble. He was still there when dawn broke, still unable to believe that the lifeless body he had pulled from the water was actually breathing.

She stirred restlessly and he put out a hand to settle her. 'Lie still, my love, my life, my own, you are safe at home.'

She opened her eyes, but there was no

recognition in their blue depths. 'Home?'

'Yes.'

'Am I ill?'

'You nearly drowned. Lie still, I will call your maid.'

Reluctantly he left her side and went to the door, to find Prue dozing in a chair on the other side of it. She was fully awake the moment he touched her. 'She does not know me.'

Prue smiled and whispered. 'Never you mind that, sir, all that matters is that she is alive. Go you and find a bed now, there are plenty of people to watch over her.'

Christmas came and went and the new year of 1646 was ushered in, but Garret hardly noticed; his whole world revolved around watching Alys's slow progress back to the land of the living. Somewhere along the way she lost part of herself, part of her memory, and was like a child again. He ached to hold her in his arms, to kiss her, to breathe warmth and life back into her body simply by willing it so. She did exactly as she was bid, eating and getting dressed and taking a little exercise as Prue directed her, but she had no will of her own. She lived in a kind of limbo, unable to feel pain or anger or love. His tenderness touched her no more than his rage had once done.

She knew who he was and accepted that they were married, in the same way as she accepted the distasteful medicine Prue concocted for her; something to be endured for her own good. They made love but there was no fire in her, no passion. And though he had raved against it at the time, he wished she could regain some of that rebelliousness which had stirred his heart in the first place and made him love her. She was lost to him and it was no consolation to know that she was also lost to that Royalist puppy, Damian Forrester; when last seen he had been stumbling back to Heronlea, dripping water. But she did not remember that and had never once asked after him.

'Will she ever be the same again?' he asked Prue in the first days of spring, as the water receded from the fen, revealing once again the rich dark soil.

'I do not know.' Prue herself was not so sure that Alys would ever come out of her cabbage - like existence. 'We must have patience. Perhaps if she went home to the manor—'

'This is her home.' He spoke angrily because he did not want to admit she might be right, that perhaps it was his presence which was causing the barrier to his wife's recovery. Ought he to let her go? Ought he to sacrifice his own happiness for hers?

While he pondered on the problem, Aldous, newly promoted, led his men to meet the enemy at Bovey Tracey. He wrote a letter which did not reach Waterlea until April, when the summer grounds had been dry for a month and the cattle were grazing on the new grass.

The weather was bitterly cold. The snow had been falling all day and the sound of marching feet, carts rumbling by with their loads and the hooves of the cavalry were so muffled, it seemed like a world of silence. It was not fighting weather, but, in truth, the men were becoming bored with nothing to do but drink and quarrel among themselves. I was much relieved when we were ordered to march out.

We took a great many prisoners and horses, which frightened the enemy into lifting the blockade of Plymouth, and we marched to meet them at Torrington. There was fighting in the streets at push of pike and the gunpowder store blew up and nearly killed Sir Thomas Fairfax, but, praise be, he escaped. Truro fell to us on March the fourteenth and on the twenty-first the King's last army in the field, commanded by old Jacob Astley, surrendered at Stow-on-the-Wold. He is a brave man, as so many of our adversaries are; 'tis a pity that they are, like their master, so stubborn, but stubbornness itself will not win battles. Can Charles not see he is beaten?

Garret read the letter with scant interest; Aldous was perfectly capable of command and the war seemed so far away; it had no relevance to life in Waterlea and his immediate problems. But it was drawing near again and he could not ignore a letter which arrived from Cromwell.

I know your wife has been very ill, but I understand she is in no danger, and it is imperative you muster what men you can and join me. That obstinate monarch has spent the last few weeks wandering about the Welsh Marches and the Midlands with the remnants of his army and indulging in futile skirmishes. Now he has ridden north and is threatening Huntingdon.

'I suppose it is because it was Cromwell's home town and he sees Oliver as the author of all his misfortunes,' Garret told Prue. 'I fancy it is his last act of defiance before he concedes his defeat. Let us hope so.'
'You will go?'
'I will think about it.'
Garret hung about for days before he finally made the decision to obey, and then it was only after making one last attempt to get through to Alys.
She was sitting on a bench in the garden, wrapped about with blankets, reading *Romeo*

and Juliet. It seemed to have the power to move her, for tears glistened in her eyes. He sat beside her and took the book from her hands. 'Alys,' he said gently. 'I must go away again.' She did not answer and he went on, 'Believe me, I do not want to go.' He took her face in both his hands and turned it towards him. 'Do you understand me?'

'Yes, I understand.'

'Tell me you do not want me to go, tell me that.'

'I do not want you to go.' Her voice was flat; she was merely repeating his words.

'For God's sake!' he shouted, angry now. 'This is more than flesh and blood can stand. You do not care a groat whether I come or go. I do not exist for you.' He pulled her roughly to her feet and kissed her in a way he had not kissed her for months, with passion and fire and longing and even a little cruelty. He kissed her because he did not know what else to do. He released her, disgusted with himself, his anger spent. She was looking at him with wide, uncomprehending blue eyes which suddenly filled with tears. They splashed over her lids and down her cheeks. He was sobbing himself as he turned from her and strode into the house. Prue came hurrying towards him and he hated her for her nearness to Alys, for her faith, for her patience, for everything he was not, nor ever could be, towards his wife.

'I am leaving,' he said. 'Take your mistress

290

back to Waterlea Manor and care for her there.' Then he ran upstairs three at a time and called for his man to pack while he scrambled into his uniform. He was a soldier; he would live and die a soldier.

He had gone before it was realised that Alys had suddenly come out of her torpor. Prue found her crumpled on the ground beside the bench in the garden sobbing as if her heart would break.

'Ssh, ssh, my chick,' she soothed. 'Come indoors and rest, you have been out here too long.'

Alys raised a tear-streaked face. 'He has gone.'

'I know, but he will come back, you can be sure of it. Now, come inside and I will mix you up a nice soothing potion.'

'I want no more potions,' Alys was decisive for the first time since the accident. 'They make me sleepy.'

'That is all to the good, sweet child, and it is only crushed poppy seeds, after all.'

'I will have no more. I want to feel alive again, even if it hurts, because only then can I know love.' She turned to Prue, smiling through her tears. She remembered little of the previous four months; it was like waking from a dream in which she had floated aimlessly, outside herself, watching them care for her. Garret had woken her with that kiss and made her realise she could still feel hurt, could still be touched by his anger and frustration, could still love. 'I was dead, wasn't I? I died out there in the fen and now I am alive again. Garret has made me so.'

Prue guided her mistress indoors. 'He suggested we go back to the manor.'

'That I will not do. It is to Eagleholm he will come when he returns and I will be here waiting.'

She would not be moved on that point; it was the beginning of her recovery, and the emergence of a new woman, and one, she told Prue confidently, who was mistress of her own destiny. Garret had left in anger, but she understood that anger now and knew, with certainty, that nothing but death could keep him from her.

Later that month, when the sun shone and the sky was blue, Alys realised she was with child. There was no way to let Garret know the news for he had not written and they had no idea where he was. She spent her time between Eagleholm and the manor, waiting with uncharacteristic patience for her husband to come home.

There were several news sheets being printed, full of the gory details of the King's last attempts to salvage his pride. They found their way to Waterlea in the bundles of packmen, or itinerant workers, or were included in letters sent to Amy by Benedick, who had rejoined his King. And though Alys tried to hide it from Amy, she could not banish from her mind the dread of the two men she most loved facing each other in battle.

'There is only Newark and Oxford left for the King,' Amy said one day when she brought Harry to see Alys at Eagleholm. 'What will happen when they fall and there is nowhere for him to go? What will become of him and his faithful followers? Benedick's last letter was written weeks ago and I am so afraid.'

Alys knew that Amy was worried about what would happen to Benedick when the war ended and, though she shared some of that concern, she was confident that Garret would somehow save him. She smiled reassuringly. 'We need only to be patient a little longer and all will be well.'

'I wish I had your faith, Alys. I cannot sleep at night for the fear that grips me. The war is nearly at an end, but if it should come to Waterlea after all—' She burst into tears. 'I could not bear it.'

Alys ran to put her arms around her and comfort her. 'Hush, sister, we will have news soon, you will see. Garret or Benedick will find a way of sending us a message.'

The messenger was the person she least expected. He arrived one afternoon in the first week of May, dusty from travel, but still dressed in satins and lace and with his curls tied with ribbon. When Alys saw him from the

293

window, her blood ran cold and she could not stop herself shaking. How dared he ride in so openly? She ran out to the gate, ignoring Prue's cries to have a care; Prue was always warning her of the mischief she could cause herself if she did such and such a thing, or failed to do something else.

She stopped as he dismounted and turned towards her, but she did not wait for him to speak first. 'What are you doing here, Damian Forrester? Have you not caused enough trouble?'

'I bring you news.' He was smiling that self-confident smile of his, which had once beguiled her, but which could do so no longer, but she could not stop herself shaking.

'Of whom?' she asked, trying to sound cool, though she knew he was not deceived and was enjoying the moment.

'Of Colonel Hartswood, of your husband.'

'Then, pray, give it to us and be gone, for you are not welcome.'

'Oh, I will be. Rest assured, I will be.' He paused, appraising her from top to toe and she was thankful that her pregnancy did not yet show, for he would make a game of that too. 'Is there no welcome for the bringer of news? I have ridden hard to come to you; the least you can do is to offer me food and drink.' He smiled suddenly. 'No refreshment, no news.'

She could not stand bandying words with

him at the gate. 'You had best come in, then,' she said, calling for the groom to take his horse, before preceding him indoors. She called to a servant to bring him ale to slake his thirst, and another to make a room ready for him so that he could wash off the grime of travel, and when that was done she turned to ask him the question that filled her mind.

'What of Garret? What news have you?'

He did not answer immediately and she looked up at him, wondering why he hesitated. When she saw the expression of triumph in his eyes, the blood drained from her face and her heart almost seemed to stop, then began pounding in her throat. She grabbed his arm. 'Damian, for pity's sake, tell me.'

'The Roundhead is dead.'

'The Roundhead? You mean my husband?' Her voice was no more than a whisper. 'Dead?' She could not believe it, would not believe it. 'You mean he is wounded.' The thought brightened her. 'He will recover and come home, I can nurse him with Prue's help . . .'

He took her hands in both his own. 'Alys, believe me, he is dead.'

Prue, sensing from the silence in the room that she was needed, came in just in time to catch her mistress as she fell. She helped her to a stool and stood beside it, cradling Alys's head against her. 'Are you sure of this?' she demanded of Damian. 'Because if you lie—'

'I do not lie, I saw him fall. He was surrounded by Royalist cavalry and—'

'My lady does not want to hear the details,' Prue said quickly. 'Just so long as you are sure.'

'I am sure. Would I come here otherwise?'

Alys knew the truth of that. Tears flooded over her in great waves. She knew Garret had loved her, the realisation had come to her on the day he left, but now that knowledge was swamped by the agonising pain that he had never felt able to tell her so, and this was followed by the self-accusation that she had never told him how much she loved him either and now it was too late. She sobbed until her shoulders ached and her chest was sore. She wept, not only because he was dead and gone from her, but because he had gone thinking she would be glad of it. Why, oh why, had she ever said she wished him dead? How far from the truth that was! 'Garret! Oh, Garret,' she sobbed. 'Would I were with you in eternity.'

'We will have none o' that,' Prue said hastily, pulling her to her feet. 'Come up to your chamber and rest.' To Damian she said, 'Thank you for coming. It were better you left as soon as you are refreshed.'

'I cannot do that,' he said bluntly. 'The struggle is not yet over and I have work to do here.'

Prue was too concerned for her charge to

give him the retort she had on the tip of her tongue and Alys did not hear him and would not have shown an interest if she had. He ate and drank his fill and then rode up to the manor, smiling to himself. By the time he had done his work, the manor and all its land would be his and Alys would be his. There was nothing to stop him.

CHAPTER ELEVEN

Alys was brought out of the nightmare of her grief several days later, when she saw Damian in the village. She had not realised he was still in Waterlea, but then she had been unaware of anything except that she had lost the man she loved and she could not come to terms with it. The Cavalier was supervising some of the village men, who were digging into the banks alongside the New Drain, close to the sluice. Beside them she saw what looked like a barrel of explosive.

'What are you doing, Captain?'

'If the enemy comes, the banks must be pulled down and the fields flooded. These men have been very helpful in telling me how best to go about that.'

'I'll wager they have.' The irony of it was lost on him and she turned to the village men, who simply grinned at her and shrugged their shoulders. 'You must not do this. Think of Garret and all the work he put into the agreement. He would not want you to flood the fields; it is against the settlement everyone agreed to.'

'The war be ended, my lady,' one of the diggers put in. 'Mistress Van Hildt ain't proved her title.'

'It is not for you to say when the war has ended,' Alys said, wondering how she could think of defending the woman who hated her enough to try and turn her husband against her. 'She has a right to her land until the Lincoln Committee say otherwise.'

'An' we are in our rights to take back our land.'

Damian was growing impatient and wanted the men back at work. 'What care I for arrangements made by dead men?' he snapped. 'It is I who command here and I who say whether the fields will be flooded. I have posted lookouts in the upper rooms of the manor, and, if they see troops coming, they will fire the saker, and we will blow up the banks and take refuge in the manor. It will be our own island paradise where no one can reach us.'

'Are these your orders? Has Lord Carthorne instructed you to do this?'

He smiled, a thin smile without humour. 'I do not need orders. I do what I please.' He motioned the men to go back to work. 'We

298

will be ready. We will be ready whoever comes, King or Parliament.'

Alys suddenly realised that he had deserted and was as afraid of the Royalist troops as those of Parliament. Had she, in her grief, ignored the fact that he was insidiously taking over the village in the name of . . . what? King or Parliament? Or simply Damian Forrester?

It was no good appealing to him, he would not listen to her entreaties. She made a last effort to influence the men. 'Garret would not do this.'

Damian seized her arm and drew her away. 'How do you know what your husband would have done, my lady? How well did you know him? Hardly at all. Now, with us it could be different, for we would come to know each other very well, you and I. Stop grieving for him, he is gone, and I am here.'

'I do not want you, not now, not ever.'

'But I want you. It is all I have wanted, ever since I first set eyes on you. I have far more to offer you than that muddle-headed Colonel, I will give you Waterlea—all of it, because when Lord Carthorne is sent to the gallows—'

'I wish you gone,' she said, trying to keep calm. 'Leave here, leave this village. We do not want you.'

He smiled slowly. 'That is not the wish of the people, my lady. They know I want to help them.'

'You help no one but yourself, just as you

helped yourself to plunder. We do not need that kind of help.'

'One day, my lady, you will thank me. One day you will need me as I need you. You will forget Garret Hartswood.'

She wrenched herself away and stumbled from him. He had a wild look in his eye and Alys realised he was mad, mad with greed and revenge and hate. How she could ever have been taken in by him in those early days of the war she did not know, and it was her blindness then that had caused all her problems since.

But there was no time to dwell on past foolishness. Something had to be done to prevent the villagers doing something which would cost them the goodwill Garret had helped them to build up with the Lincoln Committee. If they flooded the land again, they would lose all they had gained. She needed help to stop them. She turned and hurried to the manor.

Amy had learned of Garret's death from Damian when he arrived at the Manor and, though she had hurried to offer what succour she could to Alys, she had not refused hospitality to the Cavalier, because he had claimed to be her husband's friend and filled her head with compliments and loving messages from Benedick. Amy might have heard from Benedick himself since then, and if she had, they might be able to send him an urgent message that he was needed at home.

When she arrived at the manor, Amy showed so much pleasure at seeing her that she felt guilty that she was about to heap more troubles on her head. She bent over the cradle to kiss Harry and stroke his golden curls, unsure of how Amy would view the latest developments in the village. Amy was still a Royalist at heart.

'Sit down and tell me how things are with you,' Amy said and, when Alys had done so, sat beside her on the settle. 'I am glad you decided to come and see me after all. It is not good to grieve alone.'

'Amy, have you heard from Benedick?'

'No, I wish to God I had. It seems the King has disappeared into thin air and my husband along with him.'

'Disappeared? But surely a King cannot just disappear? He would need servants and baggage and horses. Someone must surely have seen him.'

'And if they have, what then? It is like a game of cat and mouse, and I fear the trap is closing.' Amy sighed. 'It may be wrong of me, but I pray hourly that we shall hear that Charles has surrendered. But why do you ask?'

'Amy, we must do something about Captain Forrester. He is filling the New Drain banks with explosives. If he sets it off, the village will be flooded, and there is no one to stop him.'

'But why should he do that? Is he expecting

301

trouble?'

'I do not know. Benedick must be found and urged to come home. We need help and he does not know of . . .' she paused to collect herself ' . . . of Garret's death . . .'

'Oh, but he does. Captain Forrester told him before he came to tell you. They were all on the same field of battle, I believe.' She paused and laid a hand gently on Alys's arm. 'I did not like to tell you.'

'Garret and Benedick met face to face?'

'I do not think so; at least, Captain Forrester did not say so.'

Alys did not want to talk or even think about it because it would not bring Garret back, and she must put aside her personal feelings until she had put an end to Damian's dominance of the villagers. 'Do you think someone can be sent to find Benedick? Someone must know where he is; there are so few places where the King could find sanctuary now.'

'And one of them is here,' Amy said softly.

'Here? You would never welcome him?'

'If my husband brings him, then I shall, most willingly.'

'Amy, how could you!'

'Alys, dear, it grieves me to upset you so, and I did try to remind Benedick of his promise to Garret, but, you see, it is no longer important . . .'

'Because Garret is dead?'

Amy nodded. 'And because it was part of the agreement that if anything happened to Garret . . .' she paused, watching Alys's face for signs of anger ' . . . if anything happened to Garret, then Benedick's debt to him would be cancelled.' She stopped speaking, but Alys made no sign of having understood her, and she added, 'Alys, the manor is Benedick's again. The village is Royalist.'

'And you were afraid to tell me this?'

Amy nodded.

Alys smiled wearily. 'Oh, my foolish, foolish sister. What care I who owns Waterlea? I would give every groat I have, every stick and stone, just to have my husband by my side.' Her eyes filled with tears, but she blinked them away. 'But enough of that—we must decide what to do about Damian. You know, Amy, he is not a loyal subject of Charles, nor is he a true friend of Benedick. What he is doing is not in the King's name. Damian Forrester thinks of no one but himself and a mad idea he has that he is in love with me. Amy, I think he means to harm you.'

'Me?'

'He wants Waterlea Manor for himself. He was raving about an island paradise where he and I could live together.'

Amy reached out to touch her hand in a gesture of sympathy. 'Oh, my dear, I do not know what to say. You are not yourself . . .'

Alys stood up and went to the window.

'Amy, he is insane, you must believe it. We must stop him.'

'But he has been so helpful and considerate. He told me—'

'He deceived you, just as he deceived me two years ago. I asked him to leave, but he will not go.'

Amy was silent for some time, finding it difficult to believe ill of the handsome man who had charmed his way into her home. But she knew Alys would not lie and there had been small things which had made her begin to doubt him, little inconsistencies in what he said. 'Shall we send for the militia?' she asked.

'I hate to do that, because it means the villagers will be in trouble as well.'

'Not if he forced them to do whatever they are doing.' She paused, watching her sister-in-law's face. 'I'll send John, shall I?'

Reluctantly Alys agreed and took her leave. She went home and spent the rest of the day wondering what she would do if the militia did not come. She went into the little room which she had been preparing as a nursery and sat beside the cradle. Garret would never see his child, but she derived some comfort from the thought that the child would be an ever-present reminder of the husband she had loved; Garret would continue to live in her heart and in the body of the infant she carried.

It was some time after dark when she was roused by the clanging of the church bell. She rose stiffly from her cramped position on the floor beside the cradle and went to the window. There was nothing to see, nothing appeared to be stirring out in the lane. She threw a cloak about her shoulders and hurried downstairs.

'Where are you going, my lady?' Prue asked her.

'To see why the bells are ringing.'

'No, my lady, stay indoors, where it is safe,' Prue begged her. 'It is Ingram Martin rousing the men.'

Alys, with her hand on the front door, turned towards her. 'What are they about to do?'

'Ingram is determined to set off the charges. He won't wait for the signal from the saker.'

'When did you hear this?'

'This afternoon, while you were at the manor.'

'Why did you not tell me?'

Prue shrugged. 'You have troubles enough, my lady.'

'But don't you realise that if Goodman Martin breaks the banks of the New Drain we will all be inundated? It won't be like the ordinary floods of old, which only covered the summer fields; this will be a great flood, even worse than the one Ingram Martin caused two years ago. The New Drain is high above the level of the fields and it carries water from dozens of miles away. You are wrong to say we will be safe here. Take all the women and children up to the manor and warn Lady Carthorne that she might have guests. If Ingram Martin succeeds, only the manor will be dry. I must try and stop him.' Ignoring Prue's protests, she set off up the lane, towards the sound of a beating drum.

Some of the more hot-headed men had assembled outside the church and were drawn up in ranks, each man carrying the musket with which he had been issued to fight the war. Breathlessly, she watched as the ragged column marched off through the village.

At the first cottage they stopped and Ingram banged on the door and shouted. 'Come out, Joshua, and join us or have the roof pulled from your house.' He signalled to one of the men who had a hook on a long pole, the sort of implement used for pulling down burning thatch when cottages caught fire, as they often did. Alys ran forward and pulled on his arm. 'Ingram Martin, do not do this thing. Do not do it.'

He shrugged her off as Joshua left his cottage and joined them, sending his family to the safety of the manor. It was the same at every dwelling, until the whole male population of the village had joined the march, too terrified to do anything else. When they reached the Van Hildt farm, they set to with a will, breaking up ploughs and harrows and pulling down fences. Alys, fearing for Lettice, ran and banged on her door to warn her, but no one answered. She walked all round the house, looking for signs of life, but it was in darkness. The men set light to the new barn and left, presumably to go to the dyke banks. She hurried after them.

Lettice was on the bridge by the sluice, facing the mob like a stag at bay, shouting at them and daring them to blow up the sluice and her along with it. Alys tried to push her way through the crowd to stand beside her. 'Stop this madness!' she cried. 'Do not take the law into your own hands!'

'The law does not care for us nor we for it,' Ingram shouted. 'Waterlea belongs to Waterlea men.'

'I have sent for the militia,' Alys said, in desperation. 'They will be here at any moment. Go back to your homes before they arrive.'

They murmured and looked from one to the other. Putting up a show was one thing, facing soldiers another. They looked from Alys to Ingram and then to Lettice.

'I believe Mistress Van Hildt wishes to sell her farm and move away,' Alys said, as a new idea struck her. 'I will buy the farm from her and take over her bond. Your agreement will be with me.'

'What difference will that make?' Ingram demanded.

'I will give the land to the village.'

'Give it?' The men were showing an interest at last. 'You would do that for us?'

'Why not? I am one of you, I belong to Waterlea.'

'And that is more than the widow does,' one said, and she knew they were weakening.

'It would be on the understanding you kept the fields drained,' she added. 'Do you agree?'

Ingram could see he had lost the initiative. 'Are you afraid of a handful of soldiers?' he cried. 'If you are not with me, then die here!' And he scrambled down the bank with his torch in his hand and lit the match cord attached to the explosive. When they saw what he was doing, they dived for the nearest cover.

Alys was blown off her feet, and found herself sprawled in the middle of the road amid a pile of muddy soil. She scrambled up, just as everyone else was doing, and looked to see what damage had been done. The bank had been breached quite high up and the water was only just lipping over it, but even as she looked she saw the earth moving. It would break at any minute.

And then they heard the saker, and no one knew whether it warned of Royalists, Parliamentarians or simply a band of militia come to arrest the troublemakers; as far as the men of Waterlea were concerned all were equally unwelcome. They began digging furiously.

Alys knew Prue would have obeyed her and that all the women and children had been sent to the manor. Leaving the diggers, she began to run. Passing the end of the lane to the ferry, she was suddenly reminded of Hannah, who would be marooned out there on the edge of the fen; she could not leave her. There was a boat below a small bridge which spanned a narrow dyke separating one of the fields from the common pasture. In summer it held very little water, but in winter it was full to bursting, keeping the water off the fields. And now it was rushing along in a craze of white foam, and she knew the men had succeeded in breaching the banks and soon the whole village would be under water. She heard someone pounding up the road behind her as she bent over the rope to release the boat. She did not even wonder who it might be, as she struggled to hold the small craft against the current so that she could climb aboard.

'Where are you going?' Damian was standing on the road above her, his chest heaving.

'I must go to Hannah. Her thoughtless husband has not considered her safety.'

He jumped down the bank and untied the boat, holding it steady for her to climb in. He was the last person she wanted to help her, but there was no time to argue and she realised that she would find it very difficult to control the boat alone. She climbed in and he pushed the boat from the bank and jumped in after her. 'Let us be off, then,' he said, sitting facing her and picking up the oars. 'I said you would need me, didn't I?'

She remained silent, as he pushed them away from the bank with an oar and then set to rowing them upstream to the place where the dyke ran into the fen proper. It was hard work but he managed to hold the boat on course until they met the rush of water released from the New Drain and were hurled across what had once been meadow and was now a lake two or three feet deep.

'It will be better when we reach deep water,' he grunted, pulling hard.

A few minutes later the turbulence subsided and they found themselves on the mere. Alys pointed the way to Ingram's cottage, but he ignored her and began pulling for the far side, where the path to Heronlea was still just passable.

'The cottage is that way,' she said, assuming he had not understood her signal.

'She won't be there,' he said. 'Ingram Martin will have made sure she was safe before he left her.'

'Then where are you taking me?'

'To safety. The saker warned of troops, so we will slip away until they have gone and it is safe to return.'

'It will never be safe for you to go back to

Waterlea. Even Amy knows you for what you are.'

'Then I will take you away and keep you. We will go somewhere where you are not always haunted by the ghost of the man you married, where you will learn to love me as I love you.'

She laughed to cover her terror, for the gleam in his eye told her, even in the dark, that his self-control was balanced on a knife-edge. 'You will never replace my husband, Captain Forrester, wherever you take me. Please row to the ferry.'

'You do not think I did what I did to let you go that easily, do you?'

It was happening again, this nightmare of cold and water, only this time there would be no Garret to save her. She stood up and the boat rocked, but it was not flat-bottomed like the ferry and there were no horses to upset it. She reached across and tried to take the oar from him.

He pushed her back and she sprawled in the bottom in the few inches of muddy water they had shipped. 'Be still! Would you have us over?'

'I do not care.'

'I will make you care. I will make you come out of that block of ice you have shut yourself in. You would have everyone believe you are cold, that nothing, no one, can touch you. I will kindle a fire in your belly, see if I don't.'

He dropped the oars into the bottom of the boat and threw himself on top of her. 'You are mine.' He began tearing at her clothing. 'I hated Garret Hartswood because he had you, because you loved him and he was too blind to see it. I killed for you and I will have you.' He pushed her down as she tried to rise. 'You don't believe me, do you? You don't believe I killed your husband.'

She was shocked enough to stop struggling, and he laughed. 'I had no wish to die for a cause that was lost and was on my way from the field when I saw him. We were surrounded and he was fighting like a demon, as if he did not care what became of him. He was so strong, so sure of himself, so invulnerable. I failed to put an end to him when I blew up the lighter, but now I had been given a second chance and this time I made sure I did not miss. I rode up behind him just before the Royalist cavalry charge, I ran him through and left him lying where his body would be trampled to pulp under the hooves of the horses. Then I came back to you, for you and Waterlea Manor are all I wanted.' He paused triumphant. 'Now, has that melted the ice in your heart? Do you rage with anger, or quiver with fear?'

It was an extraordinary effort of will which made her answer him at all. 'I pity you,' she said, pulling herself free and scrambling into a sitting position. 'I pity you. Now, be so good as to row to the cottage because I can see Hannah against the sky perched on its roof.' Was that her voice, so calm, so controlled? She did not think it could be, and yet there was no one else in the craft, except perhaps her guardian angel.

Damian remained slumped in the water in the bottom of the boat, doing nothing to obey, but nothing to stop her either; his passion seemed spent, leaving him weak and helpless. She picked up the oars and began to row.

The current was much stronger than usual and she felt its pull towards the Devil's Hole. 'This way!' shouted Hannah, who had seen them coming. 'Steer to this side!'

Alys obeyed and brought the small craft under the overhanging roof of the cottage, where Hannah slid down and scrambled into it.

'Oh, you don't know how glad I am you came,' she said. 'I don't think I could have hung on much longer.' Then seeing Damian. 'What is he doing down there?'

'Overcome by grief and loss,' Alys said, pulling away. 'Which is the best way to go?'

Before Hannah could answer, they heard a loud halloo from the far bank, and, looking up, saw the outline of a man on the path to Heronlea.

'What fool is that to be out and expecting a ferry on such a night as this?' Hannah said. 'The path is already under a foot of water.'

She stood up and cupped her hands to shout. 'Go back! Waterlea is inundated. There are no paths. Go back!'

'I must cross.' The man's voice was whipped away in the wind. 'Bring the ferry.'

'The ferry is swept away.'

'We can't leave him there,' Alys said. 'The water is rising all the time; there will be no paths at all soon. To be honest I shall be glad of someone to help row—my arms are all but pulled from their sockets.' She began to pull across the mere towards the man, whose voice had reminded her of Garret whom she had loved, Garret, who was dead, killed by a sword-thrust in the back. What an ignominious end for a brave soldier! She shook herself. What thoughts to be thinking at such a time.

'Here, let me row,' Hannah suggested, moving across to take the oar. 'I am more used to it than you are.'

Damian stirred in the bottom of the boat and shook his head, like a child coming out of a bad dream. He was still sitting there with his elbows on his knees and his head in his hands when they touched the far bank.

The man on the path was outlined against the sky as he stepped towards the boat. He was tall, Alys could see that, and there was something about the set of his shoulders and way he wore the uniform of a Parliamentary soldier which was familiar. She cried out when the wraith spoke. 'Thank heaven you saw me. I was beginning to think I would have to turn back. I—' He stopped suddenly in the act of clambering over the gunwale. 'Alys! Can it be you?'

It was no ghost that scrambled over the other two to reach her. 'Oh, Alys, Alys, my dear, my love.' He sank down beside her and took her in his arms to kiss her. 'But what are you doing out here on such a night? You could not possibly have known I was coming.'

She was shaking like an aspen and could not speak. Hannah picked up the oars and began to row. 'The sooner we all get back to a warm hearth the better, or we are all like to die of the ague,' she said.

No one, least of all Alys and Garret, noticed Damian until he was towering above them. In the dark his face glowed with a kind of white light of rage and fear. 'When a man is killed, he should stay dead,' he muttered, producing a knife from his boot top and lifting it above his head. 'Dead, I say!'

The knife never found its mark because Hannah hit out with the one of the oars and caught his legs, toppling him off balance. He shrieked as he fell overboard into the cold water and disappeared into the blackness.

They spent some minutes rowing round in the dark trying to find him, but in the end they all realised that the Devil's Hole had claimed another victim.

'I didn't mean him to drown,' Hannah said, as Garret rowed them home. 'I only wanted to stop him.'

'You saved my life,' Garret said. 'He was intent on murder.'

Alys looked up from his encircling arms. 'He told me he had killed you.'

'He tried, but, as you see, I survived. I shall tell you all about it, but not now, because I need to concentrate on finding my way home.'

'I am afraid we shall have to go to the manor; Eagleholm will be under water,' Alys said, then remembering the earlier events. 'And I am not sure if it is in Royalist or Parliament's hands; there was an alarm.'

'Take that channel,' Hannah advised. 'It leads directly to the moat.'

The manor, when they reached it, was ablaze with candles, torches and rushlights and its tables had disappeared under the food heaped on them. Amy, who saw the newcomers first, jumped up from her seat and ran them.

'Alys! Garret! Both of you safe! Oh, praise be!' She was laughing and crying together. 'Benedick is here too. And the war is at an end.' She drew them into the circle of people who gathered about Benedick, while everyone talked and shouted and laughed, all trying to explain what had happened. It seemed that Simon, at the window of the manor, had fired the saker in sheer jubilation when he saw his master returning, expecting it to bring everyone running to greet him; it had not occurred to him that they would break the banks before they came.

The militia would not be paying a visit until the floods died down and by that time Garret and Benedick would have everything in order again. Apart from Damian, the only casualty had been Ingram who had died in the explosion. Alys comforted Hannah as well as she could, but she was too overcome by her own overflowing emotions to be much help to her, and she knew Hannah would understand that. She left her in the capable hands of Prue, who always knew the right thing to say, and went to put her hand in Garret's.

Now that her husband was back at her side, she would hold nothing back, not her love, nor her fears; there would be no more barriers, no more battles, only an abiding love and understanding, she would make sure of it. 'Come,' she said, leading him to her old bedchamber, now made ready for them. 'I have some good news for you and it were better told in the privacy of our chamber.'

They were alone at last, and she suddenly felt shy, as if it were the first time, and in many ways it was. It was the first time they had come together as true lovers, as two people who had no doubts about each other. There was a rightness about their union which had not been there before. He undressed her

317

carefully, kissing every part of her and making her whole body shiver in ecstasy. He put his head down on the roundness of her belly and smiled. 'He will be a fine boy,' he said. 'I know it.'

*   *   *

Much, much later, lying in bed in the secure circle of Garret's arms, Alys heard how he had been picked up from the battlefield and taken to Oxford as a prisoner. 'My captors treated me well and looked after my wounds, but I was in no condition to think of escape,' he told her. 'I was there throughout the siege, which was more than could be said of the King. He had his hair cut short, put on a false beard and slipped out through our lines disguised as a servant. I was released by our people when Oxford surrendered.'

'We heard the King had disappeared,' she said. 'Amy thought Benedick might bring him here. He hasn't, has he? He is not hiding in the manor?'

He laughed and kissed her. 'No. He told your brother he was going abroad to seek help from France—'

'Merciful heaven!' she cried. 'Is there to be no end to it?'

'Fortunately wiser counsel prevailed and he surrendered to our Scots allies who were besieging Newark. The war is over, my lovely

318

Alys, the war between King and Parliament, the war between you and me.'

'Oh, Garret, when that madman said you were dead, I wanted to die too.' She turned in his arms to look up into his face. 'I knew I had been selfish and foolish and the thought that I could never tell you so or ask for your forgiveness was more than I could bear.' She stopped speaking because he had covered her lips with his own to silence her.

'Can you forgive me?' she asked finally.

'There is nothing to forgive. Let us blame the war, which split many a family and turned brother against brother and friend against friend.'

'To my eternal shame I believed you were our enemy.'

'I know—you made no secret of the fact you wished me dead.' He was smiling in that teasing way of his. 'Damian Forrester said he was carrying out your wishes in killing me. I was fool enough to believe it.'

She reached to kiss him. 'I was a rebel,' she said. 'I did not have the sense to recognise love for what it was.'

'Dear rebel,' he said, ruffling her hair. 'I had the same problem when my father told me what he had in mind.'

'You did not want me?'

He laughed. 'Not when you were still only fourteen and I was already a man, or so I thought. I hit out in the only way I knew—I took a mistress to spite my father.'

'Lettice Van Hildt.'

'Yes, only she was not married then. She took Jan Van Hildt only when she realised I had tired of her and would obey my father. I believe she persuaded her husband to invest in the Waterlea drainage in order to be near me.'

She turned to kiss him. 'When did you decide you would obey your father?'

'You were fifteen, I think, perhaps sixteen, and you went out on the fen to fish with Benedick. We met out there on the water, me in my boat and you in yours, and I could not take my eyes off you. My rebellion ended right then and there.'

'Why did you never tell me this?'

He smiled. 'Would you have, in my place? After all, you had never given marriage a thought, had you? And later, when the war started, I thought it prudent not to press my suit; after all, your family was Royalist. But in London . . .? He stopped to kiss her throat, sending a tingle of pleasure through her. 'You thought your father had used the fact of our betrothal to save you all—is it any wonder you rebelled? To find yourself betrothed to a man you had hardly seen before must have come as a shock. I wanted to give you time. And it seemed the more time you had, the more we quarrelled.'

'I took too long to come to my senses and

when I did I could not tell you so. But after you went away that last time, it was as if I had wakened from a long sleep, and when I looked round for you, you had gone.' She flung her arms round his neck again and kissed him with joyful abandonment. 'Garret, never leave me again, never, never.'

'And will you promise never to rebel again?'

She smiled and punched his chest playfully. 'Oh, I don't know about that . . .'

Her words were stopped as he covered her mouth with his own. He did not want to extract a promise from her that he knew she could not keep. Besides, he loved her just the way she was.